Jayded

A Forbidden Romance Series Novel
by Shevaun DeLucia

Words Written, LLC
Rochester, New York

Words Written, LLC
Rochester, New York
www.shevaundelucia.com

Publisher's Note: This is a work of fiction. Names, characters, places, and incidents are a product of the author's imagination. Locales and public names are sometimes used for atmospheric purposes. Any resemblance to actual people, living or dead, or to businesses, companies, events, institutions, or locales is completely coincidental.

Book Layout by Amy Donnelly
http://www.alchemyandwords.com/

Cover Art by Sommer Stein
https://www.facebook.com/PerfectPearCreative/?pnref=lhc

Jayded / Shevaun DeLucia
ISBN 978-0-9863951-0-9

To my number one fans—you give me a reason to

follow my dreams – Dom & Ang

jayded [ˈjā-dəd] adjective:
1. to sexually pleasure to the extreme
2. to be sexually pleasured to the point
   where all other lovers would
   be inferior

CHAPTER ONE

Kyle

A breeze rushes over me, sending goose bumps across the surface of my skin and chilling me to the bone. I pull my tangled covers up over my shoulder and bury my face deep into the warmth. Ahh, so snug.

Just then, my alarm shrieks loudly through the room. I don't want to move. Fuck work today. Ugh! If only I could lie in bed all day and get paid for it, life would be perfect. On second thought, I could do that as a male escort! I laugh at my dirty mind, shake my head, and smile. The things I come up with.

I take one last breath and blow it out forcefully before I push the covers off and feel the breeze glide over me once more. Brr! I jump across my bed to shut the darn thing off, almost falling on my face when my foot catches on the sheet.

It's the middle of January, and still, to this day, I cannot fall asleep without my fan on. It is an old habit acquired from childhood. The sounds of the whipping blades drowned out the noise of Junior, my older brother, snoring —something I had to endure when sharing a room with him as a kid. I've needed it ever since. It's one of my weird addictions.

I rub the sleep from my eyes, a parting gift from the

good ole Sandman. I just hate morning time. I think I've been up no more than five minutes before my phone rings. I don't even need to look at the caller ID to know who it is.

I press the green button and put the phone up to my ear as I walk to the bathroom. "Hey, Ma. Why must you always call me this early in the morning?" I grumble. I grab the washcloth from the towel rack and hold it under the hot, steaming water.

"Well good morning to you too, son! I just wanted to remind you to dress up today. We have a possible partner coming in to visit. Your father is going to be on his shitstorm-rampage getting the office prepared," my mother says. I sigh knowing today will be a rough one. I can hear her take the phone from her ear as she orders her french vanilla coffee with sugar and extra cream. She stops at the Dunkin Donuts drive-thru each morning. "Did you need me to grab you one?" she asks.

I finish wiping off my face with the steamy washcloth. "Nah. I'm good, Ma. I'll grab one on my way there."

"Ok, love. I'll see you in a few."

I put my phone on the counter and finish my normal morning bathroom routine. I can't help but feel a little stoked that it's business casual dress attire today. That means the girls are going to be on fire, dressed in pumps, tight dress pants, or maybe even some nice, tight ass-grabbing skirts—*yeah buddy*!

I work down the street at my parents' publishing

company: Saunders Literary Agency. My parents both built the company from the ground up. They have made it into a very successful business that's going on ten years now. Just last year, I decided to join the team after finishing my last semester at college.

Believe me, being twenty-four and working for my parents is not my ultimate goal in life, but I had to keep the money flowing. There was no way in hell I was going back home to live under my parents' roof while I figured out what to do with myself.

There are a couple of girls at the office who have caught my eye, but nothing worth talking about. They were more like wham-bam-thank-you-ma'ams. Elizabeth, the long-legged wonder with a nice rack—I just had to get my mouth on that. I dated her on and off for a couple of months, but she wanted too much from me. She wanted to be exclusive, and when I told her we needed to cool off for a while, she went all stalker-mode on me. She turned into a stage-five clinger! So I ran.

Bottom line is I'm twenty-four, for Christ's sake! Who the hell wants to settle down at twenty-four? One piece of ass for the rest of my life? That shit isn't happening! At least, not anytime soon. I've been lucky enough to have parents who've stayed together all these years. I've gotten to watch what true love looks like through them. But for me—I'm just happy living as a bachelor.

My parents met at the same age I'm at now, and they are the small percentage who've made it, stuck with it. They've been together almost thirty years, and they're still going strong. My childhood was nice. It was textbook normal, with some occasional hiccups. But marriage and family is pretty much non-existent in my future, at least for now.

I finish a quick shave and head back to my closet to put on my dress clothes. I have a studio apartment. It's small but efficient, and the rent is cheap. I have my bed, leather sofa, breakfast nook looking over the small kitchen, and a nice big window looking out on the busy downtown streets. But the best part of it is—there are no parents!

I check the thermostat before I head out, making sure it's set to turn on by five in the evening so I can come home to a nice, snug apartment, and then I head out the door.

Work's going to be a little crazy today. It always is when we have clients or prospective agents who may join our company. My parents have some big clients that are very loyal because my father is very good at what he does. He is usually extra tense and extra snippy on these days. He's fighting for traditional publishing versus the self-publishing trend that authors seem to take to lately. So keeping our clients happy is extremely important to our company.

Me, I try to stay out of Dodge when my father is in his moods, and my mother gets the short end of the deal. She has no choice but to deal with the lion head-on.

I hustle my butt getting into my car. It feels like ten below outside. Really, it's only about thirty-two degrees. At least that is what the radio man just said. Mental note: Get a car starter installed! I say this every winter. And each time I finally get down to making a move on it, it's already spring and I let it wait until the next winter. Yes, I know; I am a major procrastinator.

What can I say?

I turn the key and the motor hums to life. I pat the dashboard and whisper her sweet nothings. My car is a beauty: a black 2014 Cadillac, CTS-V luxury sports coupe. It was a graduation gift from my parents. They may have gone a little overboard, but nothing's too good for their "little baby boy," as my mom would say.

I pull up to work and park to the back. The less cars, the better. I would crush someone if they scratched or nicked this baby. Now, if only I could find a girl who is just as sleek and sexy, my world would be perfect. Yeah, I'm a little crazy. I shake my head with a grin while looking around to make sure no one is seeing my craziness.

I buzz myself in and walk past the secretary, Elise. She's quiet and shy—pretty in a natural, bland sort of way. Every time I walk past her, I make sure to give her an extra special smile. "*Hello*, Elise. You're looking very pretty today," I tell her as I walk by. I like to see her cheeks redden.

She giggles. "Thank you, Kyle." I give her a wink, she buzzes me in, and I stroll toward my desk.

As I walk past my coworkers, I nod my head and charm my way through the office. I finally reach my desk and clock in. Jeff Bauer, a longtime friend, comes to visit, hanging against the outside of my cubicle. "Hey, man.

What's up?"

Jeff's my dude. He's a blast to party with. We've known each other since eighth grade when he moved here from South Carolina with his mom. He is one loyal friend. When he's got your back, he's got your back. He's proved this many times during our drunken party nights. He never leaves a soldier behind, and he has bailed my ass out a thousand times. A true wingman.

I slap him up. "So, we still on for tonight?"

His face lights up with the thought of some free booze. "Hell yeah! I'm totally in. Where we at tonight?" Jeff asks.

I can't help but laugh. He kills me. "It's a McGregor's night tonight. My parents have to schmooze a possible new agent. You know how that shit goes," I say, rolling my eyes to add some extra affect.

"Alright, man. It's on and poppin'!" He smacks the back of my head and takes off.

"Douche!" I yell as quietly as possible. I get smacked upside the head again. "Ouch! What the—?"

"Watch the language, Kyle. We have a guest!" my mother whispers vehemently.

"Yeah, yeah," I respond, annoyed. I have to find another job. Getting scolded at work at eight thirty in the morning fucking sucks!

My mother eases up a bit, noticing my reaction. "I have Maxine in my office. Do you mind showing her around a little? Take her to the kitchen to grab some coffee, please?"

She always makes me the errand boy while Junior, my

older brother, gets to be in on the important meetings and conferences. Yes, he's worked here since right out of high school and knows the business in and out, but *I* have a degree under my belt now. I am way more qualified than he could ever be. My father tells me I need to earn my spot in the business, which, in my opinion, is total bullshit. I could go work at any one of these top agencies with my background. I may be the baby of the family, but sometimes I feel more like the black sheep.

I grunt like a child about to throw a tantrum. "Fine. Not a problem."

My mother gives me a pat on my shoulder and walks away. I push my chair in a little harder than normal and begin my touring duty.

Before I can make it to my mom's office, Elizabeth stops me. She sticks her chest out just enough for "the girls" to poke out, front and center. I can't help but look for just a quick moment. "Good morning, Kyle," she greets me with what she thinks is a seductive smile. I'm totally on to her, and her smile irks me like nails on a chalkboard.

"Morning, Beth. Listen, I can't talk right now." I try to scoot around her, hoping she'll get the hint.

"Kyle, wait! Will you be at McGregor's tonight?" she asks. Great. Stalker chick's gonna be there. Awesome.

"Yeah." I turn and walk away.

"I'll see you there!" she yells from behind.

I stroll up to my mother's office and knock on the door before opening it. A woman sits in front of my mom's desk with her back to me, typing furiously on her laptop. I look at her boringly. Most agents seem to be dull, boring, snooty, and all about business. Their idea of fun is reading a book. Or maybe it's just that any woman dressed in a dress suit reminds me of my mother.

"Uh, good *morning*," I say, trying not to startle her. She looks to be very concentrated on her work.

Maxine turns in her seat. My mouth hangs open. It's like time freezes, and all I can think is *holy fuck*! I'm speechless. Never in my life have I been speechless or caught off-guard to this magnitude. The woman in front of me is fucking hot! On fire! I slowly take her in, starting with her high red pumps, long legs, and tight red skirt reaching her knees, hugging one amazing ass and some unGodly shaped hips. Man, those hips though. I can already see my hands being at home on those hips. My eyes drift up to her tiny waist and voluptuous breasts. *Yum.* Her face is flawless: lips plush and eyes a beautiful iridescent blue, which completely contrasts against her darker complexion and the brown of her hair. Simple perfection.

I must be standing here like a doof, making an ass of myself, because she smiles with a tiny bit of amusement. She reaches her hand out to me. "Hello. You must be Kyle?"

I continue to stare, completely mesmerized. It takes me a moment to snap out of it. "Uh, yes, I'm Kyle. You must be Maxine." I grab her hand, immediately feeling the softness of her skin. "It's nice to meet you," I say with a smile.

"It's just Max," she informs me.

I scream at myself from within, trying to get a grip. She's just a woman, for God's sake! An amazingly attractive woman who undoubtedly has already, within seconds, caused a stir from down below. A woman with long, shapely legs that I would kill to trail kisses up and have wrapped around me. A woman with hips I could grab perfectly while watching her grind on top of me.

Her amusement has now traveled to her sparkling eyes. "Your mother, Connie, told me you would be giving me a tour?"

She turns to close her laptop. I almost reach my hand out to grab that beautiful ass of hers, but I slap it away before she turns back around. Man, what I could do with that ass in my hands. Shit! Okay, okay. Stay focused.

I pull the door wider and hold out my hand for her to go first. "After you," I say.

She walks past me, her eyes meeting mine as she crosses my path. Our eyes stay connected for a moment, energy rampages through every limb of my body, gathering at the southern region. I'm unable to part from her gaze until she finally disconnects from me. The air whirls around me, leaving me with the fragrance of flowers and cucumber melon. It's intoxicating. I lean in, without realizing it, to smell the air left from her trail. Shit! What the hell am I doing? I'm losing my mind, that's what I'm doing. I can't help it, though. I've only spent a couple minutes in her presence, and I'm already addicted.

CHAPTER TWO

"Wow" is the only word I can seem to come up with. I knew Connie's sons worked here, but when I pictured her younger son, for some reason I pictured a young teenage boy with acne and a socially awkward presence, not this beautiful, sexy, confident man I want to ravage like a beast standing in front of me. Just the sight of him has my juices flowing!

He is full of manly muscle, and his clothes hug him in just the right places. I can already feel my hands itching to give that tight ass a nice squeeze. I can't see it, but I can only imagine. Those luscious lips and dark brown piercing eyes have me melting like butter. *Mmm!* With just one look from him, my nipples pucker to a salute, begging to be played with. My temperature rises and settles below the belt. All of this in just a matter of minutes? Damn! I am in trouble. Maybe taking the job is not in my best interest.

I follow him toward the door, and he waits for me to exit first. I don't know if he wants to look at my ass, or if he's really just a gentleman. I walk past him, immediately locking eyes with him. A *zing* races through my body, giving me chills. My hair is literally standing up from my skin as though I just got jolted with a ten volt. This is some crazy shit! The worst part is he's wearing my favorite cologne: Versace. I can pick out that smell from a lineup any day. Ugh! So freaking hot!

Keep it cool, Max. Keep it cool. He's just a kid, for Christ's sake! What am I thinking, anyway? He may be a sexified stud muffin, but reality is, he *is* just a kid. What is he, twenty? Twenty-one? Let's also not forget I am trying to merge my company with his parents'. Become partner, and fucking the young son of my new partners would probably be frowned upon.

I can't help but put a little extra swing in my hips, and by the look on his face, I can tell he's really enjoying it. "Where to?" I ask, allowing him to take lead. Actually, *making* him take the lead so I can violate that tight ass of his with my eyes. This may be wrong, but it feels so right.

He steps in front of me after closing his mother's office door. "I thought maybe you might want some coffee before the tour?" he asks.

Yes! I am in dire need of some coffee. The bed in my hotel room is hard and uncomfortable. But it doesn't matter how much the room costs or how nice the hotels are, I can never get comfortable in someone else's bed. I used to tell that to my ex. We were engaged, and even then I wouldn't sleep at his house, in his bed. When he made the decision to sell his house to move into mine until we bought one together, I panicked. The thought of my bed no longer being just mine scared the shit out of me, and I ran—all the way to New York.

"Yes, please. That would be great." I can see the

eyeballs begin to follow and observe as we make our way through the company. The office has one large room with two smaller rooms attached on either side. Cubicles breaking up the rooms create maze-like pathways throughout. I quickly follow behind Kyle so I don't get lost but keep a far enough distance for the occasional ass peek.

We enter the kitchen, and thankfully we're alone. I'm intrigued by him and the way my body is reacting to him. Normally, I am in *full* control. I am always able to keep my emotions and body in check, but with him, I feel like a young high school girl. I'm completely out of my element. Even in high school, I was always in control.

Kyle grabs me a cup for my coffee and tells me where the sugar and creamer are. I can't help but feel this wild energy surrounding us. It's intense. Powerful. Instead of beating around the bush, I'm going to embrace it, clear the air a little so we can move on. I stop after fixing my coffee and turn to him. "Are you going to have any coffee?" What the—? Did that really just come out of my mouth? What the heck happened to confronting the giant elephant in the room head-on?

"No, I'm good. Thanks, though. So tell me something about yourself. I mean, since we're going to be spending most of the day together—why New York?" Kyle asks, getting right down to it, which is usually my thing. "You're from South Carolina, right?"

I take a sip of my coffee. "Yup, that I am. I just needed a change. This great opportunity kind of fell in my lap and, well, I couldn't resist at least considering it. So here I am! I'll be here for another week or two. Or at least until I've thoroughly gone over the proposal. If all works out, then my next step will be house hunting."

A girl enters the room just as he's about to respond. She's beautiful and young. I can feel the air thick with discomfort. Kyle's body has gone rigid, and his hands are now clenched into fists. Interesting. The girl smiles at him, hoping to get his attention, but I can only see a cold gaze looking back at her. She walks past me and smiles, though the smile never reflects in her eyes. I can tell she is sizing me up as she looks me up and down.

It's clear that she has a thing for him, and it's definitely possible they might have had a thing together in the past. Obviously, whatever went down ended badly for her, and she never intended on being this distant from him.

It's funny how women can tell all of this by just a simple smile. I feel a little bad for her. I can see the longing and lust as she looks at him, hoping he may look back at her the same. But he's made it very clear, without using words, that it's never going to happen. At least not at this moment.

"Kyle, can I talk to you for a moment?" she asks, eyes almost begging. She looks back to me, hoping I might get the hint and leave.

Kyle rolls his eyes. Even when he does this childish act, he still looks adorable. "Actually, I don't have time. I'm showing Max around. She will, hopefully soon, be added to our agent list." I smile and hold my hand out to her.

"It's nice to meet you, um—" I begin to say, and then quickly realize I haven't yet heard her name.

She extends her hand out to shake mine. "It's Elizabeth."

I nod. "Elizabeth." I let go of her hand as she does mine. "Well, I'm sure we will be meeting again in the near future." I watch as she looks back to Kyle in one last attempt at some sort of recognition from him, and then she exits.

I can't help but quietly exhale. That was just a little too intense for my liking. I will need to remind myself to stay away from the young hunk of beautifulness before I get myself in trouble.

I take a sip of coffee while looking back toward Kyle, studying him for a moment. "So, that was interesting," I say with a laugh, trying to release some of the tension.

He rubs his hand over his fuzzy head and chuckles uncomfortably. "Yeah, you could say that again. I apologize for that. She can be a little intense at times. She just never knows when to stop."

I lean my butt against the counter. "So, she a girlfriend, then?" God, why do I even care?

He stops fidgeting to look at me. "No. She's definitely *not* a girlfriend. We hung out for a while, but she got too clingy," he admits. I notice he is studying me carefully as I was doing to him a minute ago. Maybe he's trying to decipher my reaction or figure me out.

I laugh. "Ahh, I see. So she wanted a relationship, and you just wanted a piece of ass," I blurt out. I immediately cover my mouth, mortified. *Shit!* Did that really just come out of my mouth?

He looks shocked but amused. "Whoa!" he teases. "Yeah, I guess you could say it that way. I'm a guy. What can I say?" he whispers while shrugging his shoulders. Of course he's a guy. A fucking hot tamale that I can't stop checking out.

I'm still mortified. "I *so* did not mean for that to come out that way. Please, forgive me!" I beg. He moves closer to me as if he's drawn to me, moving without a thought until he is so close I can almost feel his breath. I stand here still as a statue, unable to breathe, and wonder what his next move might be. If I take a whiff of his sweet, mouthwatering aroma, it might just be the end of me. He smirks, pleased with the reaction he has arisen from me, and then reaches around me for a paper towel.

I let my breath out when he turns and shake my head with the realization that I am an actual moron. Did I really think he was drawn to me in this amount of time? I don't know what I thought, but I do know that being that close to him makes me nervous in the most girlie sort of way.

CHAPTER THREE

Kyle

The woman standing in front of me is a goddess. Is it wrong that I already want to sweep her in my arms and ravage her? I'm a hungry beast. I don't know what it is about her that's making me crazy. I'm as hard as a rock, and I've only been in her presence for ten minutes. Maybe it's the red pumps. Maybe it's those amazing blue eyes looking back at me. Can it be possible that she's just as attracted to me as I am to her? No. No way. I *need* to find out, so I close the gap between us in just three steps. I keep my eyes connected with hers as I feel out her energy. I know I've only just met her, but I feel this crazy, deep connection. Or is it lust? Whatever it is, it's turning me on. The energy surrounding us has spiked to a loud, thick buzz, and I can't help the twinges and tingles I'm feeling from down below.

She looks skeptical as I move in but that quickly turns to—hopeful, is it? Maybe just a tad hungry or lascivious? Damn, I want her! I want to lift her on top of that counter, slide her skirt up, and rip her panties off with my teeth. She probably tastes as amazing as she smells.

The closer I lean in, the more nervous she seems to get, but I still have my eyes set on hers. I'm almost afraid to keep looking. What if she's on to me? What if she slaps me? I laugh inside at this thought because any touch from her would be a good touch. Oh man. This is going to be one long day!

Ahh. I am done being a tour guide for today. Bittersweet. Max has kept me on my toes the whole day. Every movement of her body hypnotizes me. Every whiff of her scent intoxicates me, and every small glance and sly seductive smile unglues me. If I am feeling this way after only eight hours with her, what will a week or months, for that matter, do to me? I just need to fuck her to get her out of my head. Once I do the deed, I can go back to my normal self.

Of course, there may be one small problem with my solution—she may go into partnership with my parents. Damn! That may be a deal breaker right there! But, on the other hand, who has to know?

"What the *fuck*?" I snap my head around after being welted in the back of the fucking head. "Dude! Not freaking cool man!" I gripe quietly.

Jeff has an ear-to-ear dickhead grin on his face. I can tell he's ready to get his drink on, and it's only Monday night. "Sorry, bro," he chuckles. "I'm just glad it's *finally* five o'clock, man. This day has been *dragging*!" he says.

I finish clocking out and shut down my computer for the night. "I totally feel ya, my man," I agree, standing up to stretch.

Jeff looks around to make sure nobody is eavesdropping. There are a lot of nosey people in our workplace. It must be the close quarters. "All I want to know is who the fuck was that hottie you were walking around with today? She was smokin'!" Jeff barely manages to keep his voice down.

I shake my head, chuckling while putting my jacket on. "That hot piece of ass might be your boss real soon," I warn.

Jeff exhales dramatically. "I don't give a damn! If you're not going to try and tag that ass, then I will."

Brutal honesty. I wouldn't have Jeff any other way. He's not lying, either. If I don't lay claim to her, she's fair game, and there is no way in hell I'm allowing that to happen. If anyone's going to have at her, it will be me.

I plant my hand around his shoulder and squeeze. "Sorry, bro, but I already have dibs."

He stomps like a little child. As we pass through the front doors, I can't help but say goodnight to my doorwoman. "*Goodbye*, Elise." I wink and she giggles.

Jeff rolls his eyes at my nonsense. "What?" I ask, shrugging my shoulders, knowing exactly what he's going to say.

"Dude, you don't have to flirt with the underlings, too. Leave some for the little people!" Jeff explains.

He freaking kills me. "You riding with me or you following?" I ask.

"Nah, dude. I'm following. I need my own ride in case I get some play tonight," he says.

I hop into my car, shake off a quick shiver, and turn on the seat warmers. I can't wait for the warmer weather. This cold shit sucks. Warmer weather means less clothing for the woman. Yeah buddy!

I pull up to McGregor's, and I can see that most of the work gang is already here. They must have stormed out of work like lightning. I can already see Beth through the window on my way in. She doesn't even give me two seconds to breathe before grabbing my arm to pull me in her direction.

"Hey! I got you a drink already," she tells me.

I try to remain patient. I know she only means well, but she tries too hard. I guess if need be, she's a warm body to go home with tonight. "Thanks, Beth."

I grab the Heineken bottle from her and take a huge swig. I casually scope the scene and nonchalantly look for Max. I see her talking to my mother, but my father is nowhere in sight. He must still be back at work, putting in some late hours. Rarely do I ever see him out after work. He's always been the one to stroll in past dinnertime throughout my childhood years. I guess that's why he's been so successful.

My mother takes notice of me and waves me over. Thank God! An easy way out from Beth's death grip. "Hey, I'm going to go talk with my mom for a quick sec. Thanks for the beer." I begin to walk off until I'm pulled back.

"I was hoping that we can see each other after this. Leave a little early like we used to," she says, now standing in front of my view of Max.

At this point, I'm ready to say anything to get her off my back. Luckily, Jeff notices that I'm in a compromising position and yells for me. I nod my head to him and look back at Beth who is now sporting a full pout. Months ago, I would have fallen for this, but now she just looks pathetic.

"I don't know, Beth. Let's just let the night play out. We both have to be up early for work in the morning," I say, trying to turn her down as easily as I can. Who am I fooling? I just left the door cracked in case I change my mind after a few beers.

Beth looks back toward my mother's table, where Max is now sitting, and I can see her wheels turning. This calculating look is never a good look for her. It means she is trying to put two and two together, and my guess is she sees Max as competition. Unfortunately for her, Max may just end up being her boss.

I don't wait another minute for her to answer. I head toward the table. I stop and give my mother a kiss on the cheek, nod to Max, and shake Jonathan's hand. Jonathan Duke is another agent who works for my parents. He's been with the agency for about five years. He's been a friend of my father's for a while now and jumped ship from another agency when my father gave him an offer he couldn't refuse.

My father's a go-getter, and when he sees potential, he's not afraid to go after what will bring him great profit. If it means making his agents happy, he's all for it. Jonathan admires that in my father, and since he's now going through a divorce and custody battle for his kids, my father has become a listening ear for him. A mentor if you will.

"So, son, how did the day go?" my mother looks back and forth between Max and I.

I look to Max. "It was great. Max should be very comfortable in the layout of Saunders Literary Agency. She knows exactly where to get the coffee now," I reply very sarcastically.

My mother looks annoyed and Max looks a little entertained. "Yes, Connie, Kyle was a great tour guide. Actually, I was hoping he might be willing to show me around town this weekend." Max turns her attention to me. "Only if you're up for it, of course."

Did she just ask me to show her around as in "one-on-one," outside of the work environment? *Oh boy*. This could be *very* dangerous. No inquisitive eyes, no company policies or being confined by stringent rules, and ultimately, no being scrutinized under my parent's watchful eyes. Yup. Definitely dangerous, but I think I'll take my chances.

"Um, I think I can clear my schedule. Is Saturday at one o'clock okay for you?" I ask Max.

Jonathan cuts in. "Kyle, you must have a date or friends you want to go hang out with. I would be more than happy to show you around, Maxine," he says, stepping right on my toes. Fuckface! If he wasn't my superior and well-acquainted with my family, I would pound him in his head for this.

Max looks a little caught off-guard and unsure of exactly how to answer his offer. "No, Jonathan, I would be more than happy to show her around. No plans for me on Saturday. My schedule is clear," I inform him. "I assume you are staying at a hotel?"

"Yes, the Sheraton," Max answers.

"Great, right down the street from me. I'll be at your door at one, then," I say, staking my claim. Jonathan knows he has lost this battle.

What's his deal, anyway? This dude isn't even divorced yet, and he's already on to the next piece of ass? Mental note: ask Dad exactly what the cause of his divorce was. I can only imagine, since he's already on the prowl. Douchebag. Let's face it, I can hate the player, but I can't hate the game. I'm just pissed he's trying to pee on my tree.

My mother just watches us from the sidelines as we battle over Max. I see a glimmer of recognition in her eyes. Not good. The last thing I need is her on my ass when I haven't even done a thing yet. I guess "yet" is the key word. I'm not so sure I'm going to be able to keep my mind from wandering when I'm with Max, and I'm not so sure I want to, either. I'm a twenty-four-year-old guy and that's just how we are.

Max's eyes sparkle with triumph as she smiles at me. "Sounds perfect." Is it me or does she actually seem pleased that I stepped up to the plate and hit a homerun?

I get snapped out of my thoughts by my mother's clap. "Well great! I'm glad that's all settled!" she chimes in. She calls for the waitress. "Get us some shots of Patrón over here!" she orders. "So, Max—"

"Yes?"

"I just wanted to say that I am extremely happy that you are even considering a collaboration with us. You have an amazing eye for talent, and we would be extremely lucky to have you with us. Just so you know, Kyle here has graduated with his MBA in business, and if you do decide to take us on, I would be honored if you could take my son under your wing and show him the ropes.

"Junior began with us directly out of high school, and though he doesn't have a college degree, he is also a great asset to us. My sons both have made a great step in the next chapter of their lives. Junior will also be a great help to you in learning the ins and outs of our company."

My mother's speech was sweet, but really? We're at a bar, not giving confessions at church. But, I am more than happy to be under Max as long as it takes, and with the things that are running through my mind, it won't take long before she gets off. I chuckle to myself.

"Thank you, Connie, and I would be more than happy to teach Kyle everything I know. He'll be partner in no time," she says.

I take a swig of my beer first. "Yeah, not so sure about all of that," I comment.

Both my mother and Max look to me. "Oh? Have you made plans that I am unaware of?" my mother questions. I hate when she switches to "the mom glare." When I was younger, I could never squirm my way out of interrogation with that look pounding down on me. Lucky for me, I have had years of practice in diverting my attention away from her trap.

Shit! This is not what I had in mind for tonight. Time to deviate and turn the conversation to another topic. I quickly look for Jeff, but I see him at the bar, grabbing the requested shots.

"No, Ma! I haven't, but like I told you before, I'm not so sure if Rochester is my last stop," I answer only to satisfy her and take another swig of my beer, hoping Jeff gets his ass over here.

Max jumps in. "Where would you like to go if you left here?"

After here, as in this bar? I would love to take you back to my place so I could have my way with you all night long. I give her the more appropriate answer: "Somewhere warm, that's for sure!"

She laughs. "Yes, coming from South Carolina's warm, salty air, I can understand that."

"So why leave?" Jonathan sweeps in to ask Max.

I hear a pause, or maybe a stall, as she quickly tries to answer. "I needed a change and, of course, there came an offer I might not be able to refuse," Max says, smiling at my mother.

"Shots!" Jeff yells. Thank God! He sets the tray down on the table gently and begins to hand out the clear shots of Patrón. Straight man-juice. It puts hair on the chest and grows balls for the weak—just what the doctor prescribed in a room full of night-prowlers.

My mother raises her shot glass, and we all follow. "To prospering relationships and new ties that may bring us great wealth and much happiness. To Maxine!" she finishes and throws back the power liquid.

"To Maxine!" we all follow in unison.

The Patrón glides down my throat, leaving a trail of blazing fire behind. I feel warm and tingly inside. I glace over to Max, and her cheeks are now a light pink. She looks slightly embarrassed—or maybe just a little warm from the liquor.

Max and I lock eyes for a split second, and then she looks away. I glance around to see if anyone saw it, but it doesn't seem so.

"Maxine, I'm Jeff," Jeff says, holding out his hand across the table with his most charming smile. What a dick. I see he's already trying to ruffle my feathers. "I've been part of the Saunders family since middle school. I hope to have the chance to work under you. I've heard some good things from Kyle here." He gives me a noogie, purposely trying to embarrass me. I am *so* beating his ass for this.

"Have you?" Max asks, bemused. She looks to me with a sexy ass grin, and I think my cheeks have now turned a light shade of pink.

I wrap my arm around Jeff and squeeze his shoulder extra tight. "Don't mind Jeff, here. He's a major brown-noser. A kiss-ass, if you will."

Jonathan laughs out loud and takes another swig of his beer. "These two boys are something else. Hey, Kyle, I see Beth over there. It looks like she's trying to get your attention." He turns to Max. "Throw a bunch of kids together in a workplace and, in no time, they couple up," he tells her.

What the fuck is this dude's problem? I clench my teeth together in order to keep myself from opening my mouth.

He looks at me. "How long have you two been dating now?" he asks me.

My whole body stiffens. "We're not."

Jonathan chuckles. "Man, I forgot how it is to be twenty. When I was your age, I was blowing through women, too."

"Is that right?" Max asks him. "They say some things never change." She shakes her head, and my mother laughs along with her.

Way to go, Mom. Way to stick up for your son!

"No, you're wrong about that. It only takes one woman to come along and change a man's ways," Jonathan says to Max, *clearly* trying charm her. Well, his charming sucks!

"That must have been what your wife did, huh?" I throw in there.

He sneers at me, completely catching on to what is happening. "That's *ex*-wife, and yes, it was something like that."

Jeff grabs my shoulder and squeezes. "I think it's time for another shot, bro. Come on, it's on me. Let's go to the bar."

"Nah, I'm good." I know he's just trying to get me out of a situation before I insert my foot in my mouth. Jonathan still has seniority at work and is technically one of my bosses.

"I need another drink, son, before I call it a night." My mother raises her glass with one brow lifted as to tell me to leave—now. I take the hint and walk to the bar.

CHAPTER FOUR

I watch Kyle walk away with his friend Jeff, and I start to feel a little unsettled and a little curious. I could feel the testosterone building up between him and Jonathan. It's sort of entertaining to watch. Kyle gets hot-tempered quickly when he's feeling threatened. Whether he feels threatened by Jonathan because of me or just in general, that's still to be determined.

Without realizing it, I am watching Kyle intently at the bar. He's already glanced back at me a couple of times. I get butterflies in my stomach each time our eyes connect. As I stand in deep thought, Jonathan is trying to get my attention. "Uh, Maxine?" I can hear in the distance.

I snap out of it. "Yes?"

"How long will you be here in town?" he asks.

"Yes, are you planning on heading back as soon as your decision is made?" Connie chimes in.

"I thought I would stay a couple of weeks. If I decide to stay, I'll need to go house shopping before I head back and pack up."

"Well you let me know if you need any help. I know a couple of great realtors," Connie offers.

"Actually, I have a really good friend that shows houses, and I would be more than happy to take you around to look. I'm sure you'll need more than just one day to get the lay of the land," Jonathan offers.

I take a sip of my beer. He's actually really sweet for offering and kind of cute, too, in that Clark Kent sort of way. Not quite my type. Maybe it will be nice to have a friend that I'm not attracted to.

"Okay, sounds great, Jonathan! Thanks to both of you for offering to help. And Connie, this welcome has been warm and thoughtful. Everyone at the agency is very nice."

"I am so glad to hear that. Greg is so happy to have you here. He's been a pain in my ass getting everything perfect for you," Connie admits with a smile.

My eyes drift to Kyle quickly, and I see Beth leaning into him, extremely close and intimately. This time Kyle doesn't look so disinterested. He actually looks intrigued and willing to take the bait. I snap my eyes off of him and look back to Connie.

I've only just met Kyle today. He's still a child for Christ's sake. Why in the *hell* do I feel burned and slightly jealous of the sight of them together? This is freaking ridiculous! Of course he has a couple drinks and is interested in the first thing that strolls up and puts her chest in his face. He's freaking twenty-something! That's what boys do at that age, and the fact that I am even contemplating this is insane. He's nine years younger than me.

My phone rings. I look at the caller ID; it's Cody. My heart drops. Cody is my ex-fiancé who I left in the dust. I didn't even tell him I was leaving. I know that was wrong; I feel some guilt over that, but I also feel free. I can breathe now. I immediately ignore his call. It's not the time or place to answer.

"Well, tell Greg I said thank you. I really appreciate it."

"Greg's a good man. Whatever you need, he'll get it. I've known him personally for a while now. He actually recruited me just like he did you. Of course, I didn't have my own agency, but I worked for one of the best," Jonathan explains.

"Oh yeah? What agency were you at?" I ask.

I look back toward the bar and see Jeff conversing with the bartender, but Kyle and Elizabeth are no longer there. I glance around the rest of the bar, and they're nowhere in sight. My gut drops just a little with disappointment. Oh well, time to move on from this little crush. Just get over it, Max.

"I was at the Bailey Agency."

I finish my beer. "Wow! The one in New York City, right?"

"Yup, that's the one."

"They have two others, right?"

Connie jumps in. "Yes, there's one in Los Angeles and one in Miami. I think they're expanding even more and heading internationally, from what I've heard."

My eyes pop. "Really? Greg must have given you the deal of your life to give up a spot in that type of booming agency," I say with a laugh.

Both Connie and Jonathan chuckle as well. "Back then,

it was just the New York agency. They hadn't expanded yet. That happened about two years ago," Jonathan says. "I was already well-invested in the Saunders Agency," he finishes and lifts up his beer toward Connie.

"Well, since my son seems to have disappeared and never brought me my drink, I think it's time for me to hit the road. I'm sure Greg is still at the office, so I'll have to do some convincing to get his butt home," Connie jokes.

We say our goodbyes, and she heads out the front door. Jonathan offers me another drink, so I take him up on his offer. Why not? I'll just be heading off to an empty, lonely hotel room.

"So, Kyle said you're married or, I'm sorry, you *were* married—"

I watch as he ponders a moment. In the background, I can hear the jukebox playing Hinder's "Better Than Me." The words bring Cody to my mind; he loved Hinder. But as fast as I can blink, he's removed from my thoughts.

"Yes, I am. We're actually in the middle of a pretty rough divorce. I thought she was the love of my life, but I found out she was having an affair."

"Oh my gosh! I am *so* sorry to hear that." A wave of sadness rushes over me. I can almost see him in a whole new light. He's a survivor of sorts. He looks heartbroken.

"Thanks. I'm coping the best way I know how. We were married ten years, and we have two beautiful daughters. They haven't been coping very well." His heads droops just a little. I want to hold him and comfort him. I almost forget

I've only known him a couple of hours now.

"Yes, that must be rough on them. My parents got divorced when I was a teenager. It was the hardest time in my life, watching them fight and having my life torn apart. If I can give you any advice it would be to keep the routine as normal as possible and find a way to get along for the children's sake. There's nothing worse than seeing your parents go at each other's throat," I tell him.

"That's very true. I just want what's best for them. Have you been married or have any kids?" he asks, turning the tables on to me. I freeze up for a moment, caught off-guard. I haven't had many people ask those questions before.

I chug the rest of my beer and slam the bottle down a little too hard. "Nope. I've never been married and no kids."

He looks surprised. "*Wow*. I'm shocked. A beautiful woman like you—I was sure someone had snagged you up."

I blush just a little. I have to admit, he can definitely put on the charm. If I was attracted to him, I just may have fallen for it. "No. Came close once, but didn't work out. I'm married to my work, and that's probably been my downfall. Men don't seem to like take-charge, independent women."

"Oh, I beg to differ," he says.

I smile, but also realize this conversation is just getting a little too personal. I'm definitely at fault for this one. I should have kept the personal questions to a minimum. I look at the clock on the wall and realize it's almost eight o'clock. I've been here way longer than I anticipated.

"Well, it's getting pretty late, and I have a day's worth of information to go over."

"Let me walk you out then," Jonathan says, standing up from his seat.

I nod my head in agreement. My car is parked on the darker side of the building, so I'm thankful for his offer. We head out the side door. I bundle up as I push the door open. As soon as I step out of the door, I am greeted by two lovebirds making out against the building. I clear my throat to warn them of my presence, and just as Jonathan follows behind, placing his hand on the small of my back, the man's head lifts up and meets my gaze. I pause but quickly gather my composure. It's Kyle, with Elizabeth's body wrapped around his and his hands all over her. She gives me a look of pure satisfaction and triumph. Him, not so much.

This is nothing out of the ordinary in a bar setting. I think I had just hoped or thought for one split second that we had a connection of some sort. That maybe for one moment he was attracted to a woman like me—a woman that's almost ten years his senior. It made me feel young again, and a little badass, but I should have known. I must be getting old if I can't even read a man's vibes correctly.

Kyle immediately removes his hands, straightening himself up, and begins to unglue her body from his. I reach my car and turn to thank Jonathan. He gives me a quick kiss on the cheek, and I get into my car. As I pull away from my parking spot, I realize I am being watched. I shake my head, reminding myself to get over my "boy crush," and I continue to drive off. Tomorrow's a new day. I have a big decision to make ahead of me, and I'll be damned if I'll allow my schoolgirl hormones to cloud my judgment.

CHAPTER FIVE

Kyle

Shit! *Shit!* I can't believe I just allowed this to happen. What the hell was I thinking, locking lips with Beth? I knew I should have laid off on those shots. Now I have awaken the clinger and given her more of a reason to latch on. And then there's Max. *Damn!*

I don't know why it's bothering me so much, but the fact that she just saw me in that predicament is killing me. Why the hell do I care so much? I saw her eyes. I saw something that I recognized as disappointment.

I begin to walk toward her before she drives off, but Beth stops me. She grips my upper arm and pulls me back.

"Hey, where are you going? Your car is over there," she says, pointing to the main parking lot.

I watch as Max pulls off, and when I can't see her taillights any longer, I begin to walk to my car. Beth follows. I turn to stop her dead in her tracks. "Where are you parked?"

"I thought I would go home with you—"

I shake my head. "No, Beth. I'm sorry. I should have never—"

"Never what? Never put your tongue down my throat? Put your hands all over my body?" she finishes, crossing her arms and putting all of her weight on one foot.

I sigh. "Yes. We shouldn't have done that. It was the drinks. I'm sorry." I turn to open my car door. I hear her huff, turn, and stomp off to her car.

The night didn't end up how I expected. And watching Jonathan with his hands all over Max really pissed me off. Where does that dude get off? He's still freaking married. I'll be damned if he's going to get his claws into her.

I do have to admit, I feel a little guilty about Beth. But she threw herself at me—what does she expect? Does she expect me to marry her because of a kiss and some wandering hands? She already banged Matt, one of my coworkers, just a month ago to get me jealous. Did she really think having someone else inside her was going to make me want her back? Disgusting.

In order for me to get any sort of chance with Max now, I'm going to have to work overtime. This might just be impossible, considering how classy she seems to be. She's not just some normal girl. She's a woman, a woman with purpose and charge. A woman who likes to be in control instead of being controlled.

I'm not too sure how I feel about that, considering I'm always the one holding all the cards, but this change might be exhilarating and, honestly, a bit of a turn-on. I think in this case I just might allow her to think she holds all the reins. This should be interesting to see played out. I can't wait to mention my plan to Jeff. He's going to get a kick out of all this.

I pull up to my apartment and turn off the ignition.

Before I step out of my car, I see headlights pulling up behind me through my rearview mirror. The car parks right next to mine. I look over and see Beth. My stomach drops. This is *not* good.

I step out of my car and walk around to her driver side window. "What are you doing here, Beth?" I ask, completely aggravated.

A tear slides down her cheek. Great. I hate seeing a girl cry. I never know what to do or say, and I always panic. I'm sure she's counting on this reaction.

"I don't know. I was driving and I ended up here. I just want an explanation. What did I do that's so wrong? We were so close, and then you just pushed me away without even explaining why," she answers. Tears are now flowing steadily down her cheeks.

I run my hand over the top of my head, stalling to come up with a reply. I can't just pinpoint *one* thing she did. It was just a feeling that came over me. She just wasn't the one, and once I realized this, everything about her began to bother me. Instead of hurting her feelings, I just distanced myself, and that's when her other side came out. A side I never saw, a side that she obviously kept hidden from me so I wouldn't think she was crazy. Well, too late now, because I've already seen and witnessed the real her—and it's not pretty.

Now, seeing her here uninvited and crying just proves to me that I made the right decision. I don't care how fucking hot she is—and she is *smoking*—it's a complete turn-off.

Once I'm turned off, there is no turning me back on.

It's clear that I am going to have to be abrupt and a little painful in order to get my point across this time. "Listen Beth, we just aren't right for each other. I don't want to be in a relationship right now. You have to just accept it. We are *not* going to be together," I say, raising my voice. "Like I said before, I'm sorry for earlier. It was the liquor. I know that's no excuse, but it's the truth. That's all I got for you," I say.

I wait quietly for her response as she thinks it over. She looks up at me as though the devil has just entered her body. Oh no! This is *not* good. "You told me I was special! You told me you cared for me!"

"Beth, I *did* care for you. I didn't lie, but I realized we just weren't meant to be! Just accept it and move on! I mean, geez, you even fucked my friend Matt for God's sake! You're fucking crazy!" I yell.

Normally, yelling at a girl is something I am extremely against, but enough is enough. I don't know how else to get it through her crazy, thick head. She's left me no choice.

"I'm not *crazy* Kyle. I'm hurt. There's a difference! Matt meant nothing to me. I was upset and he comforted me. That's it."

I throw my arms up. "I don't care! I don't care who or what you fuck or why you fucked, ok? Just leave me the fuck alone! I can't believe this has even gotten to this point," I scream.

She slams her car in reverse. I back up. "You're such a

dick, Kyle. This isn't over! You and I are not over!" She pounds her foot on the gas to back up and takes off at full speed. Her wheels screech like nails on a chalkboard through the night.

I blow out a deep breath and head to my door. This is just crazy. I've never in my life been through this or have had to deal with girls like this. I might just have to talk with my mother about all of this if it doesn't get any better. My mother will go on a firing rampage.

I just need a good night's sleep. And thank goodness my apartment is still cozy and warm. This has been one hell of a day. Good and bad.

CHAPTER SIX

I spent a long part of the night going over the Saunders Literary Agency company policies. In order to combine our companies together, there are a few things that will have to be changed for it to work. My company is small, nowhere near the size of this one, but that's only because I have always been against partners. I've always liked to have full control over all decisions. I like to do things my way, without any conflict or opinions butting in. Let's face it, partnering is all about compromise, and I've never handled giving in very well. That could be why I was a horrible fiancée.

I've done a lot of thinking over the past couple of months, though. I love my clients. They are *very* loyal and most of them have been with me since day one, but I want better for them. With a bigger company comes bigger opportunities, and because I have been limited to the number of clients I can take on, I've been limited in the amount of talent I am able to help prosper. That's why I'm in this business.

So with that being said, I've thought long and hard about change. I am willing to change for the better of me and the better of my clients. They trust me. I have already spoken one-on-one with each of them privately, and almost all of them are looking forward to this collaboration.

I am growing as a person and learning how to accept compromise. *Wow*. I can't believe that I'm thinking this way. Never in a million years would I have expected it, but it sort of feels good. And by joining such an amazing company like Saunders Literary Agency, I think this might just be an easy transition. Let's not forget about the eye candy I'm about to encounter on a daily basis! Shit! I told myself I was going to leave that situation alone. I'll have to get better at that.

My phone rings. Ugh! I look at the number and immediately relax. It's Kinsey, my assistant.

"Hey, girl! How's the home front?" I ask.

She sighs. "Busy. How was the first day?"

"Oh my God, you sound like a mother should," I say with a laugh. "It was busy. I'm going over the proposal now."

I hear her clap. "Is it worth the move?" she questions.

"Um, yes, very worth it. You would definitely be getting a promotion along with more job responsibilities. Are you up for that?"

In a high-pitched voice, she answers, "Hell yeah! Count me in!"

"Okay, let me get back to this. I have to be up early. Oh, and give J.P. Dover a call. He had some things to go over with the editors, and he wants you to be on the call as well."

"Will do! Talk with you tomorrow."

I head into my second day of meetings and conferences. I have this stupid rental with no electric start, and it's less than forty degrees out this morning. How am I doing? Thank goodness for the hotel's complimentary coffee. I slept horrible. Tossed and turned all night. Without this, I would be one bitchy mess.

I head through the agency's doors and say hello to the adorable receptionist, Elise. She is, without a doubt, shy and lacks confidence. Sadly, this just radiates off of her. She clearly underestimates how beautiful she actually is. Yes, she's a little bit of a plain Jane, but I don't think anyone's actually taken the time to help her find her inner self, her inner Goddess.

We as women all have that "it" factor, but sometimes it's just hidden under a protective coat just as an oyster shell hides a pearl. I went through it. Growing up, I was a tomboy. I came home from school every day with dirty fingernails and scuffed-up knees. I never played with the girls. I would rather catch snakes and hold frogs than play house and dress Barbie dolls.

I have one older brother, Luke, and one younger brother, Justin. So being surrounded by boys was a given. My mother was too busy on social lunches and shopping sprees to spend any time with me. That meant I was left in the care of my older brother; make-up and dresses weren't part of the deal. Honestly, I didn't care during my younger years, because I didn't know what I was missing.

As I got older, things began to change. My body began to change as I went through that awkward phase that all teens seem to go through. The girls at school became mean, and I became a social outcast because I dressed and acted like a boy. It wasn't until college when I met my roommate, Kinsey, that I began to blossom.

I remember the first day we met. I was setting up my side of the dorm, wearing sweats and an oversized, grungy T-shirt when she came strolling in—Miss Pretty-in-Pink with fair skin and blond hair. I almost threw up in my mouth. I was ready to switch dorm rooms with someone else right then and there.

Kinsey Balterson looked me up and down in disgust, clucked her tongue at me, and shook her head. She said, without hesitation, "We need to work on you immediately. When I fix you up, men aren't going to know what hit them."

To this day, we still laugh over that. She fixed me, all right. She brought out my inner Goddess and made me a diva! And man was she right about the boys! Most of all, though, she gave me confidence and the power to face the world head-on. After years of being torn down throughout high school, she was exactly what I needed. To this day, we are still best friends.

So maybe it's time I gave a little back and helped another sister on the road to Goddess-hood.

"Good morning, Elise," I say with a warm smile.

She looks up at me, seeming a little surprised that I

remembered her name. "Good morning, Miss Daniels."

She buzzes me in, and I head to my temporary office. It's quiet; there's very little action going on in the office at seven thirty in the morning, which I like. I work better in an office setting. It grounds me and forces me to concentrate. At home, I tend to get distracted easy. That's why I pretty much lived at the office back home, making it difficult to spend time on my relationship with Cody, but for whatever reason, he stayed and was willing to work around it. He'd bring the candlelight dinners to me at the office constantly.

I get startled from the knock at the door. I look up and see Kyle leaning against the doorjamb. When I look at the clock, it's already eight thirty. I've been in major work mode and completely lost track of time.

Butterflies begin to flutter in my stomach, but I force myself to stomp them down. "Good morning, Kyle. What can I do for you?" I keep my tone strictly business.

He smiles. My insides melt. "My mother told me to come grab you so we can head over to the conference room. I thought you might want to grab some coffee first."

I close my laptop and grab my company coffee mug I was given yesterday. Before walking around my desk, I straighten out my skirt and pull down my blazer. When I look up, Kyle is watching me intently. I feel heat creep through my cheeks, but I refuse to show him he has affected me one bit. I hold my chin high and look straight ahead.

"Okay, let's go. I'll grab my laptop on the way back," I tell him.

I keep my distance, making sure not to rub against him or get close enough to enter his personal space. This is the only way I can assure myself that our energies won't meld into each other. Once that happens, I'm afraid all hope will be lost.

"Did you enjoy yourself last night?" Kyle asks. He doesn't play around. He gets right to it.

As we walk, I look at everything but him. I figure this is a good way for me to see the faces of the employees who may be working under me. "Yes, I did actually. Your mother is great, and Jonathan was extremely friendly and welcoming," I answer blandly.

"You can say that again—" Kyle says under his breath.

I look at him this time. "What was that?" I ask.

"I'm glad you had a good time," he lies. "We go there every Monday and Thursday to get some release. It can be intense around here, so it's a good way to wind down during the week."

"Most agencies as prospering as your parents' get intense," I add. "How about you? You looked like you were having a good time. Is locking lips with coworkers a normal escapade for someone your age?" Yup, I just inserted my foot into my mouth.

Kyle realizes what I've just asked him and smirks. Did I sound jealous? I must have because he looks as though he's enjoying my jealousy. "Uh yeah, about that—I was a little mortified by my actions at the end of the night. I'm sorry you had to see that. I guess I just drank a little too much," he explains.

"No, no. You don't owe me an explanation. Believe me, I do remember being your age once upon a time; it's just that sometimes I tend to forget. I've been in the adult world so long that I forget what it's like to be carefree. Please, don't apologize for it. I sort of envy you for it," I admit.

"How's that?"

Before I can answer, we enter the kitchen and it is jam-packed. The first person I see upon entering the room is Elizabeth, and she sees us. She's made direct eye contact. Kyle and I are clearly on her radar, so before things get any more awkward, I walk past him to grab my coffee.

CHAPTER SEVEN

Kyle

I watch in slow motion as Beth gives me that grimy look she gives when she's about to do something disastrous. She then walks over to Max and begins a conversation, fake smiles and all. This is not good. After last night, I have no idea what she is capable of. I'm afraid to even find out, but I have a sick inkling that she's about to show me.

I pour my coffee while watching the two of them laughing through my peripheral vision. It looks to me that Beth is trying to get into Max's good graces for some reason or another. Just yesterday, Beth was sizing her up, and now she is trying to be all buddy-buddy with her. What is she trying to accomplish?

I walk over to the two of them, chuckling like hyenas. "Good morning, Beth," I greet her without so much as looking at her. "Max, are you ready to get going? The meeting should be starting any minute—"

She says goodbye to Beth and joins me out the door.

"Wow, you two looked like you were hitting it off," I comment, expecting an answer.

"Yes, girl talk. A good pair of shoes can get any two girls talking in no time," she jokes.

I like this side of her. When she's not concentrating on her every word and rehearsing everything she wants to say in her head before she says it, she radiates a warm invitation to hear the real her. I wonder if she even realizes she does this or if it's just a habit she's turned into a trait. I think the only time I've had to rehearse what I was going to say was when I was high on the ganja during my younger years. Other than that, I've mastered just letting it flow. Sometimes my words flow too fluently without thinking, which never seems to work in my favor.

"Yes, those are some killer shoes," I joke back.

She smiles but looks away. "Thank you."

We stop into her office first to grab her laptop, and then we head over to the conference room. Everyone is just filing in. Junior, of course, is already sitting next to my father at the head of the table. I get left sitting five seats down and jealousy kicks in, but when Max takes the seat next to me, all aggravation is gone. My brother can keep his seat as long as it means breathing in this intoxicating aroma of hers all day long.

By the time the meeting is breaking, it's already lunchtime. My father takes Max out to lunch, along with my mother and Jonathan. Every nerve in my body is screaming to invite myself along, but I stop myself. I know it's just business, and the last thing I want to do is put my parents on alert.

I head out with Jeff to grab something to eat. I haven't spoken with him since he left the bar, and I need to talk with someone about Beth's crazy activity last night.

We get to Wise Guys and order some burgers. I didn't realize how starving I was until I stepped in and smelled that delicious smell.

We take a seat with our drinks.

"Dude, I have to tell you about last night!" I say. "This chick is *crazy*!"

"Wait, you mean Beth?"

"Yeah, man."

Jeff leans in closer. "When I left, you guys were lip-locked. How can that possibly turn out bad?"

I shake my head and sip my pop. "Max walked out and saw us. After that, I realized I was messing up and told Beth to go home."

"Dude—"

"Yeah, man. I know. What was I thinking sending her home, huh?"

Our number comes up, and I grab the tray. We both take some huge bites of double-loaded burgers, and I continue.

"I pulled up to my apartment, and she showed up right after. She was crying and begging, asking why I did this and why I did that," I say with a loud sigh.

"Bro, you said she was a stage-five clinger. I can't stand chicks like that."

"I haven't even told you the best part—when I told her it was over, she told me it wasn't and drove off like a madwoman."

Jeff throws his hands up and busts out laughing. "Aww man! You are in some trouble! You must have gave it to her real good. I should just call you Magic Mike from now on!" he laughs, cracking himself up. I'm not laughing. "Okay, okay, sorry bro! I shouldn't be laughing. This is some serious shit. What are you going to do?" he asks.

I lean my elbows on the table and put my head in my hands. "I don't know, man. I have no idea."

"Just tell the boss-woman. She'll can her butt and voila—problem over with!"

"Believe me, I've already thought of that. But it doesn't sit well with me. She's got bills to pay, too. I don't want that hanging over my conscience," I tell him.

We're finished, and we pack up to leave. Jeff pats me on the back on the way out to the car. "I wouldn't worry about it. She'll get the hint eventually. Let me know if you need anything or need me to come cuddle with you."

I catch his arm with my fist as he tries to run off. "Real funny, fuckface!"

This kid kills me. There's never a dull moment with him.

CHAPTER EIGHT

Max

Lunch was all business. Not what I really wanted after a morning full of work, but it was still enjoyable. I think Greg and Connie are going to be great partners. We went over all my concerns this morning and the things I need added or want changed in the policies. I went over all the concerns my clients have, too, and I think they're going to be happy with the results.

Compromise most definitely came into play. I had to choose my battles, and I'm happy with the ones I chose. This decision was a hard one, but this morning's meeting is making it much easier to accept. Let's just hope the rest of the week plays out as good. I may be hitting the goldmine here.

I stroll back in the office, waving to Elise as she buzzes me in. I have no choice but to pass Kyle's desk on the way to my office. Jeff is hanging over Kyle's cubicle wall, and when I pass by, their conversation quiets. I wave to say hello and continue walking.

That wasn't awkward, now was it? There's only one reason they would have quieted down when I walked by, and that's because their conversation was about me. I can't believe I even give a damn, but there's just something about Kyle that makes me care. Maybe I should just fuck him and get it over with. Maybe it's just sexual tension, and if we can get that out of the way, I can get him off my mind.

I hear a knock at the door, and when I look up this time, it's Junior.

"Hi Junior, what can I do for you?"

He looks around and then quietly closes the door. I begin to feel a little unsettled. This has to be something major if he needs to close the door. We barely know each other, so I'm preparing myself for anything.

"Please, have a seat," I ask, pointing to the chair in front of my desk.

I wait for him to speak. "Maxine, I know that maybe this isn't my place, but I'm going to say it anyway because he is my brother. I see the way he looks at you, and I know what comes next. He's not ready for commitment, and he's definitely not ready for someone like you."

My brows furrow. "Someone like me?" I ask, a little confused.

"Yes. A beautiful, knowledgeable, all-around catch. Regardless, you're taking a big step in your career, and I don't want to see it ruined because of my brother. So, I know you may have never considered him as anything more than a coworker, but I'm just giving you a heads up anyway. I know my brother, and I know he will make a move on you," he says.

I sit for a moment, soaking in what he has said, and I'm really not sure how to respond. "Junior, I really appreciate the warning, but I can assure you the only relationship your brother and I will have is that of coworkers. Nothing more, nothing less."

He nods his head, taking in my response. He smiles and stands, but before he exits my office, he asks that the conversation remain within these walls. I agree, and he leaves. That was not the kind of discussion I was expecting.

I can't move. I keep replaying the conversation in my head, trying to see if maybe I misunderstood him. Maybe I'm going crazy and this conversation didn't even happen. But it did, and trying to believe it didn't isn't going to change anything.

I just can't help but feel his brother is wrong about him. Something tells me his brother doesn't really know him at all. Kyle's allowed to have fun, allowed to be a player. He's twenty-four, for God's sake. If it's anyone's problem, it should be the girls who get involved with him. They've got to know at least a little of what they're getting into. I bet they just decide not to look or listen to the signs.

CHAPTER NINE

Kyle

"Man, did you see that ass on her? Holy cow, man!" Jeff remarks as he follows her with his eyes and bites his pointer finger.

I slap the finger out of his mouth. "Dude, she's gonna hear you!" I screech quietly.

"The only thing I'm going to say is—Beth who?" he says. I crack up. He's killing me.

"Later, man." I wave him off.

I get out of my seat to head to the kitchen for a drink. I have a perfect view of Max's office door. At the moment, it's closed, which seems a little strange. Usually if something important needs to be discussed, it's either handled in my dad's office or the conference room. Before I turn the corner to the kitchen, I catch a glimpse of Junior leaving her office. I halt dead in my tracks. I'm gonna freaking *kill* him! I know *exactly* what he's up to. He's such a little bitch! I can't believe he is doing this to me again!

I turn around and storm right into his office, almost slamming the door shut behind me. It's a good thing his office is the last one down the hall. Only a handful of people are able to view it.

"What the *hell* were you doing in her office, Junior?" I yell. At this point, I don't even care who hears me. I am so sick of him butting into my life!

He stands up, throwing his chair back. It hits the wall with a loud bang. "Someone's got to warn her about you. You're out of control, Kyle. I see the way you look at her like a piece of meat, and I'll be damned if I'm going to sit by and watch you ruin something Mom and Dad have been working so hard for—or sit and watch you ruin Maxine!" Junior says with a snarl.

I get right up to his desk, leaning over so I am face-to-face with him. I can feel his hot breath against my face. "You don't know shit! Keep your fucking business to yourself and leave my name out of your mouth!"

I must have been louder than I thought because my mom comes rushing in, closing the door tightly behind her. "What is going on here, you two? You have the whole office in an uproar!" she screeches in a whisper.

Neither of us answers; we just hold the death stare between us.

"Fine! If you two won't talk about it, then maybe I should have your father come in here. Is that what the two of you want?" she asks with her arms folded and her badass "mom glare."

Junior cracks first. "There's no need for that, Mom. I promise this won't happen again. *Right*, Kyle?" he says with eyes like daggers.

I glare back at him. "Right."

"Then I suggest you two gather your composure and meet us back in the conference room." She leaves the office and closes the door behind her.

I turn around to face him again. "Just stay out of my life," I demand before I walk out.

I hear the whispers and can feel the eyes on me as I walk down the hall from Junior's office. It's clear that this will be the talk of the day, but I honestly couldn't give two fucks. My brother has done this all my life. He's never on my side; he's always against me. I've never been able to pinpoint it—whether it's jealousy or hatred or a little of both.

He's always been on the straight and narrow, even as a kid. He did as he was asked—nothing more, nothing less—and always aimed to please. I was the complete opposite: free-spirited and continuously learning everything the hard way. Rules were never an option for me, and when I was told "no," it only made me want it that much more. I think he's always resented me for it. Because of my bad behavior, I was constantly getting the attention; even though it wasn't good attention, it was attention, plain and simple.

Once I cleaned up my act and decided to go off to college, I think that was the happiest I've ever seen my brother. He was able to be seen again without any distractions. He had my parents' undivided attention and obviously took full advantage of it career-wise. Even though I now have a piece of paper to show that I know what I'm doing in this business, he has the experience. And now, I almost feel the tables have turned a little; I sort of envy him now.

I head into the conference room and take my seat next to Max again. I can feel the thick tension around us, and once Junior enters the room, it magnifies by ten. We spend the next couple of hours going over numbers and statistics. I have to admit, by the time the meeting is over, my head is spinning. I don't know how people do this all day.

By six o'clock, almost everyone has left the building. It's quiet; there's only a small humming noise coming from the voices that are still here. I punch out on my time clock and shut my computer down. I take a quick glance toward Max's office and can see her back to work already. I almost want to stop by before I take off just to see her for a split second, but I think twice and head out.

Working with my family just may be the death of me.

CHAPTER TEN

The last couple of days have been packed. By the time I get back to the hotel, it is a little past midnight. The lobby is alive and vivacious on a perfect Friday night. Laughter and conversations are flowing, and there is dancing throughout the halls. Even though I am exhausted, it feels a little magical. Couples are holding hands and groups of friends are hyped up and ready for a fun night out on the town. The buzz is almost addicting.

Once I close the door to my room, all sound and reality disappears. I power off my phone and all connection to the outside world, and I'm sucked into my cave, burying myself under my covers for a much-needed sleep. I don't care what it takes; I am sleeping in tomorrow morning.

I crack my eyes open in the morning and glance at the alarm clock next to my bed. It's now eleven thirty. The room is still dark, with slices of light creeping through the curtains. I feel as tired as I did when I laid my head down. These damn beds. Now I understand what people mean when they say they're homesick. I wouldn't care where I was, though, as long as my bed was there with me.

I forgot I turned off my phone last night. When I power it on, it sounds like the coin board on the *Super Mario Brothers* game. It's ringing and dinging non-stop. I go through my text messages and see one from an unfamiliar number. I open it and see that it's a text from Kyle. Shit! He's going to be here in an hour and a half. Look at me: I'm a hot mess!

I spring out of bed and immediately jump into the shower. I turn it to boiling hot, standing for a moment and letting the hot water hit the back of my neck. I'm trying to relieve all my tension from the week and lack of sleep. It feels wonderful. Just what I need.

Today's temperature is in the low forties. It's sunny, but looks are deceiving—especially in Rochester. This weather is definitely something I'm going to need to get used to. I'm going to have to go on a major cold-weather-clothing shopping spree if I decide to move here for good.

I finish with my makeup and hair. Today, I'm going with a nude, natural look for my makeup with large, loose curls. This hair will look cute with my beige winter cap and my tan boots. I hear a knock at the door. My stomach drops. I take one last look in the mirror before answering.

I glance through the peephole and take one last deep breath. I have no idea why I'm so nervous. I feel like a teenager going on a date for the very first time.

I open the door. He looks adorable. I'm breathless. Speechless. He's holding two steaming coffees, and he's wearing a smile to die for. "Are you ready?" he asks, handing me a coffee.

I take it, closing my eyes and smelling the rich, awakening aroma. "Mmm, this is just what I needed." I open my eyes back up, and he's watching me intently.

"Wow, you need to be in a coffee commercial. After what I just witnessed, people would be stomping over each other to get a mug of that," he jokes. I blush. "You might want to put on a scarf. It looks warm but the wind chill is killer."

I turn back into my room and add a scarf to my neck. He smiles, satisfied. We head out of the hotel to his car in the parking lot. "So where are you taking me?" I ask, taking a sip of my delicious coffee.

"Well, since it's freezing out, that knocks out any outdoor activity. So I was thinking something more indoors." We reach his car, and he opens the door for me. We lock eyes for a moment. I can feel something stirring deep inside of me; I look away, tucking myself into the car.

"That narrows it down," I reply sarcastically.

He chuckles, snapping his seatbelt. "What would be your most ideal day spent inside?" he asks.

I squint my eyes and tighten my lips in thinking mode. My most ideal day spent inside, huh? Oh there are a *bunch* of things I think we could do inside, and those thoughts should be illegal. I should be arrested for all the naughtiness that's running through my mind right now!

I look over at him, and he is waiting patiently with a big smirk on his face. "What?" I ask. What does he thinks so funny?

"You. Do you always think before you speak?" He starts the ignition and backs out of the parking spot.

I'm a little perplexed. "Do I? Well, you did ask me a question, so it makes sense to think of the right answer."

"Touché," he says. "But you tend to do that a lot. It's really fascinating to watch. I can almost read your thoughts sometimes."

Huh. Weird. I guess I do tend to do that a lot.

I turn toward him. "Okay, what am I thinking right now?" I'm totally being a smartass now.

He keeps his eyes on the road, but occasionally glances over to me. In those quick moments, my breath halts. "You're thinking I am one *fine* piece of ass," he says. I immediately burst out into a laugh. "That's funny, is it? Don't be embarrassed. They're just your thoughts," he adds. He seems pretty pleased with himself.

"*Wow!* Aren't we a little sure of ourselves? I'll admit, you made me laugh, but 'hot piece of ass'? I'm not so sure of that," I say, playing back. I shake my head. I still can't believe that just came out of his mouth. And speaking of that mouth, I'd like to nibble on it and claim it with mine.

This is a bad idea. I should have never asked him for his time.

"I see I might just have to change that mind of yours, won't I?"

"Oh no! I give in. You're right. You are one piece of fine ass!" I confess, both of us now snickering.

"So, back to my question—"

"I love museums, but I love the aquariums even more. Where I'm from, they have one of the biggest indoor aquariums. It's filled with all kinds of sharks, stingrays, and beautiful iridescent fish. I could stay and watch them for hours."

"Hmm, then you might just enjoy where I'm about to take you," he says, seeming a little relieved.

It's clear we're still in the downtown area. Aged buildings and skyscrapers are surrounding us, covering us under a blanket of shadow. Kyle pays the five-dollar parking fee to the attendant, and we head to the only building that's covered in large glass windowpanes. It looks out of place but still has some history to it.

"What is this place?" I ask.

He directs me to the front door, putting his hand on the small of my back and allowing me to enter first. "This is Rochester's gallery. It shows only local artists. Today, they're showing Tessa McLean. Her work is amazing. She went to school for marine biology but ended up following her passion, which is photography," he explains.

We begin to look around. The photos are breathtaking. I feel as though I'm right there in the water. The way she captured the beauty of these large powerful fish is incredible. The colors are brilliant and magnificent. I can't seem to tear my eyes away from them.

"She ended up combining the two, and this is the outcome of that," he adds.

We continue to walk around, looking from photo to photo, spending many minutes gazing and studying each and every one. I'm a little shocked. I wouldn't have expected this from him, something intellectual and mature. I thought we might end up at a jump house place or at the mall. But this, this is just awesome.

"She has some *amazing* talent. I've never seen anything quite like it. Do you know her?" I ask, still looking at the pieces.

He stands directly behind me, so close that I can feel his breath on my neck. The energy between us is increasing by the minute, engulfing me from head to toe. I stay completely still, not wanting to move an inch in fear I might melt at his feet. It's like he has some sort of hold over my body, and I'm losing all control.

"Kyle?" a small voice asks from behind, ripping us out of this vortex we seem to be falling in.

We both turn around. I see his face light up with recognition as he walks to embrace this girl. She giggles. She's beautiful and young. I taste a bit of bitterness in my mouth, a sliver of jealousy over her innocent youthfulness. It's clear they were close at one time or another, but how close is what I want to know.

After they release each other, she looks to me and then back at him. "Tessa, this is Max. Max this is Tessa." I now understand. She kindly shakes my hand.

"It's so nice to meet you. Your work is out of this world," I compliment her.

She smiles shyly. "Thank you. I'm so glad you like it."

I simmer my jealousy down to an ember. "Like it? I *love* it! How much do your pieces run?" I ask.

Her eyes grow wide. She looks at Kyle and then back at me. "Um, which one are you interested in?"

I know the exact photo. The moment I set eyes on it, it clicked. I bring her over to the piece. "This one. I don't want to part ways with it."

"Ah, yes. This one is my favorite as well. I was off the coast of Belize in Central America. They have the second largest reef in the world. There's this amazing spot called Shark Alley where this baby whale shark crossed my path. He was about fifteen feet long and was unbelievably magnificent! I'd never seen anything like it. I was lucky enough to get him on film—that's where this shot came from."

"Belize is actually on my bucket list of places to visit. Kyle said you travel all around the world for these shots?"

"Yes, I'm fortunate enough to have a great team behind me. We've traveled to some very remote places to capture the beauty that not many have experienced," she explains.

Despite my jealousy, I like her. Her charisma is pure and good. She hasn't been tainted by life or altered by lies. I can see this just by one meeting and a deep down feeling I get. She pours all this positive energy into her work by simply bringing out the beauty through a lens.

"By looking at the photos, I can only imagine."

Kyle has been kind enough to hang in the background, letting us converse with no interruptions.

"This photo I have priced at $7,500, but since you're a friend of Kyle's, I can give it to you for $5,000."

"Can you have it shipped? I actually am just here on business—"

Before I can finish my sentence, Kyle jumps in. "How about I keep it at my place until you make your decision about moving here. If you decide not to stay, I can ship it myself," he offers.

I stare at him for a moment, speechless. I'm not too sure if this is a set-up or just a kind gesture. Tessa waits quietly for my answer. "Um, yes, I think that should be fine," I respond, still unsure.

"Okay, great! I will have Stan wrap it up for you, or I could deliver it personally to your place, Kyle?" she offers. I see the lust in her eyes.

Oh hell no! Just because I like her does not mean I am going to play wingman to a hookup. "No, that's quite alright. You can wrap it up now," I answer.

She smiles. "It was great meeting you," she says to me. She turns to give Kyle a lingering kiss on the cheek. I pretend not to notice and walk over to the cashier to pay.

Once the photo is wrapped, Kyle carries it to his car. I follow. He's a gentleman—something you don't see often these days.

CHAPTER ELEVEN

Kyle

It was nice seeing Tessa. It's been a long time. We were friends back in high school—almost had a romance before leaving for college but never actually got the chance. Life kept getting in the way. I knew I would get that reaction from her, but what I wasn't expecting was Max's reaction. I did hope for that, though.

My answer was confirmed once Tessa offered to stop by my house. Max went on claiming-stakes mode. I laugh to myself because I'm not quite sure she even realized she did it.

I drive us back to my apartment to unload the artwork. It's an expensive piece, and I would hate for anything to happen to it. I run through my checklist in my head. Bed made? Check. Dishes done? Check. Kitchen clean? Check. Bathroom picked up and plugin inserted? Check. Phew! I think that about covers it. I just never know when I might bring somebody back to my pad, so it's always been important for me to keep up with the housecleaning.

"Here we are. Do you want to come up?" I ask. I'm expecting a no, but to my surprise she says yes.

I carry the art to the elevator and give her the keys to open my apartment door. I hear her gasp quietly. Not the response I was looking for.

"Is something wrong?"

She continues to look around. "No. I guess I was expecting something completely different."

"Different how?"

"I don't know. More like a bachelor pad: beer cans and pizza boxes strewn about. Maybe a messy bed and some dirty laundry on the floor."

She walks around and examines things, picking up knickknacks and putting them back. "I guess I'm not the average bachelor now, am I?"

I place the artwork against the wall in the living room.

She laughs. "No, I guess not."

"Do you want a beer? And yes, I do have beer in the refrigerator, but it's in a bottle, not a can," I say, teasing her. She laughs.

"Sure. I could go for an afternoon drink."

I pop the top and walk over to the window she is looking out of to hand her the beer. The view from my loft is sort of amazing. I'm on the top floor, which towers over most of the buildings in the area. In the mornings, the sun hits my window just so, and the whole place lights up. I had to buy the thickest drapes I could find to keep it out.

The evening sunsets are why I rented out this place. How could I pass up a view like that? The ladies love that sort of stuff. Plus, this building was just newly renovated. They stripped it and rebuilt it from scratch. It was calling my name.

We both take a nice long swig of beer. "This view is

definitely one-of-a-kind. I bet the girls love it, huh?" she teases again with an adorable, wicked smile.

I love it. I love when she lets her hair down. She's spunky and can take my bullshit. A match made in heaven.

"Well, you seem to."

She laughs. "Yes, yes I do. So, what else do you have in store for me today? I think we got side-tracked with the photo I bought."

I look back at the wrapped artwork against the wall. "That was a pretty big purchase."

"What can I say—when I like something, I get it. Plain and simple," she states, taking another swig. And what a statement it is. It's heavy and loaded with innuendo. Sounds like something I'd say. "I'm sorry. That sounded pretty bad, didn't it?" She blushes.

"No, it sounds like you know what you want in life. That's not a bad thing. Look at you; you're your own boss. Not many people can say they started up their own business and became highly successful at it."

Man, the way she licks those lips when she's looking at me is driving me insane. And those baby-blue eyes are such a magnetic force; I can't look away. She looks so sexy with her loose curls and tight jeans. It's nice to see her in something other than suits. I mean, the skirts are nice and the high pumps are even nicer, don't get me wrong. Now, if I could just get her to stay long enough to get to know her. This is a big step coming from someone like me.

"I know I sound like I have it all together, but believe

me, there are things I need to work on. So tell me, why your parents' agency and not some hot-shot agency in NYC?" She walks over and takes a seat on my brown leather sofa and motions for me to sit as well.

I take a seat at the other end and place my beer on the glass-top coffee table. "Honestly, I'd been away from my family for some years, only coming back on holidays. I graduated early because I packed my summer with classes." I see her studying me, watching my every move. "I figured it would be good to get some experience under my belt rather than starting from the bottom at another agency," I say.

"I think that was definitely a smart move. So, that's your plan? Where do you think you'll end up?" she asks.

"Boy, you're asking some tough questions." I feel put on the spot a little, but it's nice to talk real for a moment. The girls I usually bring back here don't want to do any sort of talking unless we're in bed.

I watch her face drop. "Oh, I'm sorry. I didn't mean to pry—"

I put my hand on her thigh and immediately I begin to tingle at my fingertips, all the way up my arm. "No, it's fine," I tell her, chuckling, trying to ignore the invasion of energy that's now swarming my body. I remove my hand, but it's still tingling. Things are now stirred awake by just that one touch. "I've thought about New York, but I think it just might be too fast-paced for me. I love the idea of the warmth of the South. Rochester's weather is just out of control."

"I'm understanding exactly what you mean," she says, shaking her head.

I grab my beer and lean back into the couch. "I guess it will come to me, eventually. In time, I will figure it out. I'm young."

"Yes. That you are," she agrees. "In woman years, I'm old. I should be married and on my way to having kids now."

"And is that something you want? To be married and have kids?" I'm not so sure why I'm interested in hearing the answer to this question, because usually when a girl brings this topic up, I avoid it or run. With Max, I'm intrigued.

"I think every girl my age thinks about it at least once or twice in their lives. I'm just too preoccupied with my business to dwell over it. I'm a workaholic. That equals bad girlfriend, wife, and mother material. If it happens, it happens," she says with a shrug.

I can't help but wonder if she's really okay with that. I guess the good thing is it seems as though she's not looking for anything serious, which is fine by me. I'm down with being friends with benefits.

"Well, to be honest, I feel the same way. So, why don't we cheers to a life of freedom and no boundaries," I say, holding up my beer. She laughs and we clink our bottles together.

We sit in silence for a moment. Not an awkward silence,

but an intense silence. The energy in the room has shifted again, and it's buzzing loudly around us. I see the recognition on her face, and I know that she can feel it too. My lips are aching to touch hers and my hands are itching to feel her. I have to rub my head with my hands just to keep them occupied and keep them from wandering over to her side of the couch.

I see her fiddle with her fingers as though she is doing the same. She's so beautiful in all the right ways. I no longer want to just fuck her. I want to caress her. I want to learn everything about her. I want to take my time on each and every part of her. And just by the look she is giving me right now, I can only imagine she may be feeling the same.

I'm new at this. I never had a deep urge for all that other stuff until right now, with her. Usually, I am the guy who says all the right things just to get into a girl's pants. And maybe my brother is right about my past behavior, but I'm not so sure Max would even let that fly—she's different. Yes, more mature than what I usually go for, but it has absolutely nothing to do with age.

"Are you hungry?" I ask, trying to concentrate on something other than what's running through my mind right now.

She flings her head back. "Ugh! Starving. I thought you would *never* ask."

I laugh. "Good, because I can cook a mean steak."

CHAPTER TWELVE

Kyle hops up from the couch like a little kid. It's cute and endearing that he wants to cook for me. He continues to surprise me by the minute. Most guys his age would have jumped all over the chance to start a make-out session on the couch just now. The last couple of minutes were pretty intense. The more I try to tell myself to stay away, the more of him I want.

God, I don't even know why I am entertaining the idea of doing anything with him. I'm going to be partnering up with his parents, for goodness sake! What would they think if they found out we were sexually involved? Would they tell me to leave? I have years on their son; would they blame me as the coercer? Or do they know of his past as his brother knows? There are just so many scenarios that could make this union go into left field.

Junior did warn me about this very thing. But to be honest, I am an adult and if anything were to go further than a friendship, it wouldn't be all on Kyle—I know what I'm doing.

I take a seat at the kitchen table. I shake my head to myself from the thoughts that have been entering my mind. I can't seem to control them, and the way Kyle works that kitchen is sexy as hell. He's sure not helping any. He looks like a man on a mission who knows exactly what he is doing. And he's cutting up vegetables with such precision that I can't help but wonder what those hands could do to me.

"Hey, over there! Do you want some help?" I ask.

He's now rubbing seasoning all over the steaks, concentrating extremely hard. The crease between his brows is adorable. "How about you grab us some more beers?"

"Coming right up!" I jump out of my seat and scoot behind him. Our shoulders rub as I pass him to get to the refrigerator. I feel him stiffen just as I do for a moment, and then he releases his muscles as I release mine.

The electricity between us has just intensified. If this happens with just an accidental touch, I can't imagine how our bodies would react if it was purposeful. I shiver at the thought, and then a warm heat glides over the most sensitive parts of me. Shit! Not good. I have to stay in control. Why can't I stay in control?

I pop off the tops and leave his beer next to him on the counter. His hands are covered in seasoning and meat juice. I turn on the sink, and he washes his hands off. "Thanks," he says. Our eyes lock again. It's like time halts and the rest of the world disappears. We stay this way for a long time, both breathing heavily. Thoughts completely vanish. No questions; no concerns. All worries just slip out of my head. It's just him and me. He slowly begins to lean in to me, and for one split moment, I let my heart lead. I almost follow through, but reality comes crashing back to me like a wrecking ball, and I chicken out.

I back up and step aside. I quickly recover by taking a sip of beer and walking to the table. "Are you going to grill those or broil them?" I ask him.

"Most definitely grilling them."

I look around for a grill. "Where do you grill?" He takes the top off of the stove and points. "Ah, I see. Top of the line, huh?"

"Only the best," he says.

I watch him prepare the vegetables with olive oil and salt and pepper, and then he puts them in the oven. He warms up the grill, places them on once it's hot enough, and then turns to me. He smiles before taking a sip of his beer.

"I'm really impressed, Kyle. How did you learn to do all of this?"

He flips the steaks. "My mother. She's the griller of the house. She kind of had to be. My dad always worked late. If we waited for him, we would have never ate," he says with a laugh.

That saddens me; even though I know his father is a great man. I could only imagine how lonely Connie had to have been. Those evening hours are essential for families to connect and bond. I would know, because I lacked that my whole life.

"And was your mother okay with that?" I ask, hoping I'm not prying too much.

He flips the steaks one more time and takes the vegetables out from the oven. "You know, I'm not so sure. When I was young, that never even crossed my mind that she could be unhappy. She always had a smile on her face. But then when I was about sixteen, I remember walking in their room without knocking, I needed some cash, and she was sitting on her bed crying—alone. My dad was at work.

"She told me not to worry. She had just received some bad news. It wasn't anything I should be concerned about. I think back to that night every now and then and wonder if I should have done more. I also wonder, now that I'm old enough to realize, if she was crying because she was unhappy." He places the steaks and vegetables on plates and brings them over to the table for us.

"Once my brother and I moved out, my mother took on my father's hours. I'm guessing that's the only way she could spend time with him," he finishes.

I take a nice long whiff of the plate. "This looks amazing, Kyle."

"Thanks."

We both take our first bites, and mine melts in my mouth. "Mmmm." I close my eyes without thought and moan. "This is *so* good!" I open my eyes, and he's staring at me with a cockeyed grin.

He shakes his head. "There you go again with your commercial skills."

I giggle. "Listen, if it's any consolation, I think your parents adore each other. I also think couples need to go through hard times to appreciate their happy times. You were a kid; there was nothing you could have done. Look at them now. Those years molded them into who they are today."

He finishes chewing. "You're pretty wise for your age." I stop chewing.

Did he really just say that? "My age?" I sneer. I just couldn't help the way that came out.

He chuckles and is cool as a cucumber. "Yes, *your* age. You're young, and then there's the fact that you haven't been married yet. How do you have all these words of wisdom? It's like you're an old soul trapped in a new body."

Huh. I guess I never thought of it that way. But the fact is I learned it all from watching my parents, from watching them fail at the whole idea of love and family. "I actually could say the same to you," I reply.

It's true. Within these couple of hours I've spent with him today, he doesn't feel like the twenty-four-year-old kid that I saw before. He's different. Most thirty-year-old men aren't as put together as him.

"My parents divorced when I was a teenager. I've learned some through watching them. I don't have very many good memories, but I do like to take the positive out of it. I know what I don't want in a relationship, and I know who I don't want to end up like. I've made a conscious effort to *not* be anything like them."

"I'm sorry for that. That must have been hard for you, but look at you now—look at all you have overcome. I admire your strength in not playing the victim."

I blush. I'm not too sure why the praise feels so good coming from him, but it does. Cody praised me a lot, but it just didn't feel the same as how I feel now. How is that possible? I loved Cody. I really did, but years in our relationship together doesn't even compare to five minutes with Kyle.

"Thank you, really."

We both clean up the mess. I wash the dishes and he dries. We naturally become comfortable as we sync into a rhythmic flow. He splashes me with water, and I splash him back. He has bubbles hanging off his chin, and I can't stop laughing. My stomach hurts. I feel as though I've just done a thousand sit-ups. I haven't laughed this hard in such a long time.

It's now quarter past eight. Our laughter settles into a calm silence. I walk around the couch as he stands on the other side. We stare at each other for a moment, a buzz of energy ignites, but I am the first to look away.

It's taking everything in me not to walk straight over to him, slide my fingers through the back of his hair, pull him to me, and kiss him. Every button in me is being pushed, every limit I have made for myself is being tested, and yet I somehow am able to find the control to stop. Just barely.

I don't know what I'm so afraid of. Maybe what his brother said is sinking in. Or maybe it's because I have just ran from one relationship, and I know I shouldn't even consider jumping into another. *Or* maybe it's because I know the moment he touches me, all hope of keeping control will be lost, and I will come completely undone at the seams.

I walk over to my wrapped artwork to get some distance. I bend down and take a peek inside. It doesn't matter how much of a distance I put in between us, I can still feel him as though he is directly behind me. My stomach flutters and the hairs on my arms stand straight up. My body feels euphoric as though it's not even mine.

I stand and quickly turn to say something, but I run straight into him. My hands are now on his chest. I can feel the beat of his heart thoroughly pounding through his shirt. Heat now rushes to every inch of my body and in between my thighs is now pulsing. Everything inside of me is screaming for more. I look up at him, and he gazes into my eyes, scalding me with an intense desire. I almost stop breathing. I almost follow my feelings and give in to my need. But I don't. I just can't.

I back away from him, removing my hands to disconnect from him completely.

"I think it's getting late."

He clears his throat, obviously out of sorts. "Okay." He claps his hands together, grabs my coat, and holds it open for me. I hesitate for a moment and then realize how stupid I am being. I push my hands through my sleeves, and he turns to slide his on. "Button up. It's gonna be cold out."

"This is going to be one tough thing to get used to. Rochester's weather definitely keeps you on your toes," I tell him.

"You ain't lying. This place can get downright depressing. The winters are way too long, and the summers are barely existent." He holds the car door open for me. "And here you are, possibly moving here," he teases.

I snicker. He walks around and jumps in the driver's seat. "I can definitely understand why you might want to move somewhere warm," I say, "but *if* I do decide to move here, maybe we can do this more often. It sure does pass the time."

He grins ear to ear. He is unbelievably adorable. I reach for his face. I can't seem to stop myself this time. I slowly caress my fingers down his cheek to his jawline. His eyes don't leave mine. The stubble from his five o'clock shadow tickles in a hot, rough sort of way.

"Thanks for today. I really had a good time," I admit.

His voice is scratchy. "You're welcome."

I remove my fingers from his skin. The rest of the ride back to the hotel is quiet and full of sexual tension. I've never felt anything of this magnitude before. It's the ultimate foreplay without the play.

Kyle pulls up to the front of the hotel and parks. "Thank you for allowing me to be the one to show you around a little. I know we didn't go too far, but I'd like to take you out on the town again sometime. Maybe next weekend if you're up for it?" he asks.

I thought he would never ask. "I would love that." I open the car door and step out halfway. "I'll see you

Monday." I shut the door and watch him pull off.

Today was an exhilarating day filled with surprises. In the last couple of hours, I have experienced a multitude of emotions I never knew were in me. I've also realized that while my self-control can be my downfall, it was my savior tonight for stopping me from doing something that I could possibly regret in the long run.

I change into my night clothes and check my phone to remove it off of vibrate. I have missed six calls and have four unopened text messages, all from Cody. The last one fills me with guilt.

"Why did you leave me?"

CHAPTER THIRTEEN

Kyle

I lay in bed for hours last night, just thinking about Max. I couldn't get her out of my head: her smile, gorgeous blue eyes, the way she smelled, the sound of her laugh, but most importantly—she made me feel alive. Not the kind of feeling a guy gets when he scores. She made me for once consider my future, wanting something more than just a career and the bachelor life. And to be honest, this scares the shit out of me.

I never wanted to be the guy that gets swooped up in a fairy tale. It just isn't me. And for a while, I just thought it wasn't in my DNA. Some people are just wired differently; I thought I was one of them, and I was okay with that. But something has changed. The earth has shifted somehow, and it is Max that has bumped it off track. Now I just need to figure out how to get it back into alignment.

"What's up, bro? You look like you just got ran over by a Mack truck," Jeff says.

I feel like it too. "Thanks, man. Nice to see you too."

Every Sunday, Jeff and I meet at the gym for an early morning workout. We work all the demons out from the weekend so we can start fresh on Monday mornings. It's a regiment we've had since we were teenagers.

We stretch and then start out with cardio to get our

juices pumping. "I didn't sleep much last night."

Jeff smiles proudly. "Nice! Who'd you hook up with? Tell me it isn't that girl Trish from accounting—I see the way she looks at you. You're like a God to her," he says, rolling his eyes.

Man, is he freaking serious right now? He thinks I'm going to hook up with one of Beth's friends?

"*Dude!* She's Beth's friend. Come on; I'm not that desperate. I'm trying to get Beth out of my life, and that sure wouldn't help," I argue, half out of breath.

"Yeah, but she's hot!"

"Then *you* do her. The last thing I need is any more drama at work. My mom would kill me," I tell him, out of breath.

"Yeah, the whole office was talking about what happened in Junior's office. They said you two were going at it. What was that all about?" he asks.

Damn, I knew everyone would be gossiping about it, but I was being optimistic and hoping they would forget. With my luck, they'll probably still be talking about it on Monday. If it was anyone else in the company, the buzz would have dwindled down, but since it's me, the boss's son, it's big news. That shit drives me nuts.

I shake my head. We move on to the weights. "He's up to his old shit again. I don't know what his problem is. He told Max about my past. I wanted to kill him!" I growl. I pick up the fifty pounders and start taking it out on my triceps.

"I just don't understand why he does that," Jeff says. "He's such a dick! He's supposed to have your back."

"Yeah. I know, man."

I see Julian walking toward us. "Hey! Whaddup, Kyle?" he says, slapping me up.

Julian is Jeff's younger brother. He just turned twenty-one a couple of months ago. He could almost pass as Jeff's twin except for the fact that he's on the scrawny side. Jeff's swollen with muscle. No steroids, just pure hard work. He looks like a juicehead that should have grown up in New Jersey. They both have dark chocolate brown eyes and wear their hair short but long enough to slick back with some gel.

Julian looks up to Jeff—has ever since we were younger. When we took him out on his twenty-first birthday, he was ecstatic to finally be able to hang with us. He's now on the same playing field. Once you can legally drink and go anywhere you please, life levels out—age no longer matters. At least that's how I see it.

"What's up, Julian? You go out last night?" I ask.

Jeff's now on his back, doing chest presses. "Yeah, man. Me and Skylar went out to Louie's. It was mobbed. You guys should have been there. Chicks were all over the place!"

I laugh. "Yeah? Did you go home with any of them?"

Julian's hilarious, but the one thing he's not is a player. He won't admit it, but he's shy and doesn't have the balls to walk up to a girl. Believe me, Jeff and I have tried to get him to. He only had one serious girlfriend growing up, and he was heartbroken when she left him. I'm not sure if he ever fully recovered.

"Nah, man. Where am I going to bring her? Back to my mom's?" he jokes.

"Mom would freaking kill you!" Jeff chimes in, laughing.

Julian picks up the twenty pounders. "No shit, Sherlock!"

These two go at it for another thirty minutes or so. They've got my stomach sore as hell from laughing so hard. I envy their relationship because this is how Junior and I should be. Instead, I got gypped with a douche for a sibling.

"Alright guys, I'm out." I slap them both up.

"See ya Monday at work," Jeff says.

I look at the clock; it's seven in the morning. Ugh! I am so warm and comfortable; the last thing I want to do is expose myself to the cool air. I can't move because my man part is standing at full attention. I'm hard as a rock and my mind instantly drifts to Max.

Damn, the things I want to do to her. To feel her and to slide inside of her would be incredible. I can't help but grab myself and moan. I close my eyes, picturing her on top of me, feeling her warmth, smelling her lust, and hearing her small moans. I can only imagine.

I grab her hips and bring her against me, harder, deeper,

and faster until my toes curl. She's like heaven melting all over me. A flash of heat swarms my body as I stroke myself to a climax of sweet serenity. I lie still for a moment, trying to catch my breath. Man, that was intense. I *have* to have her; there's no doubt about it. She's making me go crazy. I don't care what I have to do, but I'm going to bury myself deep inside of her until she surrenders everything to me.

My phone rings. I look at the clock, and she's about five minutes late—it's a good thing, too!

"Good morning, Ma."

"You never called me back last night. How did your day with Max go?" she asks.

I head to my bathroom and turn the water on hot. "Good. I took her to the art gallery. Tessa was having a showing there."

"Oh great! How *is* Tessa? Didn't you two used to date?"

"Uh—"

"Hold on, dear," she says right before she orders her coffee.

I wet my washcloth and scrub my face. "We got close before college but never dated."

"Well, I thought she was adorable. Maybe you should consider asking her on a date?"

"Really, Mom? It's seven thirty in the morning! Listen, I have to get ready. I'll see you at work." I hang up the phone. Maybe I was a little dramatic. It was only a suggestion, but seriously Tessa is not who I want to talk about.

I finish getting ready and head out to work. It's even colder than it was this weekend. I didn't think that was possible, but then I remember where I am: Rochester. Only a couple more months until spring, and then I can shed some layers.

I park and head into the office. To my surprise, Jeff is standing at Elise's desk as I walk through the main doors. Elise looks uncomfortably shy as Jeff shoots the shit. I walk behind him and pat him on the back.

"Good morning, Elise," I greet her and nod to Jeff. "Is my friend over here annoying you at eight in the morning?" I joke.

Her face turns pink. "Oh, not at all!" she smiles. I swear I can see lust in her eyes as she looks at him. Weird. Could she have a thing for my friend? Jeff, out of all people? Everyone here knows he's a chauvinistic pig. He's my friend, but he definitely doesn't hide his love for women.

"Okay, good to hear. Come on, Jeff. You don't want to be late." I drag him away with me.

Elise buzzes us in, and as soon as the door closes and we're far enough away, I lay into him.

"What the fuck, Jeff? Elise? Really? She's sweet and naïve. You're going to ruin her," I whisper, trying to keep it down. I nod my head as we pass other employees in the office.

"Dude, I was just talking to her. It's not like I'm gonna take her out and have sex with her or anything," he says, looking a little insulted.

I shake my head as I take a seat at my desk. "You? Not have sex with a girl? What?" I tease.

He slaps me in the back of the head, playfully. "So, McGregor's tonight?"

"Yup! It's Monday. McGregor's it is!" I reply.

Jeff heads to his desk, and I head toward Max's office. I saw her light on when I walked in. I lean against the doorjamb, quietly watching her. She's so into her work that she doesn't even realize I am here.

I clear my throat. She jumps. "Oh, Kyle, you scared me!"

"Sorry, you were so into whatever you were doing, I almost didn't want to bother you," I lie. I wanted to see her. I *had* to see her. I haven't been able to keep her off of my mind since she left my apartment. "Do you want to go grab some coffee?"

She stands up and grabs her mug. I bite my lip before I say anything inappropriate. She looks so sexy in her tight black skirt and creamy silk shirt. I'm ready to shut this door and have my way with her against this very wall. I can have her screaming my name in no time.

She lifts an eyebrow at me, clearly interested in what I am thinking. "Man, that outfit you have on is hot. You're killing 'em!" I tell her. She hits me on the chest with the back of her hand and giggles. I can tell she's flirting back with me.

"You're not too bad yourself," she whispers back quietly

as we walk by employee cubicles.

"Will you be joining us at McGregor's tonight?" I ask.

We step into the kitchen. Like always, it's crowded. "I don't know. Will you be there as well?"

"Yup."

"I wouldn't miss it," she replies.

We split up to get our coffee. As I'm shaking the coffee creamer into my hot, steaming cup, another cup gets placed on the table. I look up and it's Beth. She smiles.

"Will you be at McGregor's tonight?" she asks.

I almost want to say no, but she'll know I'm lying. "Yup, I'll be there," I tell her.

"See you then," she says and walks away to talk with Max. God, she just gives me the chills when I see her, ever since last Monday night. There's just something so off with her. Thank God I noticed it before it was too late. I can't imagine how crazy she'd get if we were actually together for a long time and I broke it off with her. I shiver at the thought.

Max and I walk back to her office before our agent meeting. I take a seat in the chair in front of her desk. I sip my coffee. My whole body awakens with warmth.

"So, tell me. What's going on with you and Beth?" Max asks.

My brows furrow. "What do you mean?"

"I noticed you completely stiffened up when she was talking to you," she explains. "Did something happen other than you guys hooking up?"

I take a deep breath and run my hand over my head. "Yeah, last Monday night she wanted to come home with me. I told her to go home. I apologized for what had happened, and when I left, she followed me home. She got all crazy and told me we weren't over with. She creeped me the hell out," I confess.

She looks at me, shocked. "Wow. I can tell just by looking at her that she still has something for you, but I never thought she'd act like that. She's too beautiful to get all crazy."

"Yeah, well, looks are deceiving. She's turning into a nut."

Max laughs as though I'm taking this way out of proportion. "Just give her some time. I mean, you did have your tongue down her throat and hands God-knows-where just a week ago."

Great. Now Max is making excuses for her. I shouldn't have even said anything. She obviously thinks I am overreacting. This was not the kind of response I was looking for from her. I decide to take this in a different direction.

"Are you jealous?" I suggest with a huge smirk on my face.

Max looks at me like I'm crazy. "Um, no. Most definitely not!" she says with a smile.

"Hmm, I guess we'll just have to see about that," I comment and stand up.

"What does *that* mean?" she spits out.

"You'll see," I answer and walk out. I hear her huff as I leave, and I can't help but laugh to myself. It's sort of fun ruffling her all up, getting her panties in a bunch. Damn, Max's panties are not something that should be thought about in a work environment.

The meeting was long. I couldn't help but zone out with thoughts from earlier this morning. Max sat across from me rather than next to me, and Jonathan took full advantage of that by taking the seat next to her. I couldn't help but become completely and totally consumed with jealousy. My blood was boiling, and all I wanted to do was rip his head off.

Thank goodness it was a short meeting because I'm not so sure I would have been able to take much more of Jonathan's face. The rest of the day was dragged out for a Monday, and I'm stoked it's *finally* five o'clock.

Jeff and I drive up to McGregor's separately. I walk through the doors and the sound of Katy Perry, clinking glass, and laughter swirls around me. I see Beth near the pool table on the right, but I pay her no mind and walk over to my mother's table where Max, Jonathan, and Junior are hanging next to the jukebox.

I wave and then walk straight to the bar to order a round of Patrón shots for all of us.

"Hey, Kyle," the bartender, Jenny, greets me with a wink and a cute smile.

"Hey Jenny, can I get six shots of Patrón?"

"Sure, coming right up!"

I tip her good, since she never disappoints, and set the tray of shots on the table.

"Hell yeah, man!" Jeff shouts, all pumped and ready to drink.

I pass the shots out and lift mine up for a toast. "I want to make a toast to old friends and new friends. And to Mondays—without these, we would never look forward to Fridays," I say with a laugh. We all laugh, clink our shot glasses together, and let the warming liquid slide down our throats.

"Whooo!" Jeff yells, shaking his head and letting the Patrón sink in.

I slap him on the back. "Don't tell me you're getting all weak on me?"

"Nah, bro, never that."

I look across the table to my brother. I catch his attention for one short moment until he looks away. At some point, we're going to have to hash it out. We can't be like this for the rest of our lives. He's going to have to come clean and tell me what I did, why he hates me so much. This just isn't healthy. What happened in his office is nothing compared to what could possibly happen if we keep this up.

I take another long pull at my beer, listening to my mother and Max's conversation. They're discussing neighborhoods and good places to purchase a house. This is definitely a positive move in the right direction—until

Jonathan jumps in.

"Listen, I talked to my friend, and she gave me a list of houses to show you. She'll have some time this Saturday to show us around if you're up for it," Jonathan offers. I can't take this. Hearing this is just straight disgusting me, and before I make a fool of myself, I walk over to the pool table. I know I'm asking for trouble, but just seeing the way Max is smiling at him is making me go to extremes. I'm strung out on a woman who's just out of my reach.

CHAPTER FOURTEEN

Max

I see Kyle walk away from the table out of the corner of my eye. I'm trying hard to pay attention to Jonathan, but it's nearly impossible when I see Kyle is walking straight toward Elizabeth. He's making a mistake. He's about to sink his ship, and it's killing me to watch. How do I stop him? *Why* should I stop him? Why is it even my business?

Ugh! There are a million things running through my mind. It isn't what he's about to do, it's who he's doing it with. My heart pings with pain just thinking about his lips, his hands, his eyes being on someone else—I want them on me.

Jonathan's voice is muffled. It's faded all the way to the back, melding in with the music and all the other voices surrounding me while my eyes are solely on Kyle. I can't tear them away. I see Elizabeth twirling her hair and giggling like a little schoolgirl, and I'm fuming. This is just crazy! He's not mine. He's Connie and Greg's son. What the *hell* am I doing? How did this get so out of control in just a week's time? I'm not supposed to have feelings like this for him; it's wrong. But a small part of me doesn't care.

Kyle turns around, immediately searches through the crowd, and then he locks eyes with me. Neither of us can look away. It's as though there's this magnetic force keeping us bound together. Every nerve in my body is lit up by this invisible connection that's flowing through us.

"Excuse me. I'll be right back," I tell Jonathan in mid-conversation.

I get up, not waiting for his response, grab my small purse, and begin walking toward the ladies' room, never breaking eye contact with Kyle. An urge so intense, so desperate comes over me: I want him to ravage me like a hungry savage. I walk by the pool table, and his eyes follow. I go down the hallway and turn left toward the girls' bathroom, but before I can enter, a hand pulls me back and pushes me against the wall.

I gasp softly. Kyle has me pinned against the wall with his body. His excitement pushes into my groin, hard and demanding. His face only inches from mine, his breath hot and unsteady as his eyes bore into my soul. I feel bare and vulnerable, being so open to him. My pulse races as every thought and need rushes through my mind. My body is on fire, and he is the only one who can put out my flames.

My nipples are hard and begging to be touched, standing at attention through my silk shirt. He glides his thumb softly over them, and it sends a chill through my body. My back arches, gravitating toward him and reaching for more as a moan slips softly through my lips.

"Damn, you're so sexy—" he whispers low in my ear.

A shiver consumes my body. His teeth graze along my ear lobe followed by his soft plush lips against the nape of my neck. I almost lose it. If he didn't have me pinned against this wall, I might have melted completely under his touch. My hands slide under his shirt, clawing at him uncontrollably. He reaches for my thigh and I lift it with no questions asked. He grinds his bulge against my wetness and I almost come undone.

"Kyle—" I moan.

He stops for one moment to look into my eyes before claiming my mouth with his. His actions are barbaric and fierce. I moan uncontrollably as his tongue probes, coercing me to open my mouth. I let him in slowly, gently, until his patience subsides and he thrusts his tongue inside. He tastes like heaven. I want him to take me right here, right now.

"Ahem." A man walks by, clearing his throat in warning.

Shit! I almost forgot where we are. I immediately stiffen and release Kyle in every way to straighten myself out. I begin to panic, remembering his mother, Elizabeth, and all the others we work with are just around the corner.

He's obviously not worried one bit. He's calm and collected, with a grin from ear to ear. He leans his forearm on the wall over my head and slides in real close again, gripping my chin for me to look at him. My pulse picks back up. "How about you walk out through the side entrance and I'll walk out through the front, and we can meet at my place?"

He waits for my answer, watching me intently. I can't take my eyes off those lips. I want to feel them all over my body. My mind is asking for me to be rational, and my body is throwing all rationale aside. I do something I don't usually do—I give in.

"Okay."

Kyle gives me one last kiss to remember and then releases me. I fix myself and walk swiftly to the side door. I stop to look around one last time to see if there are any onlookers. Nobody even turns my way. I take a deep breath and leave. From this moment on, things will be forever altered.

CHAPTER FIFTEEN

Kyle

I come out of the bathroom and adjust myself before I walk out. The last thing I need is for someone to look down and speculate as to why I'm practically bulging out of my pants. My mind is spinning. My body is on a complete high, and I think I may have just overdosed. I knew the moment I touched her, I would be addicted.

I slowly head down the hall and look around. Beth has found someone to occupy her time with, which means I might be able to sneak out unnoticed. I never removed my jacket, so there's no need for me to go back to the table.

I gracefully speed through the bar. I exit the front door without so much as a goodbye. Yes! I made it. I crack a smile as I descend the stairs to the parking lot.

"Kyle?" I hear a small voice say.

Damn it! I turn around, and Beth is walking toward me.

"Yeah?" I answer, completely busted and annoyed.

She's now directly in front of me. "Where are you going?" She sounds more pathetic than demanding. She looks broken. Man, maybe I am just a dick.

"Beth, I have to go. Something came up. I'll see you at work tomorrow."

I walk away, not allowing her to say another word, and jump into my car. She stands there as I drive away. I have no choice but to be stern with her until she gets the point. If that makes me an asshole, then so be it.

I speed through the downtown streets, pumping Tove Lo's "Talking Body" to the max. I'm excited, exhilarated, and totally losing my calm, collected self. I can't believe this is about to happen. Everything I have been envisioning all week will finally come true. And instead of wondering if she would reciprocate, I know one hundred percent that this is what we *both* want. It's not just one-sided or some fantasy I created in my head. She wants it just as bad as I do.

I pull up to my parking lot, and her car is still running. I park right beside her. When I look over to her, she looks back to me. I can see if I wait any longer, she might just back out. If she does pull the plug, I can accept that, but I don't want her making any hasty decisions until we're face-to-face.

I step out of the car as she does the same. We both stand in place for a moment without any words. God, she is so beautiful. She's taking my breath away. There are no words that can even compare to how I'm feeling right in this moment.

I step to the front of our cars and hold my hand out for hers. She immediately looks relieved and smiles. My hand intertwines with hers, and I instantly go hard from just one touch. She will be the death of me. I'm already hooked.

We wait for the elevator in silence. The sexual energy is building into an atomic bomb, and I'm going to explode if I don't touch her now. I grab her hand and bring it up to my lips to give her soft little mini kisses. The elevator opens, and I unlock my apartment door. My heart is beating out of my chest— pumping the blood down to my pulsating rod.

The door shuts, and I am thrown against the door. This time it is her pinning *me* in place. This is the last thing I expected. The fact that she's now the one taking initiative is hot, and I am rapidly turned on. My erection is so stiff that it will rip out of my dress pants if I wait any longer.

My hands roam to her ass. It's round and tight; fits perfect in my hands. She gives me the most tempting smile before running her tongue across my lips. Oh *God!* She's going to make me bust right here in my pants. I open for her, allowing her in. When her tongue takes control of mine, I follow her lead. I make sure to do exactly as she directs. Damn, this girl is so fucking smoking. This must be a dream.

"Pinch me," I whisper in a breathless, scratchy voice.

She stops and leans back to look at my face. "What?" she asks, curious and unsure.

"I want to make sure this isn't one of my dreams," I explain. She smiles. I can tell she wants so badly to ask questions, but her thoughts get in the way. "Ever since I first saw you I've been dreaming about you," I admit.

"Can I tell you a secret?" she asks softly.

I nod my head. "When my head is on my pillow and my fingers are sliding through the wetness under my panties every night, it's you that I'm thinking of."

Holy fuck! My eyes roll back into my head. I can't smash my lips against hers any faster. I rip her jacket open and pull the sleeves down her arms. She does the same to mine. She backs up just out of my reach, I pout, and she slowly unbuttons her blouse, driving me completely insane.

She lets it fall off her shoulders and down her arms to the floor. She's a goddess. There's no doubt about it. Her white lacy bra against her creamy, caramel skin is magnificent. I can't hold back anymore. I rush to her, pull her skirt up and lift her legs, hooking them around my back in one movement while keeping my mouth busy against all of her skin.

I set Max on top of the kitchen counter, lift her ass up to slip off her white lace panties and spread open her legs. There are no words that explain this moment. Pretty and pink, she glistens with juices, and I am *dying* to taste every inch of her.

I slide one finger through her folds and lightly graze her tiny mound. Her head snaps back as she bucks up for more. My name escapes her mouth, driving me mad. I kneel down so her legs are on either side of my head and trace my tongue from her opening all the way up to her sweet spot. She tastes *amazing*.

She moans even louder than before. Every time my name leaves her mouth, I almost come undone. I have to hold on just a bit longer until I slide inside her warmth. I slowly circle her swollen mound while entering a finger deep into her opening. She gasps as I slide one more in to get her nice and ready for me. She feels *so* tight. I'm dying to be inside of her. She feels like heaven on my fingers. I patiently work everything simultaneously in little circles until I feel her clench around my fingers. She screams my name as waves of fury take over her body, one after another.

I unzip my pants, tear them off, and kick them away. Neither of us say a word, but our eyes stay locked together. I rip open a condom with my teeth, quickly roll it on, and push inside her hard and deep. My eyes roll back into my head and a moan rips out from her so loudly, I'm sure my neighbors can hear.

"Holy fuck! *Damn*, you feel *so* good!" I groan and grunt uncontrollably.

I pump into her steady and strong, trying to hold myself back from blowing right here, right now. She moves as I move, meeting me thrust for thrust. She feels unbelievable —all silky wet and tight around me. I've never felt anything as good as this.

I lift her up, she wraps her legs around me, and I carry her to the couch in the living room. She now sits on top of me, riding me with everything she has. Our breaths are heavy but in sync as she moves over me, making my toes curl. I can't hang on. I'm going to explode.

She tightens around me. I close my eyes, bracing myself for the explosion that's about to come. "Look at me," she whispers.

I open my eyes. Immediately, I feel the intensity of our

connection. It's like we were made perfectly for each other. Max convulses around me while I watch her scream my name. She's *beautiful*. I can no longer hold back. I let out an ear-deafening grunt, crying out her name as everything inside of me releases all at once. I'm drained. We both lie here, breathless, in a heap of sweaty mess. I could remain this way forever.

CHAPTER SIXTEEN

I'm not sure what just happened, but something in my universe has just changed. Shifted. My world is no longer aligned. Everything that made sense before is no longer. I lie on top of Kyle while he's slowly tracing his fingers up and down my spine. He's still inside of me. I could stay like this forever.

I sit up so I can look at him, my chest now bare, and see my reflection through his face. No fear or regret, just pure contentment looking back.

He caresses my face with the back of his fingers. "Hey," he whispers.

"Hey," I whisper back.

"I could use a drink. How about you?"

"Yes, definitely." I laugh, but quickly stop. I forget for a split moment that he and I are connected.

I move off of Kyle and he moans. He sounds so adorable. I find his shirt thrown on the floor beneath my feet among the rest of my clothes. I button up his shirt around me and slide on my panties. He watches, completely in awe.

"What?" I ask him.

"You. You're gorgeous." My face turns a shade of red. "And you look cute when you blush."

The last thing I want is to be cute after what we've just done. He stands up, completely confident and unabashed in his nudity, and walks over to the kitchen counter where he left his pants. I'm having a hot flash watching those buns walk away. Someone *needs* to save me. This man is Godlike and the personification of perfection. Man, what have I done?

I walk over to the window, while he's pouring our drinks, to gaze at the glowing sky. The sun has now descended, but the downtown lights keep the darkness from taking over fully. It's still an amazing view. I watch Kyle come toward me through the reflection in the window.

He holds out a wineglass for me to take. "Thanks." I take a much-needed sip and feel refreshed. "Mmm, this is good. What kind of white is this?"

"It's a riesling. I have a bottle of red I have been dying to open, but I thought maybe I would save it for a night of Italian. Do you like Italian?" he asks.

"Do I like Italian? Of course! Who doesn't?" I laugh.

"Good. How about a nice plate of chicken parmesan tomorrow at Casa de la Kyle's?"

God he's sexy. He can fuck and he can cook? Houston, we have a winner! The only problem is he is nine years younger, and he's the son of my soon-to-be partners. Shit! How the hell did I get into this mess?

The shrieking ring of his phone pulls me right out of my thoughts. "Hey, Ma," he answers.

"Something came up." He takes a seat on the sofa. "Yes,

I know. I should have told you," he says. "Ok, I'll see you tomorrow." He hangs up.

I walk over and sit next to him. "Kyle? What will your parents, my business partners, think of this?" My voice breaks with this question.

"Max, we're two consenting adults. No one needs to know our business. If you don't want me to say anything, I won't," he answers, making sure to look me directly in the eyes.

"But if somehow they found out—"

He places a finger on my lips to hush me for a moment. "No one will find out. Trust me, okay?"

He waits for me to nod before removing his finger. Then he swoops in for a kiss. I'm not sure if I'm ever going to get enough of these lips.

My stomach growls loudly. He looks at me in shock and laughs. "I know exactly what you mean," he says, talking to my stomach. I smack him on the arm. "Order in?" he asks.

"Oh my God, yes! Chinese?"

"I got the number stored in my phone."

Kyle calls the restaurant and places a take-out order. I stretch my legs over his lap and—with no questions asked —he begins massaging my feet.

I close my eyes, lean my head back, and moan. "That feels amazing! Being in those damn heels all day is torture."

He chuckles. "I don't know how you women do it, but

you sure look sexy as hell in them. I'll rub these feet all day if it means I get to listen to that dick-hardening moan you do."

I snap my eyes and mouth open, completely caught off-guard. "Wow! Being brutally honest, huh?"

He shrugs his shoulders. "Hey, it's the only way I like it."

He continues to rub my feet for some time as I come up with some devilish thoughts in my head. Kyle looks at me as though he knows I am up to something. I remove my feet from his lap and slide them under me so I am now on all fours, leaning toward him.

I softly place my lips on his, and when he reaches for me, I hold his hands down. He whines in objection. I trace my kisses down his jawline to his neck and down the middle of his hairless, rock-hard chest. I'm already turned on without even a touch from him. Lord, help me!

I slide down the middle of his legs until my knees touch the floor. It isn't until this moment, when I kneel down before him, that he registers what it is I am up to. He bites his bottom lip, trying to hold back a grin. I see the twinkle of excitement in his eyes, and I can also *feel* the excitement as I unzip his pants. He watches eagerly but patiently for what is next, and as soon as I reach for him, the doorbell rings.

His head slams to the back of the couch. "Aww, man! What the fuck?" he whines. But before he gets up, he gives me a sweet kiss on the lips, adjusts himself, and then heads to the door for our food. I just chuckle to myself. I've just witnessed his first "man tantrum." It was cute, but let's hope that's the last of it.

Kyle sets our food up on the coffee table in the living room and grabs some big, cushy pillows from his bed for us to sit on. His bed is on the other side of the glass block window–wall behind us. I'm just hoping he doesn't expect me to sleep in it. I really don't see him asking, though. Most men his age are all about the perks and not about the work that's needed to hold down a relationship.

He passes me the white rice, then the lemon chicken. "Mmm, this is so needed after that workout we just had."

Kyle cranks his head back in an over-dramatic way. "Workout, huh? We might have to change that to a marathon," he says with a wink.

"I look forward to that." I wink back.

"So tell me something—"

"Anything," I respond before putting a big bite of chicken in my mouth.

He takes a sip of wine first. "Have you decided if you're going to stay here?"

I knew this question was going to come up sooner or later. "I'm not too sure yet. I'm leaning toward yes, but I still have to head back home to tie up the loose ends"

"Do you have a house you have to sell in South Carolina?" he asks.

I wiggle to adjust myself on the pillow. "No, I actually have an apartment. I wasn't too sure what my future plans were, so I thought it was best to just rent. The next move I make is going to be a permanent move."

"Jeff used to live in South Carolina when he was younger."

"Oh yeah? He moved here with his parents?" I ask.

He swallows his bite. "No, just his mom. His dad's still there though. Do you have family that you would be leaving behind?"

I take another sip of my wine. I need some liquid courage for these questions. "Yup, my two brothers. Luke is my older brother and Justin is my younger. I haven't seen my parents in years. I don't even know where they live nor am I interested in knowing," I admit.

"Aww, I'm sorry to hear that. How about your brothers—do you have a good relationship with them?"

I can't help but smile. "Yes, I do. Luke pretty much raised me. We all went through a lot together. It gave us a bond that can't be broken, no matter how far apart we are."

A tear slides down my cheek.

I haven't actually allowed myself to feel sad about leaving my brothers. I left so fast. But the longer I'm here, the more it's sinking in. I have a couple of missed calls from Luke that I haven't yet returned. I'm sort of putting it off because I know what the inevitable turnout will be: They'll be fuming, and it will be all my fault.

I'll probably get the most pushback from Luke. Justin's a little preoccupied. He's been dating this girl, Valerie, for a while now, and it seems as though things are heating up with them. Luke can't stand to be in the same room with them. I don't know if it's jealousy, or if he really just hates PDA.

Cody and I were never very affectionate in public, and that wasn't my choice; that was just how he was. He made up for it in private, which is why I stayed with him as long as I did. He's just extremely clingy and possessive, and once in a while it would make me nervous. I never knew what would set him off.

He was never abusive toward me, but he did always want to be a part of my free time. Some days, I just need a moment to myself; Cody never understood that. He would take that to mean I didn't want him or I was interested in someone else. Of course, I'm not sure how that was possible since I was always either working or he was always by my side.

Kyle scooches over to wipe the tear from my cheek. "It's a beautiful thing when you can get that connection with someone. Especially when you've been through so much with them. My brother and I were close when we were younger, but as time progressed, he always felt he needed to compete for my parents' attention. He was the good one, and I was the bad one. I'm sure you can guess who got more attention naturally—even if it wasn't the good kind.

"Junior just has some major resentment toward me, and I have no idea how to fix it. Sometimes I feel like he's out to destroy me," Kyle tells me, letting me in just a bit.

My heart goes out to him. Mostly because I saw firsthand how Junior perceives him. He has no ounce of remorse for badmouthing Kyle, and he made it very clear that he has no belief in Kyle doing anything for the right reason. I think Junior's unwillingness to let go of the past is actually hurting him in the long run. Kyle is an amazing guy, and I think his brother could see that if he just let go. Maybe I should step in and help, open his mind a little. Holding on to a grudge takes ten times more energy than just forgiving. I wonder how Kyle would feel if I were to butt in.

"Can I ask you something?"

He pushes his empty plate of food away. "Ask away!"

"That argument with your brother at work, was that about me?"

He takes a deep breath and runs his hand over his head. I've noticed he does this whenever he's put in an awkward situation.

"Man, you too?" he states, shaking his head. "To be honest—yes, it was. I saw him walk out of your office. I knew exactly what he was up to. He's done it to me a million times. The only difference is this time I cared."

Wow. Um, that was not what I was expecting to hear. But what does that even mean exactly? I don't think he even knows. I decide to ignore that part for now.

"Have you actually tried to sit down and have a heart-to-heart with him?"

Kyle begins to pick up the food and carries it over to the

kitchen. I get up and help. It's obvious he wants to avoid the question. We stand in the kitchen on either side of the counter. I wait for him to speak.

"I've tried to talk to him. Maybe not in the way you might, but I've tried in my own way. My mother's even tried to sit us down, but he won't budge. After a while, you just accept what is and what won't be. I've accepted it, and I'm going on with my merry life. Life's too short for this bullshit; one day he's going to realize it, and it will be too late."

Damn. I'm actually pretty impressed. I was expecting a "fuck him" or "I'm not going to do it," but the fact that he's already tried is kind of awesome.

He starts putting the covers on the leftover Chinese, but I walk around to stop him. I put my hand over his. I can see that he's upset but trying to cover it up. "We might need that later."

He looks up at me, confused. I give him the vixen smile and watch as the light bulb turns on in his head. He swoops down on me in one fast motion, crashing his lips against mine. Thank God he's shirtless already! He rips open my shirt just like a Lifetime movie and goes right for my chest. My nipples pucker under him, begging to be touched. I slide my hands down his swollen chest, past his rippled stomach, and down to his zipper to unleash the dragon. I quiver at the thought.

Kyle bends down, grabs underneath my thighs, and lifts me up so my legs are around him. He waddles over to his bed and drops us down. He waits for me to look at him before he kisses me. This time there's no demand or rush; it's gentle and patient.

He coaxes my mouth open and glides his tongue with mine. It's all emotion that I feel. Not hot, sweaty sex emotion but the mind-blowing emotion. I don't know how this is possible. Where is all of this feeling coming from?

He explores down my neck, leaving trails of kisses behind. I dig deep into his back with my fingernails, trying to get a grasp of this all. Every inch of skin he touches is burning me alive. I feel his tongue glide over my chest until he finally draws each breast into his mouth. I buck up, rubbing against his hard shaft with my dripping wet sex.

I can't take it anymore. I'm going to catastrophically combust if he doesn't get inside me right now. "I need you. I need you inside of me, please?" I beg.

"Me too, baby. I want to feel your tightness around me. I'm *dying* to be inside of you," he reaches quickly for a condom, and within seconds, he enters me.

CHAPTER SEVENTEEN

Kyle

I crack my eyes open from the sound of rustling and the cold air that's now touching my arms. Max is gone. I look at the clock; it's three thirty in the morning. I see her shadow tiptoe across the living room. It's clear to me that she's trying to sneak out.

I flip on the light, immediately squinting until my eyes can adjust. She freezes and slowly turns around with her heels in hand. "Where are you going?" I question, voice rugged.

"I didn't want to wake you. I have to go back to my hotel so I can shower and change for today. I'm sorry. I would have woken you up, but you looked so peaceful sleeping," she tells me.

I can't tell whether she's telling the truth or lying. She has one up on me because of our lack of history. I don't want to force her to stay, and I know she is right. I'm sure the people at the office would start talking if she came in wearing the same clothes from the night before. So, instead of asking any more questions, I get up to walk her out. I give her a kiss that she won't forget and return back to bed.

The next time I wake up is from the alarm shrieking in my ear. I hit the snooze button. I just need fifteen more minutes of sleep. I close my eyes, but I can't nod back off.

The vision of Max screaming my name echoes in my head. I immediately get hard, but there's no way I'm spoiling myself. I have plans for her later tonight.

My phone rings. "Morning, Ma."

"You sound terrible. Are you sick?" she asks, worried.

"Nah, just tired. Can you grab me a coffee?"

"Sure, honey."

"Grab Max one, too. It's always overcrowded in that kitchen in the mornings," I tell her, sharing the half-truth. I really don't want my mood ruined this morning by seeing Beth's face.

I hear the speaker come on. "Okay, I'm ordering now. See you soon."

I drag myself over to the bathroom and turn on the shower. After last night's escapade, it's definitely needed. I let the steaming hot water beat on my back for a while, loosening up all my over-worked muscles. After twenty minutes of scorching water and thick steam, I am finally ready to get dressed and head out into the cold. The only reason I am doing this with a smile on is because in ten minutes I will be in the company of Max.

I walk into work, past Elise. "Good morning, Elise." I wink at her as I swipe my key. She smiles, and her cheeks turn a light shade of pink.

"Morning, Kyle," she responds softly.

I'm happy to see Jeff isn't hovering over her this morning. Jeff's a great guy, but he'll eat her alive. She wouldn't even know what hit her. She just looks so fragile and naïve.

I head straight for my mother's office without clocking in. That coffee is screaming my name. Once I inhale the bitter sweetness, I will feel much better and my day will be manageable. When I walk into her office, she is already on the phone. I grab both coffees, but before I can head out she holds her finger up for me to wait.

I take a seat in front of her desk. I sip the hot liquid and my body releases some tired tension. My mom finally hangs up the phone. "I've been meaning to ask you about the other day—the fight with Junior." She waits for me to explain.

"Ma, you know how he is toward me. I'm sick of him butting into my life all the time when he's not even a part of it!" This was not the conversation I needed at eight in the morning. Ugh!

"I know Kyle. I'll try to talk with him. Maybe your father needs to step in this time. I know Junior loves you. Just don't take it upon yourself to confront him in the office next time, okay?" She walks around her desk to give me one of her famous Mom hugs. The little boy in me smiles and hugs her tight.

I head over to Max's office with her coffee in hand, but when I get to her door, I see Jonathan inside. I knock quietly. She looks up and smiles. Jonathan gives me a nod.

"Good morning, Kyle," Jonathan greets me. I nod back.

I look to Max. "I thought you might need some good coffee—" I hold up the Dunkin Donuts cup.

She holds up a cup back. "Jonathan just beat you to the punch. Thanks anyways, though."

I feel a little awkward still standing here. I'm secretly fuming inside. "Okay then! I'll go see if Jeff needs a cup." I nod my head to them both and bow out. That didn't go as well as I planned—totally killed my good mood.

I must be sulking when I walk over to Jeff's desk. "Dude, who died?"

"More like who's gonna die," I answer, looking back at Max's office and seeing them laugh in sync. Jeff peeks over the cubicle.

"Ah, I see what's going on. You went home with her last night. That's why you both disappeared. You lucky man, you!" Jeff pats me on the back. I smack his hand away.

"Dude, that's not what happened at all. She's different. She's not a notch on my bedpost." I can see Jeff slowly beginning to comprehend the situation.

He holds his hands up in surrender. "Okay, my bad. I just didn't realize you were that serious about her. In that case—let's go beat that dude's ass!"

I can't help but laugh at Jeff's stupid-ness. I can always count on him to cheer me up, though. "Nah, bro. It's not the time or the place. I already got my ass chewed out by my mom this morning over the whole Junior thing."

He shakes his head. "Yeah, that sucks. I shot some pool with him last night. He wasn't as douchey as he normally is. Once you left, it's like he became a whole new person."

"Awesome. So it's all me. Great."

I make sure to keep myself in a hushed tone. The people surrounding us thrive off of the gossip, as if they don't have any lives of their own.

He shrugs his shoulders. "Hey, someone's gotta take the blame."

"Thanks, man."

I walk back to my desk, pretty bummed out. When I open my email, I see one short message waiting for me from Max.

"Tonight? My place?"

I email back.

"Definitely. 6?"

Another email pops up.

"I have some work I need to get done. So, 8:30 sound good? I'll grab us a late dinner?"

She just made my day. Take *that* Mr. Jonathan!

"I'll be there!"

I read the email chain one last time with a huge smile and then hit delete.

The rest of the day couldn't go any slower. The conferences this week were between the big shots and my brother. I was not invited. I honestly didn't even mind. I have some work that needed to be caught up on from all the hours I spent last week in the conferences.

Finally. I look at the clock, and it says five thirty, but now what? I have three and a half hours to kill. What the hell am I going to do? I clock out and head to the door.

"Kyle? Wait up—"

I stop and hang my head. Fuck! I turn around to Beth and try to brush her off.

"What's up? I gotta be somewhere," I tell her sternly.

She looks nervous. "Can we just go somewhere and talk?"

I roll my eyes. She just doesn't stop! "I *really* have to be somewhere. I'm sorr—"

"Okay, okay. I get it. I guess I deserve this treatment. I just want to say I'm sorry for last week. I was just really upset. Can we just start over and be friends?" she asks. She looks sincere, but I'm not buying it. Her looks are deceiving.

"Yeah, sure. Sounds good. Let's just forget about it all, okay?"

"Okay," she responds with a small fake smile.

"I gotta go. I'll talk to you later." I turn abruptly and walk out the door.

I wish I could believe her, but there's just something off about her. She just throws off the *Fatal Attraction* vibe, and it skeeves me out.

I head to my place for a much-needed nap. I figure tonight's going to require my energy, so I better be nice and rested up. Just thinking about seeing Max outside of work completely gets me giddy and excited. I hate having to pretend all day that I haven't tasted her or felt her wrapped all around me. If only her office wasn't visible for everyone to see, I would totally sneak in there, bend her over, and have my way with her over the desk.

Damn. Just the thought of that gets me hard. I can't even think about her without getting myself excited. I thought fucking her would make my need for her go away, dissipate, but it's made me crave her even more. Maybe it will change within a couple of weeks. Who knows, boredom might eventually take over. I just better enjoy this while it lasts.

I peel my clothes off, throw them over the couch, and jump into my bed, burying myself deep under the covers. Within seconds, I am asleep.

I wake up to the sound of my phone's alarm clock. I set it for eight o'clock to give me some time to get dressed and head over to her hotel room. This feels like I'm having an affair with a married woman, meeting her at her hotel room and all. I'm not going to lie, though—it puts a little extra pep in something that's already spiced up. I am not complaining whatsoever.

I pull up to the Crown Plaza and park in the parking garage. Normally, I would park on a side street, but the wind chill tonight is freezing. I throw my hoodie over my head to protect myself from the elements and head into the garage entrance.

Immediate warmth soothes my skin. I've been in this hotel before, years back for my high school graduation. Some of my friends had a hotel party in here. We ended up getting thrown out on our asses for the noise complaints. Let's just hope that doesn't happen tonight.

I pass the reception area in the lobby and wait for the elevator. When I was here last Saturday afternoon, this place was alive and sparkling with a cheerful exuberance. Tonight it's calm and eerily still. The help at the desk looks tired and drained as though she's being over-worked, but that doesn't stop her from smirking at me like I'm a nice piece of juicy steak.

The elevator finally opens, and I hop in. I knock on Max's door quietly. I'm hoping maybe she'll have on some sexy underwear or possibly nothing at all. When she opens the door, she's still in her heels and work clothes.

She gives me a seductive smile and a kiss. "Hey," she says.

"Hi, baby." I walk over to the table set up with food. I didn't realize how hungry I am until taking a whiff. My brow lifts. "Italian?"

"Yeah, I felt bad because I forgot we were supposed to do dinner at your place tonight. Work was a little crazy today. I'm beat."

She does look exhausted, and it wasn't just her who forgot about our plans that *I* had made for us last night. I just got overly excited that she was calling the shots. And the fact that she was thinking about me instead of that douche Jonathan made me forget everything else. I figure it's my turn to leave in the frigid cold at three in the morning instead of her, anyways. Technically, I could stay until she headed into the office tomorrow morning, run home to take a shower, and still be to work on time, but something tells me I shouldn't push it.

"I honestly forgot, too. This smells great. I'm starving!" I tell her as my stomach rumbles.

I pull out her chair for her to sit. I walk over to the coffee machine on the TV stand and unwrap the clear plastic cups.

"Oh, I wasn't sure what you like to drink, so I grabbed a variety at the gas station. I would have grabbed some wine, but I'm still learning the area, and I would have gotten lost," she explains.

I lean down to kiss her on the side of the forehead. "This is fine. I'm not in the drinking mood anyways."

I take a seat across from her. Tired or not, she still looks beautiful. We both dig into our containers and begin grubbing. I watch her take her first bite of pasta, waiting for the aftermath that's about to go down.

She closes her eyes and chews. "Mmm, oh my *God*. This hits the spot!"

"Hey, I thought that was my job," I joke. We both laugh.

"No, you're dessert. I'm saving the best for last."

My pants shift. She has just awakened the beast. "Damn! And I forgot the caramel syrup!"

She lifts an eyebrow in question. "Caramel, huh? That's a new one."

"That's just the beginning." The sexual tension turns up a notch in here.

Her phone begins to ring. She looks at the caller ID, then hits the silence button. I really don't think too much about it. It's not really my business yet to know who is or isn't calling her. But then her phone rings again and without looking, she hits the silence button again. This time, a tiny red flag goes up.

"I don't mind if you answer," I say. "It won't bother me."

Then her phone vibrates. My guess would be it's a text message. She seems mildly annoyed but a little flustered as well. "No, it's fine. It's not important. They can wait until tomorrow." My gut is telling me to believe otherwise. But I'm still not jumping to any conclusions. I know we have a lot of getting to know one another to do.

"So tell me—what's up with you and Jon?"

She looks at me, seeming confused. "What do you mean? If you're talking about this morning, we were just going over some things we needed to discuss in the conference. He picked me up some coffee. That's about it." She studies me for a short minute. "Are you jealous, Kyle?"

Oh no, she is not suckering me into this one. I shouldn't have even asked; it just popped out. "Me? *Pssh!* I'm definitely not jealous over that douche." Shit! That just came flying out of my mouth.

She looks entertained this time. "Douche? That's an interesting choice of words. Why is he a douche?"

"I'm a man. I know he has a thing for you, and he still isn't fully divorced. You would think he would want to tie the loose ends up before jumping on to the next," I say.

She thinks for a moment, letting the information sink in.

"Yes, you're probably right, but sometimes divorce can take years to settle. Do you think he should wait years before looking for another relationship?"

She's got me on this one. "No, I don't think he should wait years, but I do think waiting more than three months is appropriate."

"Okay, I'll give you that one," she confesses.

I walk over to the bed and push off my boots. I pat the comforter beside me for her to come sit. When she follows my direction I scooch her up against the headboard, find the remote to turn on the TV, and remove her heels.

"How do you manage to keep these on all day and night?"

I sit beside her and yank her legs over my lap. "Believe it or not, these are the comfortable ones." I flip the channel, landing on *The Goonies*. "Don't change that channel. I absolutely *love* this movie!"

I laugh. "Okay, channel stays on." I begin to rub her feet. Within seconds, her sexified Goddess moans begin to escape her lips. I can't help but smile with pride.

"That feels *so* freaking good. You are a *very* good man," she declares.

"That sounds very good. Please continue. Moan away," I order.

She kisses her fingers, and then puts them to my lips with a drunken smile.

CHAPTER EIGHTEEN

I stretch my body like a cat does: butt sticking out and arms outstretched. I crack my eyes open, still groggy, but the lights blind me. I hear the TV on and almost forget where I am. I never sleep with the TV on. I look back to Kyle and realize we must have fallen asleep.

As I stir awake, so does Kyle. His arm is wrapped around my body, so when I begin to squirm, he holds me tighter. I nudge him and he smiles.

"Nice try. I know you're awake, mister."

He groans. "What time is it?"

I look over to the alarm clock on the nightstand. "Quarter past midnight."

"I'll be right back," I get up and drag my butt to the bathroom. I drank way too much water, and it needs to be released. While I'm washing my hands, I look to my toothbrush and figure it would probably be a good idea if I brushed my teeth after eating and then sleeping. Bad breath is not something you want to be known for in the beginning stages of whatever this is.

I turn off the light. When I turn the corner to the bedroom, I stop dead in my tracks. Boy, he does not lack any self-confidence whatsoever. Kyle is lying on the bed— naked. He has one hand behind his head, feet crossed, all while he is stroking his massive, hard self. My mouth waters. Now *this* is definitely dessert.

The grin on his face reveals satisfaction. I undress myself slowly and dramatically while he watches. His eyes caress my every curve. I remove everything but my bra and panties and then crawl up the bed, placing my body between his legs. His face is now serious and filled with thirst. That look makes me feel beautiful and desired. He watches my every move, and I'm loving every minute of it.

I replace his hand with mine. He gathers up my hair so he has full access to my face. I make eye contact while slowly taking him deep into my mouth. He sucks in his breath hard while his eyes roll back and then releases it with a moan. His fingers tangle through my hair as he guides me gently. I give him all I have until he begins to reach his limit. I feel his body lock up, and his legs shake as he groans my name. I help him release everything he has built up until his body is drained of every ounce of energy.

He lies on the bed, totally spent. "Is that all you got?" I tease while his chest is heaving in sporadic movements. "You're the youngin' here. I've got nine years on you."

An evil smirk now spreads across his face. "Is that all *I* got? Oh, I haven't even begun." He jumps up, and in one swift movement, he has me lying on my stomach with my hands behind my back.

He removes my panties, spreads my legs apart, and in one rapid thrust he is inside of me. I can't help but let out a wail. "How's that for you?" he asks, scruffy and rugged, as he's pumping deep into me.

Damn, he feels so good. "Oh *fuck*! Don't stop! *Please*, don't stop," I screech. Yup, the surrounding rooms are definitely listening to me. I have no qualms whatsoever.

He continues hard and strong, still holding my hands behind my back. It's exhilarating, trusting him with all the control and just letting myself go. I perch myself up for him so he can go deeper; he instantly moans. "Yeah, baby. Just like that—" he says, leaning back to watch his every movement.

A rush of heat begins deep in my stomach, brewing and building, until it floods my body in waves. Every muscle in my body clenches and releases as I let go, completely allowing myself to go for the ride. Everything holding me together comes unglued, and Kyle follows right after.

We lie together in a sweaty mess, breathless. He rolls off of me and gathers me in his arms. No words are spoken, we just lie together, sedated and exhausted—and one hundred percent satisfied.

I wake up to my alarm. Its six thirty, and Kyle is still lying next to me. I carefully ease out of bed, trying not to wake him. I need to be into work early. I turn the shower on and undress. The steaming water feels unbelievable, melting my muscles into goo. I begin to lather my body and a pair of hands suddenly touches my back. I jump and then smile.

"Morning," Kyle whispers.

I turn around to greet him. "Good morning," I reply. The water leaves shiny droplets glistening on his skin. He's beautiful. I look down. He's also very, *very* awake.

"Turn around. Give me the shampoo," Kyle orders. I comply.

He runs the shampoo through my hair, massaging it in, and then rinses it out. He does the same with the conditioner. He turns me around, eyes drunk with lust, and smashes his lips on mine. I stroke him as he touches me. He enters me and arouses me until he drives me over the edge. My body quivers against him, but he doesn't stop there. He falls down to his knees, water dripping down his face, and glides his tongue over my already throbbing bud.

My legs shake, wanting to give up. He lifts my thigh over his shoulder, giving my legs a break, and gains greater access. The things he can do with his tongue are inconceivable. In a matter of minutes, he has me screaming. An orgasmic tide rushes over me like a tsunami, and I am pushed over the edge by his magical tongue.

"I think I just died and went to heaven," I declare.

He stands up, proud of his accomplishment. "Then my work is done." He shuts off the water, grabs a towel, and holds it up for me. He's so thoughtful. I don't even think a man my age would do this. It's definitely the little things that make a difference.

He wraps the towel around me. "That was the best shower I've ever had," I say.

He laughs and responds, "Now I don't have to take one

at home. I just need to stop there to change."

"How am I going to concentrate at work today?" I say with a smile.

After drying himself off, he wraps the towel around his lower half and heads to the bed to gather his clothes. "That was the whole point of this. So you could concentrate at work." He winks and puts on his boxers and then his pants.

"No. You've just created a monster. I might just have to lock you in my office so we can play boss and bad employee. I might just have to reprimand you for your very bad actions," I tease. I wink at him while putting on my makeup.

"You're killing me, woman," Kyle says with his hand over his heart, pretending to hurt. "You just might end up being my addiction. I'm going to need AA after you."

I giggle. He is just so adorable. "Just as long as you don't become a stalker when I'm done with you," I joke. His face drops. I don't think he really liked that joke too much. I step toward him to give him a kiss. "Hey, that was a joke."

"I know. I just don't want to think of that day."

He puts his arms around me and draws me in. "Then let's not. Now go home and change so you can pick us up some coffee," I direct.

"Oooh, I like when you get all bossy on me," he plays.

I push him away, laughing. "Go."

He throws on his shirt and jacket, blows me a kiss, and heads out the door. This whole thing is just so crazy. No matter how much I want to tell myself to stop, because this can only end badly, I just can't. I don't want to. Eventually, he'll move on anyways. We can't do this forever.

CHAPTER NINETEEN

Kyle

I get to my apartment, and I decide to beat my mother to the punch. I dial her number while changing my clothes.

"Morning, Ma," I greet her.

"Oh, wow. Isn't this a pleasant surprise? You're up early."

"Yeah, I set my alarm clock wrong and couldn't go back to sleep," I lie. "I'm stopping at DD; did you want me to grab something for you?"

"Well, yes. That would be great! I can get to the office early. Do you—"

"Yes, Mom. I already know what you like. You haven't changed your coffee preference in twenty-four years," I say sarcastically. I grab my wallet and throw on my watch.

She chuckles. "I guess you're right. Okay, see you in a bit."

She hangs up. I spray on my cologne with a smile because I know Max loves this scent. She told me the first time she walked by me she almost wet her panties right then and there. That's the image in my head now every time I see or hear the name Versace.

I walk into work with a to-go tray full of coffee and a box of glazed donuts.

"Good morning, Elise. Would you like a doughnut?" I

put down the coffees and open the box.

She looks unsure. I know it's just because she's shy. "Um, sure. Thanks," she says with her quiet, soft voice. "You are *so* welcome!" I reply.

She buzzes me in since my hands are full. I go to my mother's office first, and then I head over to Max's. This time she's alone. This most definitely brings a smile to my face.

She looks up from her work when I walk in. A smile beams across her face. "Hey, stranger. Oooh, you brought doughnuts too? Yum! After this morning, I am starving."

"Yeah, I seem to do that to the ladies."

She gives me a disgusted look. "Oh, boy. I'm so glad to be grouped with your little flings."

"Hey, I was just getting practice in for the main event." I crack a half-grin, hoping she will as well.

She huffs. "Being a comedian just isn't your thing. I suggest you shut up before you get no ass tonight," she threatens.

I put my hands up in the air in surrender. "Okay, okay. I'm shutting my mouth up now!" I zip my lips with my hand and throw away the key. She laughs. Thank God! "So tonight, huh?"

"Yup. I figure your place so you can cook that chicken parmesan for me," she answers with a cute smirk.

"You got it," I tell her and blow her a kiss.

I head to my desk, but my father stops me on the way. "Kyle, I made reservations for seven. Your mom wants to have a family dinner. We haven't all been together in a while, so I expect you to be there," he informs me.

What the hell? A family dinner, now? Being in the same vicinity with Junior is not what I call a great night. I'd rather go to the dentist.

"Dad? I, uh, have plans already."

He waves me off. "Cancel them. Be at Stella's by seven sharp." He walks away.

I hate when he does that—acts like I'm one of his employees instead of his son. I don't ever expect special treatment in the office, but when it comes to family get-togethers, he should at least consider my feelings.

I slam my butt down on my chair and clock in. I'm pissed. This is just bullshit! Fuck this! I stand up and storm calmly into my mother's office and shut the door. She's on the phone, nothing unusual. I wait while pacing back and forth until she hangs up.

"What's the matter, sweetie?" she questions, concerned as she watches me walk back and forth.

I stop to face her. "Why the hell does Dad have to be such an asshole? I mean, *God!* He is always doing this to me!" I screech quietly.

"Doing what, Kyle?"

I finally sit. She just waits for me to speak as she always does. "Treating me as though my voice doesn't matter. He listens and respects Junior, but me—he just acts like my words don't mean a thing. I tell him I have plans tonight, and he just brushes them off as no big deal. As though what

I have going on in my life doesn't matter!" I say.

She walks around her desk to sit on the edge in front of me. "Okay, if you have plans, I'll tell him just that. I just thought it would be nice to all get together. We haven't sat at the same dinner table in a long while. I'm sorry."

I immediately feel guilty. I know she means well, and if she asked me, I wouldn't have been so upset. "Mom, I didn't mean anything about the idea. I just wish he would have considered that what I have going on in my life is just as important as what Junior has going on. If he would have asked, I might have reconsidered, but he didn't. He just demanded."

Before my mother can speak, there's a knock on the door. My mother tells Max to come in. She looks at her watch. "Oh shoot, I'm sorry. I didn't realize the time," my mom tells her.

"Oh, do you need me to come back?"

A plan begins to formulate in my head. "Max, I was just notified we're having a family dinner tonight at Stella's. Would you like to join us?" I ask.

Max looks a little taken aback. She looks to me and then to my mother. My mother smiles. "Yes, please, we would love to have you there! After all, you are pretty much part of the family now."

I know she's not just being nice. My mom genuinely means it. I know she absolutely respects and adores Max or else this partnership thing would have never been offered.

"Um, okay. What time should I meet you guys there?"

she asks.

"How about I pick you up at quarter to seven? I would hate for you to get lost," I propose.

She smirks, understanding just what I have come up with. I know; I am a sneaky guy. I get to spend time with her and make my mom happy all at once. I also know with her being there, Junior will keep his ass in check.

"Okay, sounds good to me," she agrees.

I give my mom a kiss on the cheek and leave them to their meeting. On my way back to my desk, I unfortunately have to pass Beth. She watches my every move but doesn't say a word. Maybe she has finally gotten the hint.

The rest of the day actually flies by. When I leave to grab a quick lunch, I come back to find Jeff hanging at the reception desk talking with Elise again. I shake my head as I walk by. He just tosses a crinkled up piece of paper at me as I pass by. There is definitely something up with him. He doesn't usually put too much effort into the girls he flirts with, and the girls always look like tens but are complete and total bimbos. Elise is a ten, but in the most natural, subtle sort of way.

I clock back in from my lunch. Before I can put my headphones in, Junior stops by. "You really went and invited Max to our family dinner? You're such a fucking idiot. If you don't think Mom's going to catch on to your schoolboy crush, you're wrong. Max's too smart for your ass anyways. She's way out of your league," he jabs a finger into my chest, trying his best to piss me off.

I look him straight in the eyes before he walks off. "Fuck you, Junior. Get a fucking life instead of stalking mine."

He rolls his eyes and walks away. God, he is such a dick! How is it that I am related to him?

CHAPTER TWENTY

"Elise?"

"Yes, Mrs. Daniels?"

"I wanted to see if you wanted to grab some lunch—"

"Okay, what should I order for you?" she asks, clearly misunderstanding me.

I laugh. "No, let's go together. I figure you know the places around here. I'm in the mood for a good turkey club; know any places?" I ask.

"Um, yeah, I do. There's a good café a couple streets down."

I close up my laptop. "Okay, I'll be in front in just a second," I tell her.

We ride in her car since she knows where this café is. I've already made my decision that she needs a friend who can help bring the confident, real her out, and that's going to be me.

"So, how long have you worked for the agency?" I ask her.

"It will be two years in March," Elise answers.

"Did you grow up around here?

She stops for a red light. "Yup, I grew up in Brighton. I always thought I was going to get out of this town, but things didn't work in my favor," she states.

"Why not? What stopped you from trying?"

"The summer of my senior year, my father left us. He told my mother he wanted a divorce, and the next thing I know he's moving out. I barely hear from him. He just stopped trying," she reveals.

We turn into a small parking lot. It looks busy, but I expected that since its lunchtime. "Why would he stop trying?"

She finds a parking spot in the back of the café. "He stopped because I wouldn't respond. He left my mom for another woman. I just couldn't forgive him for that. Once he left, my mom fell apart, and I couldn't leave her to go to college. She couldn't have dealt with another person she loved leaving her, so I stayed here to look after her."

Her story's even worse than I imagined. I thought maybe she got made fun of in school, which made her withdrawn, but her story hits home. Reminds me a lot of my high school years.

We head into the cramped café. It smells so delicious in here. The menu on the wall is drawn out in chalk; the glass case is full of muffins, cakes, and danishes. The room is happily filled with chatter and laughter. The environment is so warm and inviting.

"Elise, this place is so cute, and the menu looks so good. I don't know what I want now."

We both laugh. "I would stick with the club. I've had it here, and it's awesome," Elise advises me.

We order our food, then head to a two-top table. "So, do

you have any brothers or sisters?" I ask her.

"No, I'm an only child."

That explains her being the one to stay back to take care of her mother.

"Our stories have a lot of similarities. My parents got divorced when I was in high school. Those were a touchy couple of years, but it gets better. You know, I think it's time for you to start living. You don't get out much, do you?"

She looks down at her hands before answering. "No, not really. I don't have too many close friends."

I reach over to put my hand over hers. "Well you have one now." She looks up and smiles. The waitress comes over with our food. "Okay, now let's eat!"

We head back to the office after lunch. It feels good taking someone under my wing. She's a sweet girl who's got the shit end of the stick in life. I think we'll be good friends in time. Kyle stops by my office to see me and to confirm the time he'll be picking me up. I want so badly to kiss his sweet lips. I see the same thing in his eyes. Once it's announced that I will be accepting the partnership, my office will be moved to a permanent place down the hall— a lot more private and out of sight from the other employees. With a locked door, the possibilities are endless!

I accepted the partnership with the Saunders Literary Agency; we just haven't announced it to anyone yet. Greg and Connie are planning an agency brunch for the announcement in the next week. We're all very excited and just working on tying up the loose ends. I think this is definitely going to be a life-changer. Now I just have to break the news to my brothers.

My phone rings. It's Cody. I still haven't talked with him either. I do owe him an explanation, so I get up to close my door and finally answer his call.

"Hello?"

"*Wow*. You finally picked up. I thought you were dead!" he says with exasperation in his voice.

I take a deep breath. "Yeah, I'm sorry. I should have told you I was leaving."

"Why did you leave without telling me?" His voice sounds strained.

I bite on my pen cap. "Cody, I told you before I left that I couldn't marry you."

He raises his voice this time. "I thought we were just taking a break! I was giving you space. You said you needed time, so I gave you time. What the *fuck* Maxine?"

I jump from his aggression. "Yes, I *did* tell you I need time to figure things out, *but* I also told you I couldn't marry you!" This time I raise my voice.

"We were together for three years, Maxine. You can't just up and leave without talking to me face-to-face." He sounds like he's crying. I hate this. I hate that I had to do this to him, but I couldn't continue something that I knew in my heart wasn't right. I only said yes because I thought it was the right thing to do, and I thought once it sunk in, I would be okay with it. I thought I would be able to love him like he loves me, but that didn't happen. I can't delay the inevitable anymore; it's not fair to him, and it's not fair to me.

"I'm moving, Cody."

"What? What do you *mean* you're moving?"

"I'm leaving South Carolina. I got a great opportunity to partner with another successful agency, and I accepted the offer. I'm moving to New York," I finish telling him. I hear silence on the other end.

"Where in New York are you? I'm coming up there."

I immediately sit up, panicked. "Um, no! You're definitely *not* going to do that. It's over Cody. *We're* over."

"Not in my eyes, Maxine. This definitely isn't over," he states. The call ends abruptly.

Well that didn't go as well as I planned. I'm not sure I actually planned anything, but if I did, this definitely wasn't it. I have to push this to the back of my mind. I said what I needed to say, and there's not much else I can do. I do feel bad, but in the end, I have to focus on what's right for me.

I keep my door closed the rest of the day. After that phone call, I need to concentrate on work with no distractions. I know this is just the calm before the storm. I don't have a team assigned to me yet, so I can work without being bothered. Once the announcement has been made, I'm going to have managers, team leaders, and a team to actually run, on top of my authors. It won't change too drastically. I just have some new people to get to know. I just hope I don't scare them away. When I'm in my working mode, I can be quite a diva with high demands and expectations.

I take a bathroom break. When I come out of the stall, Beth is walking in.

I smile. What Kyle told me the other day pops in my head for one split second. "Hello, Elizabeth," I greet her.

"You can just call me Beth. My mother calls me Elizabeth when I've done something wrong. That's been her thing ever since I was a little girl," she says with a giggle.

I laugh. "My mother used my middle name. She would yell 'Maxine Leigh Daniels' when I upset her. I knew at that point I was a goner."

"Will you be going to McGregor's tomorrow evening?" Beth asks.

I finish washing my hands, then reach for a paper towel. "Um, I'm not too sure. I have a lot of work to do. Though, it is nice taking a break and having a drink once in a while. Do you go every Monday and Thursday night?"

"Pretty much. I usually go with Kyle, but we're just taking a break for the moment." I have a feeling she purposely brought up his name.

"Oh, I'm sorry to hear that. You're a beautiful girl; I'm sure you won't stay single for too long," I say before walking out of the bathroom.

Phew! I needed to get away from that conversation. Talking about Kyle is not something I'm interested in doing, especially with his ex who just might become one of my team members. I've got to keep it professional if I'm to have dedicated, devoted employees. But the fact that she still believes there's something left between them makes me wonder—is she crazy, or is he still stringing her along? Lord knows.

I get to my hotel room and immediately rip off my shoes. The shoes I had on today were definitely not comfortable, but they sure did look good. My feet can breathe now. They felt suffocated and stuffed like a turkey.

I can't get the situation with Beth out of my head. Once I get an off vibe from someone, it puts me on alert. I am going to dissect every little thing now because she has raised a red flag. I just can't mention it to Kyle yet. I need to form my own opinion about the situation first.

My phone breaks my thoughts. I follow the ringtone, looking for my purse. Found it. It's my brother Luke calling. Shit! I know exactly why he's calling. I'm going to *kill* Cody!

"Hey Luke," I plop my butt down, getting ready for the blows.

"You're moving to New York, Max? Why is it I have to find out from Cody and not you?" he grills me, getting straight to the point as always.

"I was going to tell you when I came back. My decision wasn't made until yesterday. I'm partnering up with a bigger agency in Rochester. It's going to be a great career move for me, and I need you to be happy for me, Luke."

I hear him take a deep breath. "I *am* happy for you, sis. I just wish I would have heard it from you. So, I'm guessing you haven't spoken with Justin either?"

I flop my back down on the bed. "No, I haven't even gotten that far yet. God, Cody is such an asshole!" I whine.

"Yeah, what the heck is going on? He said you told him you needed a break."

"I also told him I wasn't going to marry him. He thinks I'm just going through a phase. I don't think he's accepting it very well."

"Well, you need to see it from his point of view. You pretty much ran from him to another state and now another life in a matter of weeks. It might take a while to sink in. He's just in denial. I wouldn't stress it too much, sis."

When my brother's not acting like a hothead, he can be really understanding. That's the brother I know. I've seen him many of times flip his switch on others but never on me. He's always been so gentle and so loving toward Justin and I. This is probably why we didn't turn out as bad as we should have. He took most of the beatings, so to speak, and emotional damage from my parents so we wouldn't have to. He sheltered us as much as possible, and I'm forever grateful for that.

Bits and pieces are stuck in my head from childhood, and as I get older I began to understand what was going on. I hate my parents for taking his childhood away from him. They stole his youth. He deserved so much more. Sometimes, I just can't understand why he is still in contact with them. I wiped them clean from my life. They're just selfish, life-sucking vampires.

"I know. I didn't handle it the best way, but he freaking smothered me," I explain.

He chuckles. "You're not a very easy person to try to smother. No wonder why you ran. Just don't make this a habit, Max. I know your career is important to you, but don't let Mom and Dad hold your life hostage still. You deserve to be happy. You deserve to be loved and to love back."

Tears slide down my cheeks at a rapid pace. He's always been able to see right through me. Every façade I've built, he was able to knock down. "I know, Luke. I'm working on it," I admit. I hear a light knock on the door and look over to the clock on the nightstand. It's already six o'clock. Shoot! "Hey Luke, I gotta call you later. I love you."

"I love you too."

I open the door, and Kyle is holding one long-stemmed red rose for me. My heart melts just a little.

"For you, my lady." He hands me the rose and leans in to give me a soft kiss on the cheek.

I inhale his mouthwatering aroma. He's wearing my favorite scent, and I'm sure he did so on purpose. He knows how Versace turns me on. He walks in past me, and I can't help but notice his attire from head to toe. His stonewashed fitted jeans hug his ass just so, showing off his fabulous assets. My mouth waters and my hands itch to touch those tight buns. His blazer is tan and casual over a white V-neck

T-shirt, and a thin gold chain hangs from his neck. He is totally GQ'ed out, and I am the lucky lady by his side tonight. Of course, we can't have anyone knowing this, but I will enjoy the secret nonetheless.

"Thanks for the rose. It smells amazing. It's like my own little piece of spring," I say with a smile.

He brings me into his arms and squeezes me tight. "You're so cute."

I lean back and give him the stank face. "Cute? Did you really just call me cute?" I inquire, half-offended and half-joking.

He snickers. "Yes. You're cute, gorgeous, amazingly sexy, you suck a mean—" before he can continue that sentence I elbow him in the gut. "Ouch! What, you didn't like those descriptions either?" he teases.

I give him the evil eye. "Loved them. Now let me go freshen up."

He takes a seat at the table and turns on the TV to the sports channel.

I put a brush through my tangled hair and throw it up in a clip, leaving loose strands beside my face. After brushing my teeth, I touch up my makeup. "So, Junior will be there, I take it?" I yell from the bathroom over the TV.

"Yup! I can't wait," he grumbles sarcastically.

I already knew why he invited me. He didn't have to tell me, and I'm sure Connie knew as well, but if I can help ease the tension, I'm willing to be the peacemaker. This will give me a chance to see their interactions firsthand.

Maybe if I can figure out the underlying issue, I can help them move past this block that's keeping them from an amazing sibling relationship. If they only knew what they were missing, they would hate themselves for letting so much time go by.

"Does he know I will be attending as well?" I shout from the bathroom.

I hear the channels flip. "Yeah, I'm pretty sure he does. I'm guessing my mom would have told him," he replies.

I come out of the bathroom to look for my brown knee-high flat boots. I figure if he's wearing brown, I should at least match. I feel eyes on my back. When I turn around, he is gaping at me.

"What?" I put my hands on my hips and smile.

"You never cease to amaze me. It doesn't matter what you wear or how you wear your hair—you are the most beautiful woman I have ever seen," he states so matter-of-factly.

My cheeks blaze with heat. They are not pink but fire engine red. "You're not so bad yourself." I try desperately to make a joke out of it. The way he's staring at me says he's not joking. He looks like he could tear me up and eat me alive. Not only do I see the hunger but I also feel his hunger pouring out of each and every one of his pores. He's ready to devour me. We both look at the clock to see the time, but we don't have time for that, unfortunately. Damn. It's already quarter to seven, and if we don't leave now, we're most definitely going to be late.

I sit on the bed to pull on my boots, but before I can get the first one over my foot, Kyle is ripping them away from me, unbuttoning my pants, and lifting my butt to tear them off of me. I don't even have time to protest.

The next thing I know, he's spreading my thighs apart and rubbing his fingers through my wet silky folds. I immediately suck in my breath and lean my head back, tingling from the sensation. He grazes over my most sensitive spot in gentle slow circles. *Fuck!* That feels *so* good! His fingers are magical. He slips two fingers inside of me, and I can't help but buck up to him, begging for him to go deeper. He pushes my thighs down in place, and then he leans down to blow on my throbbing clit, teasing me and driving me out of this world.

"Kyle, that feels—Mmm." I can't even finish my thought without moaning.

His finger slides in and out as my wetness pours over them with each hit to my G-spot. This volcano is building and dangerously close to eruption. The moment he slides his tongue over my swollen mound, I'm a goner. I thrash and scream as the flood rushes in. I quiver uncontrollably while his tongue never leaves my skin.

"Damn babe, you taste so fucking good," he tells me, voice rugged and scratchy.

I'm spent! My body continues to twitch as he places small kisses all over the inside of my thighs. I think that was a record-breaking orgasm. He climbs up my body to give me a sweet peck on the nape of my neck.

CHAPTER TWENTY-ONE

Kyle

The sound of her moans play over in my head as we drive to the restaurant to meet my parents. This woman is a Goddess, and for the moment, she is all mine. How did I get so lucky? I grab her hand, nonchalantly entwining it with mine. She looks over questioningly but doesn't say a word. We drive in a calming silence the rest of the way.

We pull up to Stella's. It looks busy. Before I get out of the car, I look over to Max. "I'm not sure how the night's going to play out, so can you do me a favor?" I ask her.

"Sure, anything."

"If things get to be too much, will you leave with me?"

Without even a thought, she answers, "Of course I will."

I can't help but crack a smile. "Come here," I ask. She instantly brings her face to mine. I gaze into her beautiful blue eyes. "Thank you." I give her a long, deep kiss to show her my appreciation.

We create a distance between each other as we walk into the restaurant. My parents and brother are already sitting at the table. My father gets up to greet Max, gives me a pat on the back, and pulls out a chair for Max to sit.

He then looks at his watch. "You're late, son." It's only quarter past seven.

My mouth opens to speak, but Max jumps in first. "It

was my fault. I was having a conversation with my brother, so Kyle kindly waited until I was finished."

"Oh, how is your brother? Did you tell him the great news?" my mother asks.

I look to her and then my mom. "What news?" I ask.

"Maxine has decided to join us. We're going to be announcing it next week to the whole agency," my mother explains.

My brows lift in surprise. "Wow, that's great! When did you decide this?" I ask Max.

Through my peripheral vision, I see my brother watching as he sips on his drink. I cringe just knowing he's near me. Just the sight of him angers me.

"Actually, it was only yesterday that the decision was made. I couldn't be happier. I did tell my brother; he took it pretty well. I know he'll visit. He's just bummed I'll be so far away," she tells us.

"What does your brother do for a living?" Junior asks.

"He actually runs a marina. He makes really good money doing it. He loves the water, so it's the perfect job for him."

"And you also have a younger brother, correct?" my mother questions.

The waitress comes around for our drink orders. "Yes, Justin. I haven't gotten the chance to speak with him yet, but he's easy-going. Plus, he's busy with his girlfriend lately, so it can be difficult to reach him," she says.

"How about your parents?" Junior inquires.

I see her tense up from the question, so I decide to step in. "How about we all do a shot of Patrón?" I call the waitress back over and order five shots.

"I could definitely use one," my father agrees.

"My parents are busy with work. I'm sure you can understand how that is," Max says. "I do need to break the news to my assistant, Kinsey, though."

The waitress returns with the shots in hand. We all take one and hold it up. We wait for my father to say a little something.

He holds his shot up high. "Here's to new ventures, new relationships, and a bright future. Salute!"

"Salute!" we all repeat, throwing back the shots.

I have to admit, I froze for a split second during the "new relationships" part of the toast, but I relaxed once Max nudged my foot. I'm counting on her to be my rock for the night. I already know this is the calm before the storm.

"I'm excited to meet Kinsey! How does she feel about moving up here?" Mom asks. My mother loves meeting new people. She finds human interactions fascinating. Sometimes I think she should have studied sociology rather than working as a literary agent.

I don't recall her mentioning an assistant, but we barely know each other at this point. I realize there is still a lot that I don't know. I keep forgetting that fact because when I'm with her, it feels as though I've known her forever.

"You know, she loves traveling, and she loves her work.

She's not tied down to any one place. I know she'll be excited as well."

"Have you had time to look for a place yet?" my father asks, jumping in.

The waitress comes back to take our food order. As I'm waiting to place my order, I notice one of Beth's best friends, Carrie, at a table adjacent from us. She's in the company of a man who I can only assume is her boyfriend by watching her body language. I never really cared for Carrie. She had wandering eyes then, and she still has wandering eyes. I can only imagine who she will be dialing once she leaves here.

I'm the last to place my order. The waitress seems to be extra friendly with me, and I can see Max's displeasure. She tries her best to play it off, but I can sense it, and I'm loving it.

"I actually will be joining Jonathan this weekend to start my house hunt. I guess he has some good connections, and I need to find something quick but something that will also be a good fit," she informs.

Immediately, my blood begins to boil. The thought of her alone with him pisses me off to no end. A million and one thoughts pass through my head on how to take him out. What kills me the most is that she's willingly going with him! He's openly flirted with her. She can't be that naïve to it, can she? Maybe she feels the same about him. Maybe I'm just someone fun to pass the time with. I stand up and excuse myself from the table. I need a moment, so I head to the men's bathroom.

Carrie eyeballs me as I walk by her table to the bathroom. Disgusting. I can't stand girls like that. Reminds me of Beth.

I wash my face under the cold water. The door opens as I reach for the paper towels. I look over, and it's Max. She locks the door behind her.

"What are you doing in here?" I ask.

She comes up close to me. "Are you upset?"

Man, was it that noticeable? "Why do you ask?" I reply in a low tone.

"It's just a feeling. As soon as I mentioned Jonathan, you came in here as if you needed to get away from me." She has her arms crossed in front of her chest. "I don't like him in that way if that's what you're thinking," she says, looking sincere.

"I'm sorry, but the thought of you alone with him bothers me. I don't know why; it just does," I say honestly, still keeping an invisible wall between us.

She puts her hands on my chest, luring me in with her enticing baby blues. I fall for it. She sends my wall shattering down into a million pieces. "I'm here with you, Kyle. When I leave him on Saturday, I will be heading straight to your place. Just keep in mind that *you're* the one that will be inside of me all night long. No one else. Just you."

I instantly get hard. I grab her and pull her into me. She immediately wraps her arms around my neck, bringing her body into mine. I plunge my tongue deep into her mouth, massaging it against hers. She rubs her lower body against my bulge, driving me wild. I shove my hand down her pants, underneath her wet panties, and dive my fingers into her pulsating slit. She instantly melts under my fingers. I work her fast while kissing her fiercely.

Just as I'm about to touch her most sensitive spot, there's a knock on the door. We freeze, knowing this could possibly be it. This could be the moment where we are outed. I'm not ready for this to end. This is nowhere near finished. I don't even think I could stay away from her if I tried. Not yet at least.

She runs into the stall. I unlock the door, and I'm relieved to see an old man on the other side. "Sorry about that. The door must have got stuck," I lie. He nods when he passes me, shooting me a knowing smirk.

When he goes into a stall, I sneak Max out. She goes to the table, and I find a back door to slide out. I walk around to the front entrance to make it look like I was on a call outside for those missing minutes.

Our salads have made their way to our table already. "Hey honey, I was wondering what happened to you. I was just about to call you," my mother says with some concern.

"Sorry, I had an important call I had to take," I tell her, holding up my phone.

My father and Max are already in the midst of a conversation, as though they never missed a beat.

"Well, listen, if you need help moving your things up

here, I'm sure Kyle would be willing to help. I can give him some paid time off," my father tells Max. He then turns to me. "Would that be okay with you?"

"Yeah, I wouldn't mind," I answer. Of course I wouldn't mind being somewhere miles away, alone with Max. At this moment, she has me completely strung out by just her body alone. It's just something about her that I can't stop thinking about. The more I delve my body into hers, the more I want.

She nods at my father's offer. "Okay, that works for me. I am hoping to head back late next week if that works for the both of you?" she looks between us both.

My dad takes a sip of his whiskey before responding to her. "That works for me. Connie, when are you planning this luncheon for the announcement?" he asks my mother.

"I was thinking Wednesday, and then you could leave that night or Thursday night. What about your assistant? When is she planning on heading here?" she asks.

Max finishes chewing her salad. Junior is still stuffing his mouth. "Actually, I'm going to speak with her tonight about coming this weekend. She most likely wants an apartment. She likes to be able to call someone if something needs fixing. And I figure if I can't find a house, I can throw my things in storage and bunk with her until I do."

"That actually sounds like a great idea. You don't want to rush into buying a house. It's one of the biggest decisions you'll make in a lifetime, so it needs to speak to you. It has to be perfectly right," Mom explains.

"And Connie would know. It took us nine months to find our 'perfect' place," my father adds, full of sarcasm. He takes another sip of his whiskey.

The waitress comes in our direction, carrying a huge tray of delicious-smelling plates. She places a folding table between my father and I before passing the dishes out.

My mother smacks him on the arm. "Oh stop! We've lived in that house ever since, so it was obviously worth the time," my mom says with a smirk, standing by her decision. I see my father grinning because he knows she is right. He just likes ruffling her feathers once in a while.

"I know, love. After renovating to our liking, we ended up with a great house that we still enjoy today," my father admits. My mother gleams. She loves being right, but what woman doesn't?

"We'll have to have you over for dinner one of these nights," my mom says, inviting Max.

The waitress passes out our plates. I ordered the fettuccini alfredo with chicken—my favorite here. My father and mother got their usual: prime rib. Junior got his gnocchi, and Max has chicken French. The waitress leaves after checking that we're all satisfied.

"I would love to! Let me know when, and I'm there," Max agrees. She then turns to Junior. "Those look amazing. One of my all-time favorites, but I had to cut myself off—gnocchi go straight to my thighs!"

Junior laughs. "Yeah, I'll be working them off at the

gym in the morning."

"You'll have to tell me which one. I need to get back to it once I get settled in. Once you get past the thirty-year mark, it takes a little more work to maintain the physical appearance," Max explains with a smile.

Junior finishes chewing. "I don't think you have anything to worry about," he tells her. My radar goes off. Is my brother flirting? Yeah, this is not going down in front of me.

"I totally know what you're saying! Of course, I would give up my right pinkie if I could be in my early thirties again," Mom says, letting out a boisterous laugh.

"Yeah, me too. I would give up my pinkie to have you be thirty again," my dad jokes. My mother gives him the death look. He holds up his hands. "Okay, okay, I was just agreeing with you. Geez!" My mother rolls her eyes.

I listen while filling my mouth with fettuccini. There's no way I'm jumping into this conversation. When it comes to age and weight with women, men will always lose, no matter what we say. I've learned this from watching my father and mother over the years. I know once those two words are mentioned, it's time to change the subject. I'll be damned if I end up in the doghouse with Max so soon in our rendezvous. I'm enjoying what we have too much for it to end.

"You're lucky I stuck with you during my younger years, honey. I was a hot commodity," Mom rubs in Dad's face. She then turns to Max. "Greg, here, had to chase me down a while before I was willing to settle down. I was a wild bachelorette." This time it's my father who rolls his eyes.

"I have a visitor's pass you can use for the gym while you're here. Just let me know, and I can grab you on the way," Junior offers Max. My whole body tenses. He'd better stop while he's ahead.

The sound of her moans play over in my head as we drive to the restaurant to meet my parents. This woman is a Goddess, and for the moment, she is all mine. How did I get so lucky? I grab her hand, nonchalantly entwining it with mine. She looks over questioningly but doesn't say a word. We drive in a calming silence the rest of the way.

We pull up to Stella's. It looks busy. Before I get out of the car, I look over to Max. "I'm not sure how the night's going to play out, so can you do me a favor?" I ask her.

"Sure, anything."

"If things get to be too much, will you leave with me?"

Without even a thought, she answers, "Of course I will."

I can't help but crack a smile. "Come here," I ask. She instantly brings her face to mine. I gaze into her beautiful blue eyes. "Thank you." I give her a long, deep kiss to show her my appreciation.

We create a distance between each other as we walk into the restaurant. My parents and brother are already sitting at the table. My father gets up to greet Max, gives me a pat on the back, and pulls out a chair for Max to sit.

He then looks at his watch. "You're late, son." It's only quarter past seven.

My mouth opens to speak, but Max jumps in first. "It

was my fault. I was having a conversation with my brother, so Kyle kindly waited until I was finished."

"Oh, how is your brother? Did you tell him the great news?" my mother asks.

I look to her and then my mom. "What news?" I ask.

"Maxine has decided to join us. We're going to be announcing it next week to the whole agency," my mother explains.

My brows lift in surprise. "Wow, that's great! When did you decide this?" I ask Max.

Through my peripheral vision, I see my brother watching as he sips on his drink. I cringe just knowing he's near me. Just the sight of him angers me.

"Actually, it was only yesterday that the decision was made. I couldn't be happier. I did tell my brother; he took it pretty well. I know he'll visit. He's just bummed I'll be so far away," she tells us.

"What does your brother do for a living?" Junior asks.

"He actually runs a marina. He makes really good money doing it. He loves the water, so it's the perfect job for him."

"And you also have a younger brother, correct?" my mother questions.

The waitress comes around for our drink orders. "Yes, Justin. I haven't gotten the chance to speak with him yet, but he's easy-going. Plus, he's busy with his girlfriend lately, so it can be difficult to reach him," she says.

"How about your parents?" Junior inquires.

I see her tense up from the question, so I decide to step in. "How about we all do a shot of Patrón?" I call the waitress back over and order five shots.

"I could definitely use one," my father agrees.

"My parents are busy with work. I'm sure you can understand how that is," Max says. "I do need to break the news to my assistant, Kinsey, though."

The waitress returns with the shots in hand. We all take one and hold it up. We wait for my father to say a little something.

He holds his shot up high. "Here's to new ventures, new relationships, and a bright future. Salute!"

"Salute!" we all repeat, throwing back the shots.

I have to admit, I froze for a split second during the "new relationships" part of the toast, but I relaxed once Max nudged my foot. I'm counting on her to be my rock for the night. I already know this is the calm before the storm.

"I'm excited to meet Kinsey! How does she feel about moving up here?" Mom asks. My mother loves meeting new people. She finds human interactions fascinating. Sometimes I think she should have studied sociology rather than working as a literary agent.

I don't recall her mentioning an assistant, but we barely know each other at this point. I realize there is still a lot that I don't know. I keep forgetting that fact because when I'm with her, it feels as though I've known her forever.

"You know, she loves traveling, and she loves her work.

She's not tied down to any one place. I know she'll be excited as well."

"Have you had time to look for a place yet?" my father asks, jumping in.

The waitress comes back to take our food order. As I'm waiting to place my order, I notice one of Beth's best friends, Carrie, at a table adjacent from us. She's in the company of a man who I can only assume is her boyfriend by watching her body language. I never really cared for Carrie. She had wandering eyes then, and she still has wandering eyes. I can only imagine who she will be dialing once she leaves here.

I'm the last to place my order. The waitress seems to be extra friendly with me, and I can see Max's displeasure. She tries her best to play it off, but I can sense it, and I'm loving it.

"I actually will be joining Jonathan this weekend to start my house hunt. I guess he has some good connections, and I need to find something quick but something that will also be a good fit," she informs.

Immediately, my blood begins to boil. The thought of her alone with him pisses me off to no end. A million and one thoughts pass through my head on how to take him out. What kills me the most is that she's willingly going with him! He's openly flirted with her. She can't be that naïve to it, can she? Maybe she feels the same about him. Maybe I'm just someone fun to pass the time with. I stand up and excuse myself from the table. I need a moment, so I head to the men's bathroom.

Carrie eyeballs me as I walk by her table to the bathroom. Disgusting. I can't stand girls like that. Reminds me of Beth.

I wash my face under the cold water. The door opens as I reach for the paper towels. I look over, and it's Max. She locks the door behind her.

"What are you doing in here?" I ask.

She comes up close to me. "Are you upset?"

Man, was it that noticeable? "Why do you ask?" I reply in a low tone.

"It's just a feeling. As soon as I mentioned Jonathan, you came in here as if you needed to get away from me." She has her arms crossed in front of her chest. "I don't like him in that way if that's what you're thinking," she says, looking sincere.

"I'm sorry, but the thought of you alone with him bothers me. I don't know why; it just does," I say honestly, still keeping an invisible wall between us.

She puts her hands on my chest, luring me in with her enticing baby blues. I fall for it. She sends my wall shattering down into a million pieces. "I'm here with you, Kyle. When I leave him on Saturday, I will be heading straight to your place. Just keep in mind that *you're* the one that will be inside of me all night long. No one else. Just you."

I instantly get hard. I grab her and pull her into me. She immediately wraps her arms around my neck, bringing her body into mine. I plunge my tongue deep into her mouth, massaging it against hers. She rubs her lower body against my bulge, driving me wild. I shove my hand down her pants, underneath her wet panties, and dive my fingers into her pulsating slit. She instantly melts under my fingers. I work her fast while kissing her fiercely.

Just as I'm about to touch her most sensitive spot, there's a knock on the door. We freeze, knowing this could possibly be it. This could be the moment where we are outed. I'm not ready for this to end. This is nowhere near finished. I don't even think I could stay away from her if I tried. Not yet at least.

She runs into the stall. I unlock the door, and I'm relieved to see an old man on the other side. "Sorry about that. The door must have got stuck," I lie. He nods when he passes me, shooting me a knowing smirk.

When he goes into a stall, I sneak Max out. She goes to the table, and I find a back door to slide out. I walk around to the front entrance to make it look like I was on a call outside for those missing minutes.

Our salads have made their way to our table already. "Hey honey, I was wondering what happened to you. I was just about to call you," my mother says with some concern.

"Sorry, I had an important call I had to take," I tell her, holding up my phone.

My father and Max are already in the midst of a conversation, as though they never missed a beat.

"Well, listen, if you need help moving your things up

here, I'm sure Kyle would be willing to help. I can give him some paid time off," my father tells Max. He then turns to me. "Would that be okay with you?"

"Yeah, I wouldn't mind," I answer. Of course I wouldn't mind being somewhere miles away, alone with Max. At this moment, she has me completely strung out by just her body alone. It's just something about her that I can't stop thinking about. The more I delve my body into hers, the more I want.

She nods at my father's offer. "Okay, that works for me. I am hoping to head back late next week if that works for the both of you?" she looks between us both.

My dad takes a sip of his whiskey before responding to her. "That works for me. Connie, when are you planning this luncheon for the announcement?" he asks my mother.

"I was thinking Wednesday, and then you could leave that night or Thursday night. What about your assistant? When is she planning on heading here?" she asks.

Max finishes chewing her salad. Junior is still stuffing his mouth. "Actually, I'm going to speak with her tonight about coming this weekend. She most likely wants an apartment. She likes to be able to call someone if something needs fixing. And I figure if I can't find a house, I can throw my things in storage and bunk with her until I do."

"That actually sounds like a great idea. You don't want to rush into buying a house. It's one of the biggest decisions you'll make in a lifetime, so it needs to speak to you. It has to be perfectly right," Mom explains.

"And Connie would know. It took us nine months to find our 'perfect' place," my father adds, full of sarcasm. He takes another sip of his whiskey.

The waitress comes in our direction, carrying a huge tray of delicious-smelling plates. She places a folding table between my father and I before passing the dishes out.

My mother smacks him on the arm. "Oh stop! We've lived in that house ever since, so it was obviously worth the time," my mom says with a smirk, standing by her decision. I see my father grinning because he knows she is right. He just likes ruffling her feathers once in a while.

"I know, love. After renovating to our liking, we ended up with a great house that we still enjoy today," my father admits. My mother gleams. She loves being right, but what woman doesn't?

"We'll have to have you over for dinner one of these nights," my mom says, inviting Max.

The waitress passes out our plates. I ordered the fettuccini alfredo with chicken—my favorite here. My father and mother got their usual: prime rib. Junior got his gnocchi, and Max has chicken French. The waitress leaves after checking that we're all satisfied.

"I would love to! Let me know when, and I'm there," Max agrees. She then turns to Junior. "Those look amazing. One of my all-time favorites, but I had to cut myself off—gnocchi go straight to my thighs!"

Junior laughs. "Yeah, I'll be working them off at the

gym in the morning."

"You'll have to tell me which one. I need to get back to it once I get settled in. Once you get past the thirty-year mark, it takes a little more work to maintain the physical appearance," Max explains with a smile.

Junior finishes chewing. "I don't think you have anything to worry about," he tells her. My radar goes off. Is my brother flirting? Yeah, this is not going down in front of me.

"I totally know what you're saying! Of course, I would give up my right pinkie if I could be in my early thirties again," Mom says, letting out a boisterous laugh.

"Yeah, me too. I would give up my pinkie to have you be thirty again," my dad jokes. My mother gives him the death look. He holds up his hands. "Okay, okay, I was just agreeing with you. Geez!" My mother rolls her eyes.

I listen while filling my mouth with fettuccini. There's no way I'm jumping into this conversation. When it comes to age and weight with women, men will always lose, no matter what we say. I've learned this from watching my father and mother over the years. I know once those two words are mentioned, it's time to change the subject. I'll be damned if I end up in the doghouse with Max so soon in our rendezvous. I'm enjoying what we have too much for it to end.

"You're lucky I stuck with you during my younger years, honey. I was a hot commodity," Mom rubs in Dad's face. She then turns to Max. "Greg, here, had to chase me down a while before I was willing to settle down. I was a wild bachelorette." This time it's my father who rolls his eyes.

"I have a visitor's pass you can use for the gym while you're here. Just let me know, and I can grab you on the way," Junior offers Max. My whole body tenses. He'd better stop while he's ahead.

CHAPTER TWENTY-THREE

Kyle

I can't help but wonder who that text was from last night. I saw the words scroll across her screen before she came out to check: "This isn't over." What isn't over? There's got to be something she's hiding. I watched her read the text, and she froze up. Now that I think of it, every call and text she has received when I'm around, she pushes off. What the hell is up?

I finish changing my clothes and head out the door. My phone rings; perfect timing.

"Hey, Ma."

"Hi, honey. Your father is on a rampage. He woke up on the wrong side of the bed this morning, so I suggest you stay out of his way," she warns.

"Thanks for the 411. I'm just going to hide in my cubicle, then." I start up the car and let it sit for a moment. The morning air is crisp and the sun is bright. If it were ten degrees warmer, it would be a comfortable winter morning. I love sweater-and-jeans weather, but this is just way too cold.

My mother laughs. "Okay, honey. Just remember we have a conference at nine o'clock sharp. So don't be late."

"I won't, Ma." She's such a worrywart.

I stop and grab the coffee. It's just after eight by the time I reach the office. I enter the front doors and see Jeff hanging by Elise's desk. I don't know what's with him. It's like he can't stay away from this girl. He's so deep in conversation that he doesn't even realize I'm behind him.

"Ahem."

He turns around with a huge smile. Elise's face is flushed pink. "Hey, man. What's up?"

I raise my brow, looking between the both of them. "Not much. Just wanted to see what you two are up to this early in the morning," I admit.

"We were actually talking about hanging out this weekend—maybe going to see a band or something. You wanna go?" Jeff asks.

Before I can answer, Elise chimes in. "Oh, that's such a good idea! I will call Max to see if she might want to come out."

I look at her, a little amazed. I think this is the most I've heard her talk since she's worked here. I flash a crooked grin. "You know what? I'm in! Give me the time and place, and I'm there!"

Elise smiles contently. I smack Jeff on the back and head into the office.

I clock in first and then head over to Max's office. She looks as though something has thrown her off since I left her. She does her best to put on a smile when I walk through the door, but I've spent enough time with her to notice when her mojo is off-kilter.

"Hey, beautiful," I greet her quietly, placing her coffee on her desk.

"Morning," she replies. A slight shade of pink tints her face. I love when that happens. It makes her look softer, more feminine, rather than all boss-like.

"So Jeff and Elise are planning a night out this weekend, going to see a band or something, and invited us. Well, actually Elise mentioned she wanted to invite you, and Jeff invited me, so—"

She giggles. "Yes, she actually just emailed me."

"So, you and Elise talk?" I ask. I didn't know Elise spoke with anyone inside the office other than me and Jeff.

Max throws her phone in her drawer and shuts it. "Yeah, we went to lunch together the other day. She's sweet. I like her. She reminds me of me before my college years," she explains.

"Okay, so this weekend. It's a secret date," I joke. I zip my mouth and throw away the pretend key. "Oh, and by the way, you look hot this morning. I'm digging the royal blue color. It brings out your amazing eyes."

She looks hot in anything she puts on, but this blue is extra special because it makes her eyes pop. Those baby blues are tattooed on the inside of my eyelids. Every time I close my eyes, they are there, staring back at me.

I head back to my desk and make a quick detour as I notice my father walking out of his office. There is no way I am crossing his path this morning, especially after last night's dinner. It didn't end on a good note, and I sure don't want to rehash why.

Not even realizing it, I end up right in the lion's den.

"Hey, stranger," Beth says from her desk. I don't know how she does it, but she can scope me from anywhere.

I stop, not wanting to be rude. "Hello, Beth. How are you?"

"I'm good. Will you be at McGregor's tonight?" she asks. It feels like her everyday question lately.

I completely forgot it's Thursday. "Nah, I don't think I'll be there tonight. I have some things to do," I tell her. She looks pouty, like I just told her that her dog died.

"Are you doing anything this weekend?"

"Yeah, I have plans." I look down at my watch to see if it's almost nine.

"My friend Casey said she saw your family at dinner last night. Since when is that lady Maxine part of your family?" she asks, completely out of line. That's none of her concern, and my mind is blown that she just asked.

"Really, Beth? I didn't know my parents had rules on who they're allowed to invite to dinner," I snap. I turn and walk away. This chick has just lost her mind. I don't know why I even waste my time.

I look back at my watch. It's just minutes before nine. I stop at my desk to grab my coffee and notepad, and then I head to the conference room. Max is already there, and sitting beside her is Jonathan, talking her ear off. Never fails, I still want to bash his face in. I stroll in, taking my seat quietly. I don't want to interrupt anything.

Jonathan stops talking enough to greet me. "Hey, Kyle. Your dad letting you sit in on this meeting?" He's clearly trying to antagonize me.

I keep my face still, clear of emotion. "Yeah, man. He wants me to learn the business inside and out," I inform. He now looks pissed. Did I hit a button? Is he hoping to be the next partner? Not if I can help it. He's not getting any part of this business. Dickwad.

"I see. I guess that's the benefit of being the boss's son, huh? Being born into a business rather than having to work hard," he states.

My blood is boiling, but before everyone else walks in, I have to set him straight. "I didn't realize six years of college and a master's degree requires no work. If I wanted the silver spoon put in my mouth, I would have begun working here from high school like my brother," I inform him calmly and professionally.

Max claps. "I completely agree with you, Kyle. You in no way took the easy way to get here. Be proud of that. You earned your spot at this conference table," she praises. She then looks at Jonathan, waiting for his rebuttal.

Jonathan doesn't say another word. The others walk in and take their seats for the meeting. I make sure to sneak a wink in Max's direction. That was pretty cool how she just stuck up for me. Jonathan obviously feels like an ass after that because he doesn't say another peep except when asked during the meeting.

We break for lunch. I head out with Jeff, and I see Max walking to her car with Elise.

"Dude, tell me you don't have a thing for Elise?" I

question Jeff, putting him on the spot.

He shrugs his shoulders. "I don't know. Something just draws me to her. She's not like any other girl I've met. She has this pure beauty that just radiates from her. Is that weird?" he looks to me for some sort of approval or advice.

We jump in my car. I allow it to warm up for a moment before taking off. "Nah, that's not weird. I think that's pretty non-asshole-ish of you," I joke. "But seriously, man, if you like her, then go for it. No one's gonna judge you, especially not me."

He looks more at ease. "So, tell me the truth. What's up with you and Maxine? I see this crazy unsaid connection between you. The woman lights up when you step in her path and vice versa."

Damn, he's noticed. Does that mean everyone else does as well? No. Jeff's just extra-observant when it comes to me because we've known each other for so long. He knows what's behind my every thought and behind my every move. I seem to forget this little notion.

I hang my head in defeat, then pull out of the parking lot. "Max and I have been hanging out a lot. I totally dig her. She's a cool chick. The more I'm with her, the more I don't want to be without her. I mean, not in a girlfriend, falling-in-love way, but a good, fun, friendly way. Does that make sense?" I ask him.

Jeff snickers. "Yeah, makes plenty of sense. You guys are having hot sex. I knew it, man!"

I slap my hand over my face. "Okay, okay. Just keep it

to yourself. Can you do that?"

"Of course I can. What do you think, I'm gonna blurt it out all around work? Beth would love that one!" he says. "Is she still acting like a psycho?"

I turn into the deli down the street from work. "Max was at dinner with us last night, and I saw Casey, Beth's best friend, there. She told Beth about Max being at the family dinner, and Beth had the nerve to ask me why she was there!"

Jeff exhales loudly. "Wow. She is freaking nuts."

"Tell me about it," I respond.

We order our subs and take a seat in the booth. "So what's up with that girl Tracey you were talking to?" I question him.

"She was just something to pass the time. Tracey's already gone like a leaf in the wind," Jeff tells me.

I shove my mouth full of meatball sub. I can't help but groan. This thing tastes like a piece of heaven right now. I finish chewing. "Real poetic, man," I tease.

Jeff swallows his sub and then takes a long pull at his water. "So, what about the age thing? Max is like ten years older than you. You don't feel strange that she's a cougar?"

I knew this had to come out at some point. I just didn't think it would come out so soon. "What? A cougar? Are you out of your mind? She's nine years older, and I could give two shits about her age," I spit out, a little pissed he even asked. "Why the fuck does that even matter?"

He holds his hands up in surrender, not wanting to be

shot at anymore. "It doesn't. Relax," Jeff chuckles. "Hey, as long as it doesn't bother you, then who cares?"

I nod my head, hoping that's the truth. The last thing I want is for him to say something to make her feel uncomfortable this weekend. We get back to the office. I clock in and open my email to write to Max, but I already have an email waiting. I can't help but crack a smile.

"Tonight?" she asks.

"My place? After here?" I reply.

"I'll be there. Chicken parm tonight? "

I can't help snickering to myself. "Anything you want. " I send.

The rest of the day goes by pretty steady until my desk phone rings, and it's my father's office.

"What's up, Dad?"

"I want you to come into my office." He hangs up before I can respond.

Shit! Not exactly how I want to end my day. Maybe he's calmed down since this morning. He seemed okay during the meeting, but God only knows what he wants to speak with me about. I head over to his office and shut the door behind me.

I sit down on his couch, adjacent to him. "What's up, Dad?" I ask again.

"I'd like you to tell me what's going on between you and Junior." Phew! For a second I thought he was going to ask about Max.

"Nothing. He's just a dick."

"Watch your mouth, son," he scolds, as if talking to a little boy.

I grab the pen on his coffee table and begin twisting it in my hands. "I'm not a little kid anymore, Dad. You can't just tell me to 'watch my mouth.' You need to be asking Junior this question, not me. He's the one who has the problem with me! I am so sick of explaining this to everyone!" I screech.

My father raises his voice slightly. "You two need to find a way to figure it out. Eventually, this agency will be left to the both of you, and you have to be a united front. Our authors, as well as employees, need to see this now. It builds trust, and when it's time for you both to take over, there will be no concerns or questions asked," he clarifies.

I lean back on the couch. "Dad, that isn't going to be for years to come. I mean, seriously, you never even asked me if this is what I want. I don't even know if I'm staying in Rochester for years to come. You have Junior, and now you have Max. I don't need the pressure," I tell him honestly. I stand up and walk to the door, but before I leave, I turn to him. "Can you just be my dad for once and not my boss?" I leave it at that and walk out of his office.

CHAPTER TWENTY-FOUR

I shut down my computer and head out of the office. I hear the buzz about McGregor's as I walk through the aisles. Mondays and Thursdays are definitely a popular night with Saunders Agency employees. I'd so much rather spend a quiet night alone with Kyle. I've been dying for that chicken parmesan ever since he mentioned it, and I want to take a look at the photo I bought. I feel like I haven't seen it in so long.

I almost stop at the liquor store to grab a bottle of wine, but I remember he was saving that bottle of red for this occasion. We most definitely can't drink two bottles if we're to be on time for work tomorrow.

I pull up to his apartment. I see a tan Honda parked in the parking lot behind me. I see a shadow inside, but I can't make out anything else. I know it's not uncommon for people to sit in their cars, but something strikes me as weird. I brush the thought off as Kyle buzzes me in.

The door's unlocked, so I let myself in. Kyle is by his closet, changing out of his work clothes. He just has boxers and a white tee on. So freaking sexy. The man looks like a god. Just thinking about his body against mine makes my panties moist. How did I become this sex-crazed teenager? I've never been so in tune with my body until now.

He throws on a pair of fitted jeans and then walks toward me. "Hey, beautiful."

He pulls me in, moves my hair to the side, and kisses my neck. I moan quietly, a sound made just for him and I to hear. He nips down on my earlobe playfully. I dig my fingers into his back. The longer we stay like this, the farther dinner drifts away.

My stomach growls. I pull back, slightly out of breath. "Let's go start that dinner," Kyle says.

"I'm starving! I didn't eat much for lunch," I admit.

Kyle begins taking out the ingredients for our meal. "You went with Elise, right?"

"Yeah, we stopped at a little diner. I wasn't that hungry at the time, so I just got a piece of pie."

He grabs a frying pan and pours some oil into it. "Did she mention Jeff's name at all?" he asks, handing me the bottle of red wine and a wine opener.

I begin twisting the opener into the cork. "She just said she was shocked Jeff asked her to hang out. I guess he visits her up front every now and then, but she knows she's not his type."

I pull at the cork until a big popping noise fills the air. Kyle's throwing the chicken in the batter he just made. The oil in the frying pan is beginning to sizzle. He quickly adjusts the water for the pasta and takes out sauce from the freezer.

"I always make enough to freeze for occasions like this," he explains. "Well, let me just tell you this—he wouldn't be wasting his time up front if it wasn't for a reason. Jeff can be a real egotistical dick, but he seems to value Elise in a different sort of way."

After allowing the sauce to heat and the water to boil, Kyle throws the pasta in. "Wow. So maybe opposites do attract," I suggest. I've seen it happen more than once throughout my lifetime.

The pan awakens with the crackling of the chicken. Kyle quickly closes the top before burning himself, then tends to the sauce. "I guess we'll see. I heard the band we're going to see is good. I think their name is Crank. They're a local band that's actually getting pretty big," Kyle says.

Finally, after ten minutes or so, everything is done. It smells delicious. I grab the wineglass out of his cupboard, and he sets the food down at the table. "Salad?" he offers before he takes the lettuce out of the refrigerator.

"No, all I want is the main course," I tell him.

He smirks, looking a little devilish. "What about dessert?"

I feel my face begin to heat. "That's most definitely for later," I inform.

I just can't get enough of this guy. I'm hooked, and it's barely been two weeks. Before I can say another word, my phone rings. I rummage through my purse, which is hanging from the back of the chair. I immediately relax; it's my brother, Luke. I answer it.

"Hey!"

"Hey, sis. I just thought you should know that Dad will

be in town this weekend. He wants to have dinner with us. Can you make the drive down here?" he asks.

I can't believe I'm even hearing this come out of his mouth. "Are you kidding me, Luke? I have work to do. I won't be able to head down there until next weekend."

I hear silence for a moment. "I know your feelings on the matter, and I don't blame you one bit, but don't you think it's time to hear him out?"

"No, I really don't. I have no need to go back to the past. I've moved on from it. Just tell him I'm busy, okay?" I know it's asking a lot of him. He hates having to be in the middle of this all the time, but I never asked him to be in the middle.

He sighs. "Okay, sis. I'll do that, but just so you know, keeping this all bottled inside isn't healthy. Maybe it's time you go talk to someone about all this," he suggests.

I crinkle my forehead and shake my head at this nonsense he is talking. Kyle starts to chuckle. "Luke, that's not happening. Listen, I have to go. I'm in the middle of dinner," I tell him, trying to escape before he says any more.

He sighs again. "Okay, I love you."

"I love you, too," I tell him. I end the call.

I look up at Kyle, and he looks concerned. Damn Luke.

"Are you good?"

I shake it off and throw on a fake smile. "Yeah, he wanted to know if I would be in town this weekend. I guess my father is passing through."

I cut a piece of the chicken and direct it into my mouth. My eyes close shut in extreme pleasure. I moan as I chew in pure bliss. He is amazing in the kitchen. My stomach couldn't be happier. I open my eyes, and he is giving me a hungered look. I think I just woke up the beast.

"What?" I giggle, playing innocent.

He shakes his head. "I don't think I'm ever going to get sick of that," he says with a smile. "When's the last time you saw your father?"

It takes me a moment to think. "I don't know. Maybe ten years?"

His brows lift in shock. "Holy shit, Max. That's a *very* long time. Why did you initially stop talking to him?"

I watch him twirl his fork in the spaghetti with his spoon. "He was having an affair for years. My mom knew it, but she was too comfortable spending my father's money to even confront him. He would be off gallivanting for days. Never even took a moment to see if his kids were okay. Eventually, he ended up leaving my mother for this other woman. When he left, he didn't even look back. Then years later, he decided he wanted to be part of my life," I disclose.

Kyle looks angered but sad. "I'm so sorry he did that to you. You have every right to not speak with him. A man that does that to his family is not a man; he's a coward."

I take a much-needed sip of my wine. A tear slides down my cheek, but before Kyle sees it, I brush it away. You would think that after all these years, the pain would just fade away. But it doesn't. Every time my dad pops into our lives, the wound is reopened like it was yesterday. The only way I know how to heal is to avoid him at all costs. It may not heal pretty, but it will eventually close up the wound until the next time.

"Thank you for that," I sincerely tell him.

"So how's that chicken?"

I finish taking another sip of wine. "*Amazing!* Did you make the sauce yourself?"

He pretends to brush his shoulder off. "Yup. It's my mom's recipe, but I like to alter it a little and add my own ingredients to it."

"Well, I think you should bottle it up and sell it," I advise him before taking another bite. "So tell me something—how did your parents meet?"

Unlike me, he smiles at the thought of their story. "They met in college. They hung out with the same crowd for a couple of years, but it wasn't until their senior year that my dad got up the courage to ask her out. Of course, if you ask my father, he'll have a completely different version of the story," he says with a laugh. "They've been together ever since. My father began this business years later when Junior was a baby, and my mom's helped run it ever since. They've had their ups and downs like I mentioned before, but who doesn't? I think you have to go through down times to appreciate the great times, you know?"

I adore his positive outlook on life. I just wish I had an ounce of it to hold on to. Who the hell wants to feel negative their whole life? At first, I thought maybe Cody was my little bit of positive, but I realized quickly that he wasn't it for me. Maybe he was "it" in the beginning, but as time went on, it took too much effort to make it work. I know relationships can be hard, but I personally believe if someone's meant for someone else, it just clicks and you ride out the waves together, not separately.

"Yes, I totally agree. You know, you're pretty wise for your age," I compliment him.

He doesn't look appreciative. "Can I ask you something?"

I nod my head. "Sure, anything."

"Does our age difference bother you any?"

I take a moment to think before I answer. I want it to be said in just the right way. "As of right now, no. It's just you and I involved in some casual sex. There are moments where I think maybe I've taken advantage of you, considering I'm much older, but I also know you're not a boy. You're very much a man," I playfully joke, trying to ease the tension as he's listening extra carefully. "I'm really not sure how I would feel if your parents or people from work knew. I haven't thought of it that deeply. What about you?"

"I don't care who knows. I don't care what anyone else thinks, either. Just so we're clear, our age difference isn't even a thought in my mind. You seem a little bothered by it, though," he points out.

I smile at his boldness. "It's just because I'm the one

who's older here. Now, if this was something serious, like talking marriage and kids, I might have a bigger issue with it. But since we're just having fun, it's not really an issue," I say.

"Do you want marriage and kids?" he questions seriously.

I take a sip of my wine before responding. "No, I don't think I do. How about you?"

"I've usually been the 'hell no' type of guy, but I think if the right woman comes around, I would be willing to change that. It *has* to be the right woman though," he says with a laugh.

He pushes his plate away. I didn't even leave a drop of food on mine. I get up to clear the table. He watches me do my thing. He has a glaze over his eyes that I can't explain. It's either sexual hunger or he likes this domestic side of me. Believe me, I don't do this very often. I just figured I would clean up since he cooked.

CHAPTER TWENTY-FIVE

Kyle

I enjoy watching her. She moves around the kitchen like a ballerina. This is definitely something I could get used to. Her story saddens me deeply though. That is a lot to take on at such a young age. To turn out as well as she has says something about her character. She's not weak. She doesn't use her past as an excuse or crutch, and I admire that about her.

I've always been attracted to the easy woman, the woman that makes herself readily available. But then I get bored and go on to the next. I knew Max would be a challenge, and I was up for the chase. But what I didn't expect was how much I would enjoy being in her presence and how every time I look at her, I get hard like she was my first. She just does it for me. I don't know why or how. But how am I supposed to let go when she's done with me?

This question just lingers in my head as she pours the rest of the wine into our glasses. I get up and walk over to the couch to stretch out after the meal. I am stuffed. She looks through my CD selection near the TV. She picks one out to place into the CD player and turns to me as the room fills with Sade's "No Ordinary Love."

"Sade, huh? Isn't this before your time?" she questions with a smirk.

She comes to sit next to me. "I grew up on that. My mother loves her stuff. It just kind of grew on me. I love playing it after work when I watch the sunset with a nice glass of wine. Sound weird?"

She shakes her head and snickers. "Yeah, coming from you it does. I would have never pictured that. Now, I can picture you trying to seduce a girl while doing that, but the girls you bring back wouldn't know who the hell Sade is," I say with a laugh. The more I learn about him, the more I like. It's like he's an old soul in a new body.

"I definitely haven't played this for the girls I bring back. I gotta keep the cute bad-boy impression going, or they'll get bored of me. I can't have that happen."

She shakes her head slowly, obviously amused. "Oh no, you couldn't have that!" she teases, laughing hysterically now. I grab her wineglass from her and place it on the coffee table. She's still laughing. I start tickling her so she's almost in tears now.

"Oh my *God!* No! Wait—stop!" she screeches. "I'm gonna pee my pants!"

I immediately stop and put my palms up. "Whoa! We definitely don't want that!" I chuckle.

She sits up, straightening herself out. "That works every time," she brags, proud of herself.

I shake my head. "You are not right."

She looks at me with lust in her eyes. She crawls over my lap and straddles me. God, she is just so sexy. She unbuttons her blouse slowly. I watch, intrigued. She slides the silk off her shoulders and down her arms. Her light pink bra covers just enough to tease me as her chest heaves up and down slowly. I have to touch her. My fingers ache to feel her. I graze my fingers over the swell of her breasts. Her skin is so soft and smooth.

She unclips her bra, letting it slowly slide down her chest. My breath halts; she is so damn beautiful. She grabs my hands to place them on her breasts, her nipples taut. I lean down to suck one into my mouth; she bucks up immediately and begins to grind herself on me.

She has me hard as fuck. I unbutton her pants while still kissing her chest. I slide my fingers under her panties, through her silky wetness. I keep her breast in my mouth, biting and nibbling to drive her crazy. She rides my fingers slowly as they slip in and out of her. I can't take it anymore. I have to taste her.

I lift her up and throw her onto her back. I take off each pant leg, along with her underwear, never removing my eyes from hers. I feel a connection that is indescribable—a pull that's so magnetic, I almost can't breathe. She lies in front of me, baring it all. I can't take my eyes off of her. She's a goddess, a queen.

I lean down to taste her, grazing my tongue through her folds and over her clit. She moans as she rubs her fingers over my scalp. I can't seem to get enough. I pull away only to tease her, kissing her inner thighs. She whines in protest. I move to her other thigh and travel slowly down, leaving trails of kisses behind.

I touch her, sliding my tongue through her most intimate parts, tasting every inch of her. She moans even louder as I slip my fingers inside of her again, reaching high toward that divine spot. I work my fingers in a rhythmic pace and my tongue in small circles over her swollen skin. She moans louder and begins to scream my name as her inner walls grab ahold of my fingers, tight and pulsating, as she explodes all around me. I continue to taste her until her climax finally finishes. Beautiful.

She's spent, completely drained of energy. I lie behind her on the couch, wrapping myself around her and placing little kisses on her neck until her quick breathing subsides.

"Will you stay with me tonight?" I ask her, risking the chance of her turning me down.

She turns enough to face me. "I thought we discussed this?"

"We discussed me not spending the night when I'm at your place, but we never said anything about mine," I smirk while waiting for her response.

She shakes her head. "You are just too much."

"So, does that mean you'll stay here with me tonight?" I ask, getting excited.

She rolls her eyes. "I'll stay, but *only* because you just gave me the best orgasm ever," she agrees.

I almost want to jump up and down, ecstatic like a little kid. I get up and rummage through my drawer. I throw her one of my shirts to change into so she's comfortable. She pulls it over her head and slides her underwear back on.

She looks hot in my shirt. I don't think I've ever seen anything hotter than this.

I turn on the TV, trying to find something that we'll both like. "Do you want a movie or a reality show?" I ask, giving her the control.

"What time is it?"

I look down at my watch. "About seven thirty."

She has her pointer finger against her lips while trying to think. "Okay, so I kind of have a sick obsession when it comes to reality TV," she discloses.

I can only imagine. "Okay—"

"Don't judge me," she pleads.

She's now making me nervous. I'm afraid to say it, but I do anyways: "I won't. I promise."

"There's a *Bad Girl's Club* marathon on. I totally forgot about it until you just mentioned it!" she tells me, getting super-excited.

I burst out laughing. I can't help it. I've never heard anything so funny in my life! This corporate, business-running boss-lady loves watching the rude, crude, totally insane girls of the *Bad Girls Club*? Jeff freaking watches that show. I make fun of him every time he has it on. He's going to go crazy when I tell him.

"Oh, wow! Okay, so you like watching *that* show. What channel?"

A huge smile breaks through her face. She jumps up and down and then rushes over to give me a kiss before she sits down. I have to admit she looks so adorable when she does that. I wouldn't mind a redo on that.

"Turn to channel seventy-five," she instructs.

I spend the next hour completely blown away by how these girls act and how they project themselves to purposely be seen in a negative way. It's a complete turn off. The show is a hot mess, but more crazily, I am totally getting sucked into this shit. How the hell can this happen? It's like watching a train wreck, and I can't take my eyes off of it. I totally get it now. I still won't admit any of this to Jeff, though. He'll never let me live it up. It can be Max's and my little secret.

When the next episode is over, we take a break. She goes to the bathroom, and I open another bottle of wine. I set her glass on the coffee table and lean back against the couch, putting my feet up. She comes over and puts her feet on my lap. I don't even think twice about laying my hands on top of them like it's just something we've done forever.

We don't even have to question or calculate our moves around each other, because we just have this natural grace. We move in sync, as though we've been together forever. It's definitely a little scary, but it's also a nice change. We have no expectations, which causes no tension or the questioning of motives with one another. We can just be.

CHAPTER TWENTY-SIX

I can feel him observing me while my eyes are on the TV. It's not a scary, obsessed kind of observing; it's more like he's coming to a realization. It seems like there are things he's suddenly understanding or maybe admitting to himself. I think we all go through these emotions when getting to know one another. I also think a guy can sense early on if a woman is the one or not. The only difference is that a woman will walk away as soon as she realizes someone isn't the one. A man will stay, if only for the pleasure of getting his rocks off.

I can only imagine what he's thinking. Should I just be straightforward and ask? Or should I wait until he's ready to tell? But what man is ever open about his feelings? I don't even know if I'm ready to hear the answer if I ask.

"What are you thinking?"

Wait. Did he just beat me to the punch?

"Um, I was actually going to ask you the same thing. I just wasn't so sure I would want to hear the answer," I admit.

He chuckles. "You are just too much. You constantly overthink things. If you ever want to know something, just ask. There's no reason for us to hide anything from each other. We're not technically in a relationship, so there's no worry about stepping on each other's toes, right?"

I loosen up a little. "So, I don't really say this often, but maybe you're right," I quickly put my hand over his mouth before he can get too cocky. "But don't get too used to it," I warn him. I slowly remove my hand from his mouth. He just continues to look at me, gratified. I roll my eyes.

"So, let's get back to the question. What were you thinking?"

"I felt you looking at me. No one observes someone without a thought. I wanted to know what that thought was."

He presses his lips together while nodding. "I was just thinking about how natural you and I feel. We're like the cool breeze; we just go. It's never been this easy before. Of course, I realize now that I've always picked the wrong kind of girl before," he explains honestly.

"Before what?"

He makes sure to look me in the eyes. It seems to be a thing he does when he wants my full attention. "Before you."

I look away from him, trying to keep the conversation light. There's no need to get too deep with all this. Nothing good can come from that.

"So Beth was the wrong kind of girl, right? Is that the type of girl you usually go for?" I ask.

"She was most definitely the wrong kind of girl. Usually, that's my type. They're all the same: completely self-absorbed. It gets tiring after a while, dealing with girls like that. That's why I ended it with her," he explains.

"I saw her in the bathroom yesterday. She wanted to know if I would be at McGregor's tonight."

"She asked me the same thing today. What did you tell her?"

I grab my wineglass off the coffee table. "I told her I wasn't sure. I had to leave my options open in case someone special wanted to hang."

"As far as I'm concerned, my nights are all booked up until future notice," he states. He is adorable. He looks at me like I'm the most beautiful thing in the world. His smoldering brown eyes glisten and twinkle when he looks my way. I'm not too sure he even realizes this, but I feel as though I look at him the same.

It's getting late, pretty close to nine o'clock. He downs the rest of his wine and then stands up, offering me his hand. I place mine into his, and he pulls me up. "I think we should get warm in bed. We don't have to cuddle, but we can lie next to each other for body heat," he teases.

Did I really freak out that bad? I guess cuddling isn't that serious. Friends do it all the time. Friends with benefits do it more often than normal. But where does the line end?

I smack his shoulder after emptying my wineglass. He walks me over to the bathroom, reaches in his drawer, and hands me a brand new toothbrush. My eyebrow raises. I don't even have to ask, because he already knows.

"Yes, I keep extra toothbrushes around in case my company needs one. It's called being prepared." He puts toothpaste on his and turns on the water to wet it.

He begins brushing. "You know, this is kind of sick, but I do have to give it to you on the player meter," I say. "But what happens with the toothbrush after? Do they leave it, hoping it will be there for the next night they spend over, or do you tell them to throw it out so they know this isn't a regular thing?" I question while he rinses his mouth with water.

He holds up his finger for me to wait. After he's done spitting, he moves over and allows me to take his spot. "I tell them to throw it away or take it with them," he answers honestly.

My brows now furrow. I finish brushing and rinsing. "Wow. You're pretty ruthless. I think I'm going to take mine with me, if that's okay?" I start walking out of the bathroom, but he stops me. He takes my toothbrush out of my hand and places it in the cup next to his. He doesn't say another word. He just grabs my hand and pulls me toward the bed.

I unconsciously begin to moan. Whatever it is I'm moaning about feels so damn good. This is one *hell* of a dream, and I don't want to wake up. My body rocks with pleasure. Light kisses are applied on my skin below my neck. I want to open my eyes, but they feel so heavy. I'm stuck in a haze. Everything I feel is heightened by ten, so dream-like. The build-up in my core is going to bust at any moment. I hear a voice through the thick muck. It's far away yet so close and so familiar. I begin to crack my eyes open. I break free from the fog and everything around me is pitch black.

"Hey, there. You're awake," he says, still applying light kisses up my neck.

I can't even talk. I allow my body to guide me and take control of my emotions. I push him over and climb on top of him. He lifts me up and strips off my panties. He's already stripped himself of his own clothing. I lean down for a kiss. Our lips connect and our tongues collide. He's waiting at my entrance for me to make the move. I can't wait any longer; I need him inside of me.

I guide my weight down as he enters me. We both hiss with anticipation as I stretch to accommodate him. I don't stop until I am filled to the max with him. My sex is throbbing around him. He holds me still as we kiss so he can gain control of himself. Any small movement from me might make him combust.

His lips leave mine to travel down my neck while directing me with his hands. He rocks into me slowly, guiding me while he's deep within me. I can't take this slow shit any longer. I break free, anchoring my hands on his chest, and roll my hips in wild, untamed movements. Every thrust revvs me up and builds the tension. When his thumb grazes over my delicate skin, I can't hold back any longer. I begin to scream his name, riding him with a vengeance. As I become completely undone, he follows, filling me to the brim while yelling my name. Nothing pleasures me more than to hear his cries as his body convulses inside of me.

I drop against him, nuzzling my face into his neck. He strokes his fingers up and down my spine. We lie here together, connected, until we almost fall asleep.

"I have to clean myself up," I whisper.

"Grab me a towel."

He whines when he slips out of me. I throw him a towel and head to the bathroom. By the time I come back, he is sound asleep. He looks so peaceful and so magnificent. My heart aches with the thought of someday not being this close to him anymore. He's becoming a small fixture in my life. Who says goodbye first?

CHAPTER TWENTY-SEVEN

Kyle

I roll over to grab Max, but she's not there. The sheets beside me are cold as though she's been gone for a while now. I sit up, pissed. Her clothes and purse are gone. *She's gone.* I slam my body back down on the bed and begin sulking. Why does she do this? It's like she's always running, but why?

Just when I think we understand each other, this happens. I just don't get it. She wants boundaries and rules, but who are they for exactly? If she sets them, she doesn't get attached or she won't feel as guilty when she decides to walk away.

If she does decide to walk away, will I be able to let her go? I've never had a problem letting go before, but the big question is—will I have a problem now?

I jump in the shower and allow the steam and hot water to loosen my tension. The knots in my back begin to unravel and the anger slides away. It is what it is. She's made it clear we are friends with benefits, and I made the decision to accept that. So I'm going to stand by my word.

I dry myself off and wrap my towel around my hips. I hear my phone ring in the other room. It could be Max, so I hustle to grab it, only to find that it's my mother. Go figure.

"Hey, Ma."

"Well, good morning to you. You don't sound like your normal self. Are you not feeling well?"

No, I feel terrible. "I'm alright," I answer.

"Maybe you should stay home today," she states.

You know what, maybe I *should* stay home today. I'm aggravated and don't feel like being bothered, and the last thing I want to see is Jonathan hitting on my girl. Shit! My girl? This is worse than I thought. She's right. I should stay home.

"I guess you're right. I'm not feeling that great, actually."

"Okay, you stay home and rest. Do you need me to bring you anything? Do you have any medicine? Or I can bring you some chicken soup for lunch?" she asks, concerned. What would I do without my mother?

"I'm fine, Ma. I'm just going to sleep it off. I'll be rested for tomorrow," I tell her.

"Okay, love. Call me if you need anything."

"I will."

I end the call, throw my boxers and sweatpants on, and sprawl out on my couch. Today is going to be a don't-bother-me day. I just want to veg out in front of my TV and snooze all day. I switch my phone to silent and toss it lightly on my coffee table. I'm not looking at it until tomorrow morning. Everyone can just screw off today.

I end up drifting in and out of sleep all afternoon. It's four o'clock, and my stomach is growling. I look over at the kitchen, but I'm definitely not in the mood to cook.

Maybe I'll just order some takeout. I lift up my phone to order and realize I have five missed calls and three texts—all from Max.

The first text:

"I'm sorry I didn't say goodbye. I didn't want to wake you. You looked so peaceful."

Second text:

"Are you okay? Your mom said you're not feeling well. Text me if you need me to grab you something."

Third text:

"I'm on my way. You better answer your door."

Before I can even text back, my buzzer goes off. It's Max. I open the door and head back to the couch. She can let herself in; she sure knows how to let herself out. I hear her heels click across the room and then stop. I look up at her, and she has her hands on her hips.

"It's not even five o'clock yet. You should still be at work," I say.

She huffs. "I left early to check on you. You won't answer my calls. You won't respond to my texts! Are you even sick? You don't look sick!" she observes, slowly raising her voice.

"You would have known had you been here when I woke up," I snap.

She rolls her eyes. "So that's what the cold shoulder is all about. I texted you about why I left. I woke up early and went back to the hotel to get ready. I went into work early, and I didn't want to wake you!" she yells.

I stand up, now heated. "No, you woke up in a panic just like you did the last time and the time before that! You're running from something. What are you so scared of? That you might actually like me? That you might actually feel something for me?

"Well let me lay it all out for you: *I* like you, and I most *definitely* feel something for you. What? I don't know, but it's something, and I'm not going to run like a coward. You're worth it enough to find out what that something is exactly," I reveal to her.

I sit back down, calm. She stands in front of me, clearly unsure of what to say. I reach out for her. "Come here." She complies and takes a seat on my lap. She leans her head against my shoulder.

"Yes, I freaked out before, but not this morning. Did you really stay home because you were upset with me?" she wonders.

I chuckle. "Yes and no. I was ready to barge into your office and call you out on your bullshit, but I knew that wouldn't go over very well. So, I stayed home. I needed the rest anyways. I was feeling a little under the weather, regardless," I confess.

"So you were ready to barge into my office like I just barged into your apartment just now?" she questions, beginning to laugh.

I laugh also. "Yeah, I guess you're right. Just please don't leave me again without saying goodbye. I don't care how awesome I look sleeping, okay?"

She smacks me in the abs, and we both laugh.

"Okay, I promise."

"Are you hungry?" I ask.

"Starving."

I lift her up and place her standing on the floor as I get up from the couch. "Then let's go out and grab something. I'm sick of being in the house."

Her smile is sexy as hell. "Okay."

We head out in my car. I stop at a little burger joint that's connected to a strip mall. I figure we can eat and then go window-shopping.

I order the bacon cheeseburger, which is the best burger on earth, and she orders the same. I love a girl who can eat like me. We share some onion rings, and we both get a strawberry shake. We are in and out right before the dinner rush.

It's pretty cold out. Who am I kidding? It's fucking freezing out! I slip on my beanie, slide on my gloves, and wrap my arm around her. She pauses momentarily.

"What's up?" I ask, confused.

"We probably should keep it casual just in case we run into anyone we know," she suggests. I can't say I don't agree, because she's right—we could run into anyone from work at any second. I was just too caught up in the moment.

Thank goodness we leave next week to a whole other state. We won't have to act and pretend about anything. We can just be. "You're right. I wasn't even thinking," I agree.

We walk by an Old Navy and a couple of other clothing stores. When we get to Pier One, Max jumps up and down. "I absolutely *love* this store! I've been dying to see if this store carries anything different than the one back home."

I shake my head. "You're really this excited over a home store?"

"A home store? Let's go," she demands, holding the door open for me to enter first.

The first thing I notice when I walk in is the smell. It's an earthy sweetness that seems to calm and help center the surrounding energy. It's comforting, relaxing. Then I notice all the shiny, glittery glasses along the shelves. I'm nervous to even walk around, afraid of shattering them. There are incredibly unique knickknacks that fill the crevasses of each and every space. This style is sophisticated and sassy. I can see how this store can get addicting.

I look at Max, and she is in her glory.

"So, what do you think?" she questions.

I nod in agreement. "It's nice. I like it. I guess I know where to go now if I need to decorate. Maybe you can help me out one day and be my personal decorator?"

She giggles. "Maybe I could. That would be fun, making your apartment all girlie," she taunts.

We look around for a bit longer and then exit the building. Target is down a ways. I have to grab a few items for the apartment. Just before we're about to enter, Jonathan comes out of the exit. We're too busy laughing to notice.

"Maxine? Kyle?" he says, a little taken aback.

Max greets him first. "Oh, hey Jonathan."

I just nod.

"What are you two up to? You seem to be feeling better, Kyle," he states, eyeing me suspiciously.

"Yup, I took some medicine and got some rest. I'm feeling much better," I say proudly.

Max clears her throat. "Well it was nice running into you. We'll see you tomorrow." We begin to walk toward the doors.

"Yes, okay. We're still on, right?" Jonathan asks, raising his voice.

She turns. "Yes, we're still on!"

He smiles, then turns away. My face hardens with disgust, and jealousy boils through my veins. I try to push it down, but it just seeps out. I need to slip away for a moment to calm down.

"I have to use the restroom. I'll be right back," I announce.

"Okay. I'll be by the books."

I should have figured that's where I'd find her. We have to keep up with the trends in our industry. It's our job to figure out what's hot and what will sell. But it's kind of like playing blackjack. We all try to guess what card will be dealt next, but ultimately it's the cards themselves in control.

I hate when my temper gets the best of me. The last thing I want to do is direct it toward Max. She doesn't deserve that. I finish up in the bathroom and head out to find her. She's exactly where she said she would be, by the books.

"Did you find anything good?"

"Just my own authors up on the shelves. I know how to pick them, huh?" she brags.

I can't help but laugh. She's too adorable when she gets this way.

"So, what time will you be done with dickface tomorrow?"

She elbows me in the gut. I pretend it hurts. "I'll be done with Jonathan around five or so. What time will we be meeting Elise and Jeff?"

"I think about seven. They want to grab a bite to eat before the show."

We head over to the cleaning aisle. "Okay, I'll probably be starving by then. I have a feeling Jonathan's going to try to suck me into dinner."

I immediately respond, "If he does, just tell him you already have plans with me."

She shakes her head. "Oh no. I most definitely won't be saying that. It's enough he saw us out tonight. If I tell him I'm spending another weekend with you, he's going to think something's up," she explains.

I grab some products and candles from the shelves. "Who cares? Let him think whatever he wants." We walk back toward the registers.

She slows down. "Um, we agreed that this was going to stay between us. If Greg and Connie find out that I'm banging their son, shit's going to go down!" she screeches in a whisper.

I chuckle. "Okay, okay. Take a joke, woman! The girl I'm with has to be pretty special in order for others to think I'm with her." I wink, just playing with her.

"Ha, ha! You're too funny for your own good."

I pay for my things, and we head back to the car. My phone rings; it's my mother.

"Hey, Ma."

"Hi honey. Are you feeling any better?" she asks, clearly still worried.

I unlock the car doors. "I feel much better. I slept it all off."

"Okay, well I'll check up on you later."

"You don't have to. I'm fine. I have plans anyways that I couldn't break, so I won't be home," I lie. I'm taking Max back to my place, and I'm holding her hostage until the morning. This time we're stopping by the hotel to get some of her belongings. That way she has no excuses in the morning.

"Okay. I'll talk to you tomorrow."

I end the call and start the ignition. The leather seats are freezing this time of year. I flip both our seat heaters up to high. I catch her glancing over at me.

"I know; I'm too hot. You just couldn't resist a peek, could you?"

"Oh. My. God! You are just full of it today! I think you got way too much sleep," she says. "So, what are these big plans of yours?"

I head out of the parking lot toward her hotel. "I'm kidnapping you tonight. First, I'm taking you to your hotel so you can grab some clothes, and then we're locking ourselves in my apartment for the night. I have many, many things I want to do to you."

She sucks in her breath and bites her bottom lip. Panic has not entered her thoughts yet. They're too filled with dirty images. I can tell I've just excited her by the way her leg rocks back and forth. She's ready for me now. I should just find a place to pull over and have her ride me like she did last night. She was unbelievable.

The best part was watching her come undone. She starts with little cries while biting her bottom lip, doing her best to hold it all back. Her curves and her silky skin are like a piece of beautiful fine art that you can't help but stare at. I study her every move, burning them into my brain. She's just so mesmerizing. I can't get enough of her. Man, I think I'm in big trouble.

"So what are you waiting for? Step on it!" she demands.

I laugh out loud. I like when she's all demanding. It's sexy as hell. Maybe we should try a little role-playing; she can be my personal dominatrix.

"Okay, I'm stepping on it. Do you need me to come up with you, or should I wait out here?" I ask.

"No, you stay out here. If we both go up there, we might not come back out." She gives me a devilish smirk.

I chuckle to myself. I pull up to the hotel, parking right

in front for a fast getaway. She leans over to give me a nice long kiss, completely seducing me in every way possible. She now has me hard as a rock. She pulls away and gives me a wink before she exits the car. *Damn!* I quickly adjust myself and wait.

CHAPTER TWENTY-EIGHT

I grab my little to-go bag and fill it to the max. I need options when I get ready in the mornings. One outfit won't do. I pack the rest of my girlie stuff, and just as I'm about to head out, my phone rings. I reach into my pocket. It's Cody. Damn it! Why can't he just let me be? I've said all I can to him. There's nothing left to talk about. I press "Ignore" and head downstairs.

"You ready?" Kyle asks.

"Yup."

We pull off. I look out the window, watching the city pass by us. It's a little surreal; in just a number of weeks, this will be my new home. No family, new friends—I totally need Kinsey in my life. She grounds me, she keeps me sane, and she's the only one who totally gets me and knows me inside and out.

"Hey, what are you thinking about?" Kyle asks.

I sigh. "Kinsey. I have to call and check in with her. I was supposed to earlier, but I left the office in such a rush."

"Because of me."

I look over at him and smile. "Yes, because of you," I admit.

"Well, listen, I need to do some household stuff and get some laundry done. So, you take any part of the apartment you want and turn it into your mini travel office. I'll stay out of your way until you're ready for me," he offers.

My heart melts. "Really? You would do that for me?" He's beginning to seem too good to be true.

He grabs my head and brings it to his lips. "Of course," he responds.

Oh, he is good. He is *real* good!

We pull into his parking lot, and I look around at the cars, particularly for that gold car that was parked here the other night. It's not here. I'm just being silly. I shake the weird thought from my head. I don't even know why I focused so much on that car. I see gold cars all the time.

I pick the bar countertop for the best makeshift work area. It has a plug for my computer as well as my phone charger and seems like a good spot that Kyle can work around. I have to admit, seeing Kyle clean does something for me. I could get used to this scenario: me working and him working around the house. Oh my, I'm letting my mind drift way too far into the future. Not good. Not good at all.

I dial Kinsey's number.

"Hey, I've been waiting for your call. Where'd you go?" she asks.

I pull up my schedule on my computer. "Sorry, got a little caught up. Let's go over this month's schedule. Are you still in the office?"

"Yup, still here. What's new? Okay, I've got it up."

"Okay, so I'm coming back next weekend to pack up. I know this is last-minute, but I need you here tomorrow to come house hunting with me. I found a couple of apartments for you that seem really nice and aren't far from the office. I already booked you a flight today. I'm emailing it to you now."

"I just got it. Will there be a car picking me up?"

"No, I'm grabbing you after I leave work, and from there, we're going to be meeting Jonathan. He's one of the agents. I think he has a hard-on for me," I tell her, quickly looking around to make sure Kyle didn't overhear.

She bursts out laughing. "That's awesome. I totally need some entertainment. I've been bored out of my mind. I need some company," she confesses. "Tell me, are there any hotties there?"

I should have known this was coming next. "I don't know! I'm the boss; remember? I don't have time to be scoping out the 'hotties,'" I lie. God, if she only knew. She'd totally kill me for not telling her about Kyle and me.

"Pssh! Yeah, okay. Like I believe that!" She totally just called me out on my bullshit like she always does. "Oh, I completely forgot to tell you that Cody stopped in the office."

I sigh. "What did he want?"

"He wanted to know where in New York you are. I think he's going crazy. Did you tell him anything yet?"

"Yes! He just won't accept it. He even called Luke before I could to tell him I was moving!"

"Oh no! I'm sure that went over real well," she says sarcastically.

"Tell me about it," I huff. "I can't believe I forgot to tell you. I've been so slammed trying to redirect everything and meld the two agencies together as seamlessly as possible."

"Well, I'll be there soon to alleviate some of the workload." She always knows how to make me feel better. She's a gift from God.

We continue catching up as much as possible. I look out the window after I hang up and realize its pitch-black out. What time is it? Holy crap! It's almost seven o'clock. Kyle is lounging out on the couch with the TV on a low muffle. I didn't even realize it was this late. He's so sweet not to have bothered me.

I quietly walk over to the back of the couch and wrap my arms around Kyle's neck. He stretches and then runs his hands over my arms. The little hairs on my body stand up from his contact. His touch alone ignites my dormant embers into violent flames. I lay small kisses along the nape of his neck; he moans. I reach for his shirt and pull it up over his head.

The contours of his pecks all the way down to his rippling abs are just the beginning of my downfall. I think I've died and gone to heaven. How will I ever be able to look at another man again? He's ruined it for me. *This* is perfection. It can't get much better than this.

He turns around and kneels on the couch. He runs his hands through my hair, bringing my face to his. He kisses me with urgency, an intense need to be connected. His tongue dives into my mouth, coaxing me to follow its lead.

My body burns with desire and a dulling throb is now prominent between my legs.

He climbs over the couch and bends down, scoops me up, and wraps my legs around his waist in one movement. I feel him fully erect underneath me. Our breathing is rugged and completely sporadic. I can't get enough of him.

He lays me on my back with my legs still wrapped around his waist as he stands at the edge of the bed. My skirt is already up to my waist; he then slips my panties to the side and strokes his fingers through my throbbing folds. I close my eyes in complete bliss. His sweatpants fall down to the floor. I open my eyes and watch him stroke himself while entering his fingers inside of me.

My breath catches as he stretches me, preparing me for his width and length. I whine with impatience. I *need* him inside of me. I don't want to wait another minute. He lays the tip of his cock at my entrance, teasing me and enjoying every minute of it. He slowly eases himself in bit by bit until he's finally filled me to the max. I can't help but let out a moan of induced pleasure. He pumps deep into me, thrusting with everything he's got to drive me over the edge.

A layer of sweat coats our bodies as we work ourselves to the hilt. Each pump brings us closer to release. "Baby, I can't hold myself off much longer," he growls.

He applies more pressure to my now-hypersensitive sweet spot while plunging into me like a champ. My body responds by clenching around him in rippling effects. The tide descends only momentarily, builds intensely, and comes crashing down like a tsunami. Both of us fall over the edge, crashing into pure ecstasy.

We lie in a sweaty heap of exhausted mess until we fall asleep.

I open my eyes to the screeching beep of the alarm. It's seven thirty already. I didn't budge at all last night. I don't even remember falling asleep. Kyle quiets the wretched noise and then rolls over, closer to me.

"Hey, good morning," he whispers. His voice is scratchy and sexy.

I snuggle into him. "Morning. I can't believe we're going in to work on a Saturday!" I whine.

He wraps his arms around me. "Come on, let's go get in the shower."

"Oh my God, it's cold! Do you have to sleep with a fan on in the middle of winter?" I gripe. He laughs.

He takes my hand, and I follow his lead to the bathroom. He lifts up my T-shirt over my head and drops my panties to the floor. He washes my hair and then my body. I do the same for him. No words are really spoken; it's just a calming silence. He most definitely is not a normal twenty-four-year-old. I mean, who washes a girl from head to toe? He's romantic and thoughtful. I love it.

I take over the bathroom with all my girlie products, and he doesn't seem to mind whatsoever. I quickly text Junior to cancel our gym date before I finish up. We get ready to leave, but then I remember the situation at hand. "Wait. You need to drop me off to my car. We can't show up to work together."

He laughs and shakes his head. "Okay, I'll drop you off on the way."

"You think I'm freaking out, don't you?"

He opts not to answer this time. We jump in the car and wait for it to warm up.

"No. Well, maybe a little," he finally admits. "But I get it," he smiles. "Will you be coming back to my apartment after work?"

"Of course. I didn't pack a bag for nothing," I tease.

He pulls out of the parking lot and heads to my hotel.

Connie calls me and asks me to her office. She has a new client in the works and wants me to meet with her; she thinks we'll be a good fit. Already, we're expanding our agency. It can only get better from here. I'm excited to see our company flourish and to see where we are a year from now.

I knock on Connie's door before walking in. "Good morning," I say before taking a seat in front of her desk.

"Morning! It's only eight thirty in the morning on a Saturday, and my emails are already outrageous!" Connie gripes.

I laugh. "Yeah, I hear you on that. I haven't even looked at mine yet."

"Okay, so this client, Kelly, is a young adult fiction

writer. This is her second book of a trilogy. She already has a massive amount of followers, and she has sold over twenty thousand copies already. I don't think she expected to blow up so fast. She needs guidance and direction," Connie explains.

"Okay, what time will she be in?"

"She should be here at ten. She's actually a local author, if you can believe it. We don't usually find a lot of local talent," she says. Connie's great at multi-tasking. She's texting, checking her emails, and filling me in all at the same time.

"Great! I can't wait to meet her. Oh, Kinsey comes in later today. She'll be staying here and traveling back with me on Thursday. I'll be catching her up all next week," I inform her.

Connie's responding to an email on her laptop. "Oh good! I can have Junior catch her up on the basics," she offers.

"Yes, that would be great. She can spend the first half of each day with him and the second half with me. She should be pretty caught up by the time we head back. We're meeting up with Jonathan later to search for some houses and to look at some apartments for her. I already know it's going to be a long day."

She looks up at me from her laptop. "How about you stop over for dinner tonight?"

Shoot! She just had to pick tonight. "Actually I have plans with Kinsey tonight. Can I take a rain check?"

"Yes, of course. I'm making sauce tomorrow night. I'm going to have the boys over. Why don't you bring Kinsey with you? How does six o'clock sound?" she asks.

"Perfect. Do you need me to bring anything?"

She puts her glasses on. "Just yourselves."

"Sounds good."

I feel a little guilty sneaking around. This is normally not my thing. I'm not sure how Greg and Connie would feel, though, if they found out about my extracurricular activities with their youngest son. I should probably be safe and stop this before someone gets hurt or too attached, but every time I think of not spending time with Kyle, I panic. I don't want to stop. I *can't* stop.

Am I already too attached? This is my own doing. I should have just kept it to sex and nothing more. Lines begin to get blurred when you spend so much time together. The black and white becomes gray. Friends with benefits suddenly find themselves in a relationship without even meaning to. Things get way too complicated. I feel *we're* getting too complicated.

CHAPTER TWENTY-NINE

Kyle

Work drags by; the minutes feel like hours, and the hours feel like days. I'm just ready to chill out with Max and put in a nice afternoon movie, maybe order a pizza. It's finally almost noon. I head out to my car. I see Beth watching me as she gets into her gold Honda. I didn't even realize she comes in on Saturdays. Strange. It's like she's always creeping around.

I shake her off and jump in my car. I can't wait for this cold weather to end. I'm ready for some cookouts, beer, and outdoor fun. I'm beginning to get antsy. I can't wait to see Max in some shorts and bathing suits. I'm not going to be able to keep my hands off of her. I get hard just by the thought of this.

This whole thing has totally backfired on me. I had sex with her to get her out of my mind, but now I can't go one hour without thinking about her. Crazy. I have got to get myself together. What the hell happened to my single-guy attitude? I was so set on living the bachelor life that I never saw this coming. I never saw *her* coming. I'm in big trouble.

I head over to my apartment, and Max pulls up right after I do. I wait for her before I go up. I do my normal ritual when we get inside: throw my keys on the counter, hang my jacket up in the coat closet, remove my shoes, and grab a glass of ice-cold water.

Max follows my steps and goes through the same motions. Except for water, though, she asks for an ice-cold beer. I chuckle at her request because I was thinking the exact same thing. It's been a long week. An afternoon beer seems like heaven at the moment.

I twist off the cap on both beers. I hand her one, and we both take a nice long swig.

"Ugh! This is exactly what I needed," she says.

I smirk. "I'm going to get changed into some sweats. Do you need a pair, or do you have something to wear?" I ask.

She walks over to her packed bag and pulls out a pair of blue sweats and a matching T-shirt from Victoria's Secret.

"Got it covered," she announces. I nod my head in approval.

"Pizza for lunch?" I ask.

She takes another sip of her beer. "That sounds great. I could go for some greasy therapy to start the weekend off right!"

I call in the pizza and grab two more beers for us. We look through Movies On Demand to see what's out to rent. We decide on *Think Like a Man Too*. The first one was hysterical. I could use a good laugh, and I need something to keep my mind distracted. I know she'll be spending time with Jonathan, but I also know Kinsey will be with them. That eased my mind some when she told me that last night. Then the rest of the night, she's all mine.

I get to be the lucky man who lies with her in bed tonight and wakes up with her in the morning, not him. If only I could let that be known to him, I would feel one hundred percent better. Knowing that while he's fanaticizing about her, I actually get to act out my fantasies *with* her is also a satisfying thought.

We wait to start the movie until the pizza comes. Once it finally arrives, we grub and then put the movie on. We end up falling asleep on the couch before it ends. I wake her up and drag us into bed for a short afternoon nap. We're both exhausted. I wrap her up in my arms, and we fall back to sleep.

CHAPTER THIRTY

I stretch and feel completely rested and satisfied after our nice nap. Falling asleep in his arms without panic seems to be happening more and more lately. The sun is desperately peeking through the curtains, leaving small rays of light to illuminate the darkness. I let my eyes adjust.

It's already three o'clock. I need to be at the airport at four to pick up Kinsey, and then we're meeting Jonathan at the first house. I roll over to sneak off the bed. He looks so peaceful sleeping. This time, though, I'm not going to leave without saying goodbye.

He pulls me back to him before I can get up. "Where are you going?"

I turn to face him. He has a hungry look in his eyes. "I have to get ready. I can't be late picking up Kinsey. She hates that," I explain.

"Damn, so no afternoon sex then?" he says with a pout.

He looks adorable when he pouts. I almost want to give in, but I can't. "No afternoon sex." I giggle. He snuggles up to my neck and lays sweet sensual kisses there. "That's not helping."

He growls, knowing he is affecting me. "Go get ready. I'm going back to sleep. Wake me when you leave."

"Okay, I will."

I put on some casual winter clothes along with my brown Uggs. These things are so damn comfortable. I wrap up in my warm beige scarf, then head over to the bed. He's buried himself under the comforter. I jostle him lightly until he wakes.

"I'm leaving," I tell him.

He smiles and rubs his fingers along my cheek. "Okay baby. Good luck."

I pull up to the airport. Kinsey has already arrived. I see her at the baggage claim, waiting for her suitcase. I hit the button to pop open the trunk for her.

Kinsey jumps in the car. "Hey!" We give each other a big squeeze.

"Hey girl. These airports are getting worse and worse. It takes forever to get through these things now!" she says. "So, where are we headed?"

I pull off and head to the expressway. "We're meeting Jonathan at a house out in Spencerport. It's about twenty minutes from the office. I'm not too sure I want to be that far away, but I told him I would take a look anyways."

"Are you sure you're ready to buy a house? Why not an apartment? Or why not just bunk up with me for a while, at least until we get used to it here?" she offers.

I head west on 390. "I was weighing that as an option, actually, maybe just until I'm able to find the perfect house," I reply. "Just to forewarn you, I think Jonathan is most definitely on the prowl for some ass. He's getting divorced, and I think he's just lonely. He's a nice guy though, a really good agent."

Kinsey rubs her hands together. "Oh yeah, I'm dying for some entertainment!"

"Speaking of entertainment—has Cody contacted you again?" I question.

She sighs. "No, thank God! That was such an awkward conversation. He was almost in a crazed panic when he came in the office. I think he's a little obsessed, but I also know you kind of left him hanging," she says, scolding me slightly. This is just Kinsey being Kinsey. She doesn't hold anything back. I love and hate this part of her.

"I know, but to be fair, I *did* tell him I didn't want to marry him. I told him I needed space. You saw how clingy he was getting—"

"Yeah, he was definitely making his presence known. You don't think your brother will tell him where you are, do you?" she asks.

I don't even have to think twice. "No, no way. He actually already tried. Luke's not giving anything up, and I still haven't talked to Justin, so he doesn't know where I am, unless Luke told him."

We finally pull up to the house. It's cute. It looks like a cottage with a two-car garage. I wave to Jonathan as I pull in the driveway. I look over to Kinsey. "Here we go! You ready?"

"I'm ready to be entertained," she says, giggling.

We get out of my car to greet Jonathan and the realtor. "Hello," I say to Jonathan, giving him a quick hug. "Jonathan, this is Kinsey, my assistant."

He places his hand out to her. "Hey, it's great to meet you," Jonathan says.

Kinsey smirks. "Nice to meet you too, Jonathan." I can see the twinkle of mischief in her eyes.

He turns to the realtor. "This is Jessica; she'll be showing us the houses today." Kinsey and I both wave hello to her. "You ladies ready?" Jonathan asks, clapping his hands together.

"Yup, we're ready!" I announce. I'm actually really excited to get my new life started.

After we look at four houses, we move on to the apartments. None of the houses did it for me. I didn't get that *wow* factor. I just need more time to search. The first two apartments are nice but a little further from work than Kinsey would like. We make it to the third and final apartment, and she seems impressed. I am too, actually.

"This is amazing!" Kinsey and I say at the same time.

"Go ahead and check it out. Jonathan and I will wait here in the kitchen," Jessica tells us.

We walk through the apartment. It's a downtown loft with 1,500 square feet, two bedrooms, marble countertops, and brand-new appliances. It's on the top floor out of six, and the view is unbelievable. It even has a small deck off of the living room. This is definitely a place to die for. It's a little pricey, but if I become a roommate and chip in half, it really wouldn't be that bad at all.

"What do you think?" Kinsey says as she turns to me excitedly.

I continue to take everything in. "I think it's magnificent. It's way more than just an apartment. The price is steep though."

She stands in front of me with her huge grin. "It won't be if we become roomies!" she hints. "Will you move in with me?"

I laugh. It sounds like she just proposed to me. "Do I get a ring?"

She smacks my arm. "Do you need one?" she teases.

"Let's do it!" I agree.

She starts jumping up and down, squealing like a little kid. Jonathan and Jessica stroll over after hearing all the noise. "So—what do you think?" Jessica asks.

Kinsey immediately responds. "We'll take it!"

It only took two hours, but we finally found *the* place. I'm kind of happy about the decision. We'll be able to work late nights together in our own place, and I get to look thoroughly for the perfect house while saving some money. This is a win-win for the both of us.

We sign all the paperwork to move in on the first. This gives us enough time to pack and relocate. We head downstairs. Jessica says her goodbyes, and Jonathan sticks around to talk some.

"Hey, do you ladies want to grab something to eat?" he asks us.

We both look at each other and then back to him. "Well, we actually made plans already. We need to catch up on a lot. It's hard handling everything over the phone," I tell him, also saving Kinsey from having to make her own awkward excuse.

"Oh, well I understand," he says, a little let down.

"Definitely another time, Jonathan. We really appreciate your help. We couldn't have found this place without you," Kinsey points out.

I join in. "Yes, you've been a great help! We'll have to do lunch sometime next week, all three of us."

We begin walking toward our cars. "Okay, that sounds good. Just let me know when, and I'll be there! Enjoy the rest of your night, ladies." He waves goodbye and hops in his car. Phew! That letdown wasn't so bad. I feel a little guilty, only because he took so much time out of his day to help, but he offered.

We both get into the car and let out a sigh of relief. "That wasn't so bad, was it?" I ask her.

"No, he actually is a really nice guy. Of course he's going to hit on you—look at you! Ever since I came into your life, you've never had a problem with the opposite sex," she jokes.

"Ha-ha. Very funny," I express sarcastically.

"So where to now, captain?"

I make the drive to my hotel so she can get changed and unpack. "Well, I kind of have plans with Greg and Connie's son, Kyle. We're going out with his friend Jeff and Elise, who is the receptionist at the agency. You can come be the fifth wheel. We're just all going to get something to eat and then going to see a band."

She shakes her head. "Wait, hold on! Is this a double date you're going on? And did I just hear it's with Greg and Connie's son? Is he even old enough to hang out with us?"

I totally knew she was going to make a big deal out of this. "No, it's not a double date or a date of any kind for that matter. And yes, Kyle is old enough to drink, so he's old enough to hang. I don't know Jeff that well, but Elise is great. She reminds me a lot of me before I met you," I explain.

"Oh no, does this require another makeover?" she squeals in excitement.

I laugh. "Yup, that's exactly what this requires. She is beautiful already. She just needs a little push in the right direction, some good guidance, and some good girlfriends," I say, breaking it down for her.

"Well, she met the right set of girls for that! I can totally be the fifth wheel if there are no dates involved."

I park in the garage. "Nope, no dates," I reiterate.

We get up to the room. I relax while Kinsey freshens up. We have a little time before we have to meet up with them. Kyle's going to be a little bummed to hear I have to meet him there and also a little bummed that I won't be able to go back to his place with him later. I'm not ready to explain to Kinsey the real deal. I'm not ready to explain it out loud to anyone for that matter. I don't want any outside opinions. I'm okay with what we're doing for the moment, so there's no need to get anyone else involved.

I shoot him a quick text to inform him of the changes. He's disappointed but understands, and he is happy to meet Kinsey finally. I talk about her enough that he feels as though he already knows her. I just know Kinsey's going to take one look at us interacting together and know what's going on. She's always been so in tune with me that even though I want to keep it from her, she will see right through me.

"So, what's the dress code for tonight?" Kinsey asks, picking through her clothes.

I'm still lying on the bed. "Um, casual for sure."

She holds up a navy blue sweater and some cute ripped jeans. I nod in approval. I guess it's my turn to freshen up. I drag myself up and move toward the bathroom. I jump in the shower quickly, not wetting my hair, and jump back out. I touch up my makeup and pull out some comfy clothes as well. I'm sick of heels, and it's not an Ugg-wearing event, so I grab my flat boots.

It's now seven. We have to meet everyone at Tony D's before the show for some appetizers. I'm starving. I could eat an elephant. It's packed, and luckily we get there just as someone else is pulling out. Jeff, Elise, and Kyle are already there with a table. I introduce everyone to Kinsey, and then we order drinks. I am in need of a drink!

"So how did house shopping go?" Elise asks.

"Good! I didn't find a house yet, but Kinsey and I found

a great apartment. We're gonna be roommates for a while," I announce.

Kyle's face drops slightly but quickly recovers. "Oh, that's great," he says. "That sucks you didn't find a house though—"

"You know, it just wasn't meant to be for right now. My perfect house is out there, though. I know it," I respond with a wink.

I look over at Kinsey, and she's watching us intently. Shit! She furrows her brows and squints as though she's trying to figure us out. By the end of the night, I guarantee she will be asking what the deal is.

"So, Kinsey, did you have a good flight?" Jeff asks.

I roll my eyes. He just opened up a can of worms. "Ugh! I swear, next time I will just drive. I understand why we have to go through all the madness just to get through security, but for such a short flight it is *so* not worth it! They need to create an express lane!" she says, exasperated.

We all laugh at her madness. "Well, so sorry I asked!" Jeff jokes.

"So, someone please tell me about this band," I say.

The waitress comes around with our drinks. "They're called Crank. They're kind of a hip punk rock band. You'll like them, they're different," Jeff responds.

"Um, is there going to be a bunch of teenie boppers there?" I ask.

Kinsey joins in. "Yeah, some underage drinkers who

wipe off the 'X' on their hands?"

"Wait, what's wrong with teenie boppers?" Jeff asks.

I laugh. "Oh, that's right, you still are one."

"Um, that would make me one as well," Kyle adds. "And I am *way* past teeny," Kyle says with a smile.

Jeff throws up his hands. "Dude! No one wants to know that!"

Poor Elise doesn't know what to say. Jeff whispers something to her every now and then, and she giggles. She's got it bad. I'm not so sure it's a good thing. I don't know much about Jeff, but from what I gather, he is most definitely a bad boy. I would hate to see her get her heart broken.

"So Kyle, who are you banging at the office?" Kinsey questions, very direct and to the point. She's not a bullshiter. I learned to be so direct from her, but she's way worse than I am. Kyle just might want to walk away.

He almost spits out his drink. Kinsey looks proud. "No one at the moment. Why? Are you in line?" he teases. I personally don't find it funny.

"If I was in line, you would know it. Let's cut the crap here. I see how you look at my friend—" she begins to say. Jeff and Elise quietly watch this shit go down.

I know all too well where this is going. "Kins—" I try to interrupt. She holds her finger up to me to hold my thought.

"If you hurt her, I will wring your little neck and then stomp on your face until it's unrecognizable. Got it?" she says, pointing her finger at him.

I cover my face, completely embarrassed. She is just so over-the-top sometimes, but she means well. She's seen me hurt, and she won't have it happen again. She didn't really care for Cody, but she tolerated him for my sake. I'm sure she won't do that again.

Kyle looks her straight in the eyes. "I don't plan on breaking anything of hers. She means way too much to me," he confesses. She continues to stare him down, but then she stops. It's almost as though she can see his honesty.

I let his words sink in.

"Okay, as long as we're on the same page," she says, backing down.

Jeff holds up his beer. "On that note, salute!" he yells.

We all put our drinks up.

CHAPTER THIRTY-ONE

Kyle

Wow! That is all I'm going to say about Kinsey. She is one crazy chick, but I think I'm going to like her. Anyone who is willing to put their neck out for a friend is definitely someone I want on my side. I periodically peer at Jeff and Elise, and he seems very attentive to her. I haven't really witnessed this side of him before, so it's actually inspiring. If he can change, maybe I can too.

Geez, thinking this way seems a little foreign to me, a little domestic. Is this okay at twenty-four? Shouldn't I be on the prowl for the next easy thing? I look over at Max. No, definitely not.

We get our appetizers and inhale them down with another round of drinks. We all have to drive, so we cut ourselves off until we get to the Smoke House to see the band.

The Smoke House is a little dive bar near the beach. It's jam-packed, but the energy is upbeat and the vibe is good. Everyone seems to be having a chill time.

I grab us all a round of drinks as we squeeze into the only open bar table. The only advantage of this is I can be close to Max without even trying or seeming suspicious.

"Wow, this is some crowd. Do you go to these things a lot?" Max asks me.

I have to speak right up to her ear. "No, not really—every now and then. Before my college years, Jeff and I would sneak into these places through the back," I say, pointing to the back door. "But they obviously caught on to that." I smile as we watch the bouncer guarding the back door with his life.

The opening band begins. Some stop to listen, but most continue on with their conversations and wait for the headliner.

"This is actually great!" Kinsey screams. She's right next to us. I laugh. I'm glad everyone is having a good time.

Max just bobs her head to the music, and Elise seems to be enjoying herself. Tonight couldn't have been more perfect.

After the band ends, the bar starts to empty. We head to the parking lot. I stop Max to speak with her while Kinsey gets into the passenger's seat.

"Hey, I had a good time tonight," I tell her. God, I want to kiss her so bad.

"Me too. Kinsey really enjoyed herself."

"Can't you drop her off and sneak away?" I beg. I'm just dying to have my lips all over her body. "I'll make it worth your while," I say coyly. I will try anything to influence her decision.

She sighs. "I can't. God, I want to, but I can't," she says with a pout.

"Please don't make me beg," I plead.

She shakes her head, denying me. I drop my head in defeat. "It's only one night. We can be without each other for one night." She puts her palm against my cheek, then walks away.

I don't want to go a night without her next to me. How the hell did I become so addicted? I straighten myself up and say goodnight to Jeff and Elise before I head to my car. I can do this. I don't need anyone sleeping next to me. I was fine two weeks ago, and I'll be fine now.

As soon as I get into my apartment, I strip off my clothes and dive into my bed. No matter how much I want to deny it, I can't stop thinking about Max. I do what I never do this late at night unless it's a booty call: I text her.

"My bed's cold. I wish you were here."

I wake up early to meet Jeff at the gym. He's already there, warmed up and starting his cardio. I begin my stretches.

"Dude, you're late," he scolds. "I went to bed the same time you went to be—" He doesn't even finish before the light bulb in his head lights up. "*Unless* Maxine stopped by?"

He's digging. He's trying to get the lowdown. I should be doing the same with him and Elise. "No man, she didn't come by. I spent the night alone if that's what you're getting at."

"Well, that sucks. Are you losing your touch already?" he teases.

Before I can put in my rebuttal, Jeff's younger brother Julian comes by. "Oh my God! You should have seen the chick I snagged last night!" he brags while slapping me up.

"Oh yeah?" Jeff taunts. "Did she have a dick?"

I snicker. He's freaking crazy. Julian's face is priceless. "Nah, you dumb fuck. She has a nice pair of tits and a huge ass. Don't hate."

At this point, I am dying. I can't even contain myself. "Julian, you freaking kill me!" I tell him between laughs.

After an hour of catching up and laughing, I head out. I think I worked my ab muscles more than anything with those two guys. I drive home to shower and take a nap before heading to my parents for dinner. My mom called yesterday to say she was making sauce and wanted Junior and I there. I just couldn't say no and disappoint her. It's not her fault we're assholes. I haven't had a home-cooked meal in a while. My mom's just been too busy to find the time. Now that my brother and I are grown, there's no need for the family dinners every night. Not like my father was always a part of those, anyway.

I finally get a text back from Max. She must have just woken up.

"Hey, I slept like shit if it makes you feel any better..."

"Me too. Wanna have an afternoon nap with me?" I reply.

"Hmm, what time?"

I do a quick, excited dance.

"Now. I'm getting in the shower," I write.

"Be there in 15."

Yup. She just made my day. I rip my soaking, sweaty clothes off and jump into the shower. By the time I get out and throw some sweats on, she's already here. I buzz her in. She's also in her sweats. They're kind of sexy on her. The word "Pink" is written on the ass of her sweats. I can't stop trying to read it. She turns, trying to hide herself.

I grab her in a big hug, placing my hands right over the word on her backside. Her ass is perfect—firm but still squeezable. I sniff her hair. "Mmm, you smell so good," I tell her, still breathing her in.

She sniffs me back. "Ditto."

I bend my head down and reach my lips down to hers for a smooch. She tastes like strawberry ChapStick. "Yum," I say, licking my lips. She giggles. I graze her cheek with the back of my fingers and touch my lips to hers again. She's highly addictive. I just can't get enough.

I lead her to my unmade bed, bring her down with me, and snuggle up behind her, tangling my legs with hers. Everything just feels so right. Nothing could be any better than this moment. I feel—happy.

Is this what people die to have? Is this what a real relationship is about? If so, why would I ever want to put a name on it? Names, titles, and papers always have a way of tainting things. I don't know why, but I've seen it a million times. Of course, my parents are the exception to this.

"You're so warm and comfy," she tells me, inching her butt closer to me. I'm not so sure if that's a good idea. "Uh-oh," she says, looking back at me with a smile.

I chuckle. "I can't help it. Just seeing you and touching you drives me insane," I admit as I kiss the nape of her neck. She smells like her normal flower-and-cucumber-melon scent. It's a sweet, intoxicating mix. I can't get enough.

God, I think I'm going insane. Maybe I just need a couple of days without her to regain my sanity. Where the hell am I? What did I do with my pimp-daddy bachelor side? What's crazy is that I have fallen into this casual comfort with Max, and I don't even miss being alone or being free. What I miss now is her when she's not around.

We both close our eyes, breathing slowly until well fall into a deep sleep.

CHAPTER THIRTY-TWO

I wake up with arms around me. It takes me a moment
to figure out where I am. Kyle rustles next to me, holding
on to me tighter. I roll over to face him. He smirks cutely
without even opening his eyes.

"Hey," I say.

"Hey," he replies. "What time is it?"

I look up at the alarm clock next to his side of the bed.

"It's three thirty. I have to get going. Your mom invited
Kinsey and I for dinner. Will you be there?"

"Yeah, she told Junior and I to come also. This is going
to be interesting."

I chuckle because he's right. The last dinner didn't end
so great, and that was in a restaurant, so I can't imagine
what will possibly go down in their family home. Maybe it
won't be too bad since Kinsey will be there. Hopefully
Junior can show some manners.

"Well, I'll warn Kinsey beforehand so it won't be such a
shock if things go down," I tell him.

He shakes his head. "Thanks, babe."

"I'm gonna head out." I give him a soft kiss on the
cheek, but he doesn't accept that. He runs his hand through
my hair and brings me back to him. He plunges his tongue
deep into my mouth with hunger and raw desire. I can't

help but follow. Every stroke and every caress I feel from his tongue invokes a fire from deep within. I have to ease off or we'll never get to dinner on time.

He whines as I push off of him. "Do we have to go?"

"Um, yes, this was your mother's invite. She'll definitely think something's up if we show up late again and without Kinsey."

He smashes his head into the pillows. "Ugh! Okay, you're right."

I blow him a kiss and head out the door. This euphoric feeling comes over me. It's calming. I don't feel panicked or suffocated. I feel ... happy. That's really the only way to explain it. I have to admit, it's sort of strange to feel so okay with all of this.

I get back to the hotel and jump into the shower. Kinsey is already dressed and headed downstairs for some coffee. By the time I'm dressed and ready to go, it's nearly five o'clock.

"So, what are these boss-people like?" she asks. It's a fair question when going to someone's house you don't know.

"Well, Connie is great. She's very carefree and tolerates no bullshit. She is extremely good at keeping everything together at the agency. I really don't know how she does it with such a big clientele. You'll be working with her a lot, so get acquainted.

"Greg, on the other hand, I haven't spent much time with him other than the meetings and the one family dinner

I attended, but he's a good guy. He treats his employees very well, and they all seem pretty happy in their jobs. He's not the biggest people person, but he likes to help out when needed," I explain.

Kinsey watches out the window. "So, you said Kyle also has a brother. Where does he come into play? Does he also work at the agency?" she asks, getting the lay of the land.

Oh boy! Good thing she asked. I almost forgot about him. "Yes, Junior works at the agency. He deals with mostly the non-fiction clients. He's very direct and to-the-point. He kind of takes life a little too seriously. Oh, he and Kyle absolutely do not get along. So, I'm just warning you now. They have gotten into it multiple times in public areas in the last two weeks, so I'm not so sure what's going to happen in closed, private quarters," I warn.

Kinsey's face lights up. She's so evil. "Oh, this is going to be fun! I am in need of this. My life's been too drama-free lately. I need to spice it up. Is this Junior brother cute?"

I shake my head. She's too predictable. "Yes, but he's off limits! We all work together, so we need to keep the relationships completely platonic. We don't need a messy office," I instruct her.

I look over at her; she has her arms crossed against her chest. "Oh, okay. You mean keep it platonic like you and Kyle are doing?" she jabs back. "Maxine Leigh Daniels! Don't you dare think I'm stupid! I saw the way you two looked at each other, and I *saw* that special spark between two people who have fallen in love!"

I snap my neck back and gasp. "What the hell are you talking about?! We are not in love! Okay, yes, we may be involved more than we should be, but that's it. He's twenty-four for Christ's sake! What the hell am I going to do with a twenty-four-year-old?"

She gives me the stank face and makes a disgusted sound. "Um, you're going to do exactly what you've been doing—fuck the shit out of him. Are you seriously that concerned about his age? It sounds to me you got over it the moment you had your tongue down his throat. Stop lying to yourself, Max. You have more feelings than you're willing to admit. I don't know what he did in such a short amount of time, but he obviously does it well," she says, gleaming with satisfaction.

I still have my mouth hanging open. I'm still in shock over the "in love" comment. Kinsey always says it how she sees it, but she's got to be off on this one. Wouldn't I obviously be the first to know? I mean, they're my own emotions for goodness sake! She's just blowing this way out of proportion.

We pull up to the Saunders' house. I would have to say it's pretty massive. A little too grand for no longer having any children in it. If I was them, I would definitely downsize. This house most likely requires a huge upkeep.

I turn to Kinsey quickly before the front door opens. "Keep your mouth shut about the car ride here, okay?"

She zips her lips and throws away the key just as Kyle usually does. Connie opens the door to greet us.

"Hello ladies! Please come in!" she says in a very warm and welcoming tone. Seeing Connie in this setting makes me sad that I never had a mother like this. I'm a little envious.

"Connie, this is Kinsey."

I notice Kyle sitting on the kitchen barstool in the background.

Connie envelops Kinsey in a huge hug. It must be the casual non-office environment. "It's great to finally meet you. I hope your flight in was okay," she says to Kinsey. Oh man! Here we go. I just hope Kinsey can keep her mouth closed.

"Yes, it was fine," she responds. Thank God! She finally listened.

Connie leads us into the kitchen where Kyle and Junior are managing to sit together in harmony for the time being.

She waves at Kyle, and I introduce her to Junior. "Junior, this is my assistant Kinsey. She will be working close with you this week, so work her hard for me!" I tell him jokingly.

He smiles in her direction. "Will do. You better be ready to learn, so come to work with your 'A' game! I don't like stragglers," he informs Kinsey.

I see Kinsey's strained face as she tries to hold herself back. Kyle laughs quietly while watching from a distance. He knows all too well how Kinsey is with her words. She's a spitfire, so to have not only a man but a man she just met, who is clearly younger than her, tell her how to work is killing her inside. I can see her about to blow a gasket, but she keeps a tight lid on it so she won't explode.

"I was actually going to say the same about you. I work fast and learn fast. I hope *you* can keep up," she states.

Junior just glares in her direction. She smirks, knowing she put his boxers in a bunch. Connie seems to be enjoying the little banter from the sidelines. I hear her giggling quietly. Greg finally comes out of his office.

"Oh honey, come meet Kinsey," Connie says, directing him toward her.

He reaches out to shake her hand. "Welcome to the team. Maxine has only said great things about you. You and Junior are going to be my go-to people when in need, so be prepared; I can be a real pain sometimes," he admits.

Kinsey laughs. "I work well with 'pains in the butt,' so don't worry about me, sir."

"Please, call me Greg."

"Will do!" Kinsey responds. She's a charmer. I know they're going to love her.

We all sit down at the dining room table; it's a massive table that fits in well in this massive house. I sit next to Kinsey and across from Kyle. Junior takes a seat next to Kyle, and their parents are on either end of the table. I feel the need to shout to be heard. We begin passing around the pasta while making small conversation. I see the daggers Kinsey is mentally throwing toward Junior. It's clear she now has it out for him. Lord help him.

The sauce and meatballs smell delicious as I pile up my

plate. I can't really remember the last time I sat at a dining room table while eating a home-cooked meal. Actually, I can count on one hand how many times this has happened in my family.

"So, Kinsey, what college did you graduate from?" Junior asks.

"South Carolina State; the same as Max. We were roommates," she answers. "What about you? Harvard? Yale?"

I shake my head. Why did he even have to get her going? "Nope. I began working for my father straight out of high school. Learned all the ropes from him," he states with pride.

"Interesting," she says. She doesn't say another word; I'm assuming it's because both Greg and Connie are listening.

Kinsey stays pretty quiet for the rest of dinner. Greg and Connie tell us stories spanning the last ten years. Connie even goes into stories about Kyle and Junior when they were little. I thought for a split second that she was going to pull out the naked baby pictures. That would have been awesome!

We have dessert and coffee and chat a little while longer. Junior heads out shortly after, and Greg sneaks back to his office. I leave Kinsey to talk with Connie while I head to the bathroom. Before I can close the door, Kyle is entering behind me. He closes and locks the door, and then he steals a kiss from me.

Nice and sweet is out the window. This kiss says "fuck me right here" all over it, and even though I'm completely turned on, we're still in his parents' house.

His lips have now made it down to my neck. I put my hands between us, against his chest. "Hey, hey, we can't be doing this here. Someone can come in at any moment," I tell him.

His teeth are now grazing my earlobe. "The door's locked," he says in between nips.

"Kyle, you know what I mean," I whine.

He takes a step back to look at me. "Okay, but you're coming back to my apartment after you drop Kinsey off. I'm not taking no for an answer this time," he warns.

I can't help but laugh. He's too adorable when he's all demanding. I give in. "Okay, let's go say our goodbyes."

We head back into the kitchen. Laughter fills the room from Connie and Kinsey. It looks like they're hitting it off. I knew they would love each other. I grab Kinsey, and we say goodbye. Kyle waits a moment before leaving so he doesn't look obvious.

CHAPTER THIRTY-THREE

Kyle

The girls leave, and I stay behind to kill some time. Max has to drop Kinsey off before heading to my place. My mother finishes cleaning up and pours me a cup of coffee.

"Do you know what you're doing, son?" she asks.

I look at her, confused. "Um, I don't know what you're talking about," I tell her honestly.

She gives me the "mom look." "I'm talking about Maxine," she explains bluntly.

"Uh, what about her?" I try my best to act dumb.

"You've never been good at lying. I see the connection you two have. I saw it the first moment you two were together. I was just waiting for you two to admit it to yourselves. I'm not going to mention this to your dad. He might blow a gasket. But just remember—things could get messy if this doesn't end up working out," she advises.

"Ma, she's different. She's nothing like the rest of them. She makes me want to be a better me. Does that sound strange?" I ask her.

"No, it sounds like you're finally growing into a man. Love will do that to you."

Wait, did she just say love? What the—? "Mom, you're looking too much into it. We're just spending time together," I try to explain.

"Am I?" she asks. She comes around to give me a kiss on the cheek. "If I'm not mistaken, you have plans. You better get going." She pats me on the back and heads out of the kitchen.

My mouth just drops open.

I get to my apartment just as Max pulls up. There is no way in hell I am mentioning the conversation with my mom to her. She'll freak. We meet at the doorway, and I grab her hand as we get into the elevator. The electricity between us is at an all-time high. The sexual tension is thick between us.

As soon as we get into the apartment, I lock the door, and she slams me against it. With her eyes, she wills me to stay put as she unbuckles my pants and rips them down to my feet. I'm standing tall. She doesn't even have to warm me up. I'm ready to go.

She gives me that devilish smirk before dropping to her knees. I already want to explode, and she hasn't even touched me yet. She grabs my stiff rod and then takes me deep within her mouth. My knees almost buckle, and I groan loudly. I can't even hold it in.

She works her magic, teasing then consuming all of me over and over again. My whole body overheats, releasing waves of fury. My toes curl and my knees wobble as I erupt like a volcano down her throat. She drained my energy. This girl is a goddess.

I kick my pants off and begin stripping off her clothes.

First her sweater, then her tank top and bra, then her pants —leaving only her panties on. She's fucking gorgeous. I could stare at her for hours. I slide my hand under her panties and immediately dive into her wetness. And boy, is she wet.

She moans from my touch and digs her fingers into my back. I work her into a frenzy, sliding my thumb over her swollen mound and then diving back inside of her. I don't let up until she is about to climax, then I stop and withdraw my hand.

"No, don't stop. Please?" she begs. I love the sound of her begging.

I turn her around and direct her over the arm of the couch, ass up and everything readily available for the taking. She glistens with wetness as I stand and take the beauty all in. This is mine, all mine. Nobody else's. I'm going to make sure of that. I'm going to fuck her like no one's fucked her before—make her beg for her release.

I slide my tip in and then slide out. She moans, then whines. I push in again, a little deeper this time, feeling her walls grab on to me tightly. She feels like fucking heaven. I want to stay in her forever. This time I thrust hard and deep into her, not stopping until she screams my name. I feel her begin to quiver around me; her release is so close, so I stop.

"Oh my *God!* Please don't stop! *Please* don't stop!" she pleads.

I plunge into her again, this time not stopping until she unleashes everything she has around me, bringing me to my own release. We shake and quiver as we both come down from our climax. I don't even want to move. My whole body is tingling and weak.

I slide out of her and head to the bathroom to grab us a towel. We clean up, and I drag her back to my bed so we can lie down together. My energy is depleted, and I can barely move a limb.

"I have to go back to the hotel," she whispers.

I hold on to her tighter. "Not yet. Just lie with me."

CHAPTER THIRTY-FOUR

The week has flown by. I've spent every other night at Kyle's. Kinsey doesn't seem to mind. In the last two weeks, we have gotten close and extremely comfortable with each other. I'm not quite sure how it happened, but it has. I just don't know where to go from here. Are we supposed to continue this friends-with-benefits thing, or are we to stop before it goes too far?

What's "too far" exactly, anyways? I've never been in a situation like this, so it's all new to me. Maybe I should just wait until he ends it. It's obvious I can't do anything about it now since he will be traveling down to South Carolina with me. Not that I want to do anything about it yet. Our sexual connection is just too amazing to leave alone right now. I'm highly addicted.

I've spoken to my brother Luke, and he knows I'm coming. He's offered to help, which we totally need. I have movers boxing up and moving the office as well as Kinsey's apartment and my house. It's really going to be a big event. There are a lot of things to move between the both of us. I'm glad Kyle will be along to help, too.

During the past week, Kinsey has gotten very acquainted with the ins and outs of the Saunders Literary Agency. She and Junior have been working closely together. I was a little nervous at first, but as the week went on, they seemed to do okay. There was a lot of tension in the air between them, but all in all they still worked well together.

My partnering up with the agency was confirmed and announced yesterday. Greg and Connie set up an amazing luncheon for all of the employees to celebrate. I got familiarized with each and every one of my team members, one on one. I think that was the highlight of my day. Of course, I'm not too sure how I feel about Beth being under me. She sort of rubs me the wrong way.

I've been busy gathering all my things together in my hotel room. I took today off to get everything packed and ready to go. It's definitely been an all-day process. My hotel room was a mess. Kinsey is still back at the office. She only brought one small suitcase, so she's already packed.

I get ready to jump in the shower, but I hear a knock at the door. I look through the peephole—it's Beth. I freeze for a moment. What the hell is she doing here? Shouldn't she be at work? And why the hell would she want to see me?

I open the door. "Beth?"

She looks angry. "Can we talk?" she asks in a monotone voice.

I move out of the way so she can enter. I shut the door and follow in behind her.

"Is something wrong at the office?" I ask, not knowing

what else to ask about.

She snaps her body around to face me. "Yes, something *is* wrong at the office. My boss is fucking my ex-boyfriend!" she unveils.

I freeze for one slight moment in panic but quickly recover. "I'm sorry, but I don't know what you're talking about," I respond.

She shakes her head with a grin. "Oh, but you do. I saw you walking into Kyle's apartment the other night, and you didn't leave until the next morning. In fact, I've seen that quite a few nights. I'm sure you remember now, don't you?"

Now I'm pissed. How dare she? "Are you stalking me? Because I think you're clearly mistaken or maybe a little delusional. Who the hell in their right mind follows people around?"

She points her finger up at me. "You are not going to turn this around on me. You're disgusting, sleeping with another girl's man. How old are you anyways? You shouldn't be messing with twenty-four-year-olds."

I take a step closer to her. "First of all, your *ex-*boyfriend is *not* your man. And second of all, my age has nothing to do with this. You can't prove a damn thing anyways. I'll be contacting Connie right after you walk yourself out. You are out of line and most definitely fired!" I growl.

She holds up her phone with a smile. "Oh, I have the proof." She holds up her phone and has a picture of me exiting Kyle's apartment and one of us walking in together holding hands. Kyle was right. This girl *is* crazy, and to think I was giving her the benefit of the doubt.

"You have a gold car, don't you?"

"Yes, why?"

I shake my head in disgust. I knew there was something off about that car I saw sitting in the parking lot. I should have went with my gut feeling. "You're pathetic and sick. No wonder why Kyle didn't want to be with you. He saw right through you."

She storms past me to let herself out, but before she does, she turns to speak one last time. "I'll be contacting Connie as well. I'm on my way to the office as we speak," she informs me and walks out the door.

I am fuming! I can't believe this crazy bitch. Who the hell does that? I walk around in circles; I'm so pissed. She has some goddamn nerve. But, then it hits me. She's going to the office to tell Connie. Shit! I whip out my phone and dial Kyle's number immediately.

"Hey you."

"Kyle, we have a big problem!"

"What's the matter?" he asks quickly.

I take a deep breath. "Beth was just here. She's been stalking us, and she came here to confront me about being with you," I spit out.

I hear silence for a moment. "What?!" he screeches quietly. "Hold on." I hear him walk out of the office. "What the fuck do you mean she's been stalking us?"

I pace back and forth in my small room. "She has

pictures of us, Kyle. She's on the way to the office now to tell your mom."

"Dude, I knew that bitch was crazy. Let her go ahead and tell my mother. My mom will put her in her place," he says.

My hand flares out. "What do you mean 'let her'? Are you kidding me?" I yell. Has he lost his mind?

"Listen, calm down. My mother already knows about us," he reveals.

I stop in mid-pace. "What do you mean she already knows? How does she know? You told her?" I growl. I'm feeling a little betrayed. He promised me he wouldn't say a word.

"No, of course not. She confronted me last night about us. She said she's known for a while now; she just hasn't said anything about it. Max, it's okay. She doesn't have a problem with us seeing each other. And she won't be mentioning this to my father, if you're concerned about that."

"So your mother knew just from seeing us together?" I plop down on the bed.

"Yeah."

"Then how many others do you think have noticed?" I ask him.

"Listen, my mother is very in tune with me. She saw it coming before I even did. There's no need to worry. I'm going to speak with my mom quickly so she knows what to expect, and then I'm coming over to help you finish packing. I have my bag all set in the car. We can leave as soon as Kinsey is done. Okay?"

I nod my head as though he can see me doing it. "Okay," I agree before hanging up.

I can't pack now. I don't even know what to think or how to feel about all of this. I know it's not his fault that we have a stalker on our hands, but maybe we could have been more discreet. We should have been more careful.

I close my eyes for what seems like only a minute and wake up to my phone ringing and someone knocking at the door. I wipe my eyes from the sleepiness and head toward the door.

I see it's Kinsey calling my phone.

"Hey," I say to her while opening the door for Kyle. I walk back to the bed to sit down.

"Did you hear all the drama?" she asks, exasperated.

I look at Kyle with my brows furrowed. "What drama?" I can only imagine what she's going to say.

"That girl, Elizabeth, got fired today. I guess Kyle used to date her, and she became all stalker-ish on him. Connie had security remove her from her office," she says.

Kyle waits for me to finish. "Kinsey, Kyle just got here. Are you on your way so we can leave? We'll talk about this on the drive."

"Yeah, Jonathan's going to bring me now."

"Okay." I hang up the phone.

I turn to Kyle. "What the hell happened?"

Kyle blows out a deep breath. "She's freaking nuts. I

saw her walk into my mom's office, so I followed her in. She told my mom about us and showed her the pics. I asked to see them, and when she handed me her phone, I erased them. She went all apeshit. My mother called security to walk her out after she fired her," he finishes.

My mouth hangs open in shock. "Holy crap! What did your father say?"

"Luckily he wasn't in the office. He had a lunch meeting. I'm just hoping Junior doesn't get a whiff of what happened. He will surely tell my father if he does."

"Yeah, that would not be good. I'm lucky Connie is okay with it all." My heart's beating a mile a minute. How the hell did this get so messy?

Kyle takes a seat next to me and wraps his arm around me. "Honestly, I don't give a fuck who knows. We're two grown adults who can do whatever we want. Not my father, not anyone can tell us what to do."

I admire his strength and his bravery to want to stand up to anyone and everyone, but it's not needed. We're not even together like that. Does he think that is what's happening here? I feel like every time our line is drawn it gets blurred all over again.

"Okay, relax. Don't get all crazy on me. Beth's gone, so we don't have to worry about her any longer. Let's just get my stuff down to the car so we can leave as soon as Kinsey gets here, okay?"

He snuggles his nose into my neck sweetly. "Okay."

CHAPTER THIRTY-FIVE

Kyle

We've been on the road for about eight hours now. We have another hour or so to go. Each stop we've made, the weather gets warmer and warmer. I think it's in the high seventies now. I'm totally loving it. The girls rode together in Max's car, and I am following behind. It's been nice to be able to listen to my music and clear my mind.

Shit hit the fan right before we left. But Beth's actions reinforced something for me. I don't care who knows about Max and me. I'm actually okay with the whole world knowing, and I wouldn't mind screaming it from the rooftops for everyone to hear. That's big for me. I haven't been the commitment type, and here I am, three weeks later, ready to commit.

I *want* to be with her and only her. I can't imagine my life without her. I don't want a life without her. God, this sounds so crazy, but it's so true. What my mother said the other night has stuck in my head. She saw all this before I did, and the fact that it doesn't bother her one bit shows me I've made the right choice in going with my gut.

From the moment I laid eyes on Max, she invoked something deep within. I just hadn't known it, but I do now. I've never felt this way about anyone, and this is the kind of thing I don't expect to find or feel again with anyone else. I just know this deep in my bones. I know it by my intuition. Now if I could just know if she feels the same. That's the scary part.

We finally reach our destination and pull up in front of a nice set of townhouses on a private beach. Who the hell would want to leave this place to come to Rochester? My father must have given her one hell of an offer to pick up from here and move. Of course, he's well known for that exact thing.

I follow in behind her and park. I immediately jump out of the car to stretch. My ass is numb, and my legs are stiff. I watch the girls do the same. I pull my bag out of the trunk and head up to the door.

"This place is nice! That beach is calling my name. Do you think the water is warm?" I ask.

They both give me a crazy face. "Uh, most definitely not. You'd have to give it another month or two," Max answers.

Kinsey is next to me, doing a pee dance. I laugh. This girl is nuts. "What? I have to freaking pee!" she tells me.

I allow her to enter first, and I follow Max's footsteps as she turns on all the lights. The inside of this place is amazing. I didn't know townhouses could be so open and spacious. It sure doesn't look this way from the outside.

I look around and begin to be reminded of our little trip to Pier One last week. Some things look familiar. The atmosphere has the same calming vibe as the store.

"Okay you two, I will see you guys tomorrow, bright

and early," Kinsey announces after stepping out of the bathroom.

Max throws her the keys as she walks Kinsey out the door. I'm exhausted from the drive. We have a couple more hours of sleep to get in before the sun comes up, and I am all for it.

"Do you want to go up and get some sleep?" Max asks as she throws me a bottled water from the fridge.

"Yes, I'm so ready for a pillow under my head. You coming?"

"Yeah, I was going to get some packing done, but it won't help any if I'm exhausted later."

I follow her up the stairs, grabbing her ass as we go. She giggles and smacks my hand away. It just sort of hits me that we are in a whole other state alone. There are no eyes or lurkers around us. We can just be.

We enter her room, and I'm sort of astonished. Her room is so tranquil. She has sheer curtains hanging from the canopy of her bed. The room is decorated with warm earth tones and screams sex. I look at the bedposts and think ties and handcuffs. I look over to her, and she is watching me inquisitively.

"What are you thinking?" she asks.

"I'm thinking I have to tie you up on those posts before we leave."

She laughs. "This bed is coming with me. We'll have lots of time for that," she says.

Damn, I can't wait. She begins to change out of her

clothes. I can't help myself; I have to touch her. I stand behind her and wrap my arms around her naked belly. Her neck looks so inviting; I can't help but kiss it. I watch her reaction from the mirror on her dresser. She closes her eyes and moans lightly. That's all she needs to do to fully arouse me.

She sighs. "We have to get some sleep, baby. We have a long day ahead of us," she tells me. She's right.

"I know."

She walks to the bed and removes all the decorative pillows and pulls the blankets down. I slide in next to her and move her butt right to my hips, tangling my legs with hers. We take one long, deep, satisfying breath, and we fall asleep.

The sun comes quick. Her place doesn't have heavy curtains to keep the light out like mine does. Her shades are white and shear. The sun doesn't filter in—it bursts in. I'm almost blinded by the brightness. I look over at Max who is sleeping right through this. It feels like I'm lying on the sand at noon on the brightest day of the year with no umbrella. This is crazy.

I get out of bed and head to the bathroom to wash my face. I look for the toothpaste and finally find it in the medicine cabinet behind the mirror. Lying next to the tube of Crest are two toothbrushes, a men's Degree deodorant stick, and a Gillette razor. I would say the razor could pass as hers but the deodorant and extra toothbrush? I'm not so sure.

After freshening up, I head back to the bed. She's now awake.

I crawl back into bed next to her. "Hey beautiful."

"Hey." She stretches.

"What's with all the men's things in your bathroom?" I ask. I'm not letting this go. I need an answer.

She thinks for a moment. "Oh, those are my brother's things. He stays here sometimes when his girlfriend kicks him out," she replies.

I nod. That's definitely a doable thing. I let it go. There's no other reason to question it.

"I'm gonna go attempt to make breakfast. You want to meet me down there?" I ask.

She yawns. "Okay, let me just freshen up first."

I give her a lingering kiss, then head off downstairs.

CHAPTER THIRTY-SIX

I watch him leave the room. I exhale the breath I've been holding in. Fuck! I thought I got rid of everything. Cody just has to sneak back into my life in one way or another. I'm just glad I recovered from Kyle's question so fast.

I really don't see the issue of not telling Kyle about Cody—at least not yet. We're not together, and Cody and I aren't together any longer, so why dredge up the past? We're just having fun.

I stretch one last time and then force myself out of my bed. That couple hours of sleep was like heaven. I've missed my bed. I'm so ecstatic that I get to bring it with me this time. Of course, the thought of Kyle tying me up on it sends tingles to naughty places. I can never get my mind out of the gutter.

When I stand up, I get a little light-headed and have to sit back down. I shake it off and stand back up again. I must be overly drained. Once I get some food in my system, I'll feel much better.

I head downstairs and the whiff of bacon and eggs makes my feet move faster. My stomach growls. "Mmm, that smells magnificent!"

He's just finishing up and placing the food on both of

our plates. Kinsey comes strolling in just in time.

"Oh my God, that looks amazing! Where's my plate?" she asks.

I can't help but chuckle. God, I'm so glad she's back in my life.

"You okay, Max? You look pretty flush," Kinsey advises.

I look up at Kyle. "Do I?" I feel my face to see if it's hot.

"Yeah, you kind of do. Are you feeling okay?" Kyle asks, seeming a little concerned.

"I think the drive took a lot of energy out of me. The food will help though," I tell them honestly. I scarf the whole plate up in a matter of five minutes.

Kyle looks at my plate and then looks at his. "Wow, I guess you brought your appetite down with you," he jokes while sliding more food onto my plate. "So what's the plan for today?"

"I figured we'll pack up my house today, and then tomorrow we can pack up yours," I say, looking to Kinsey.

Kinsey scarfs down the food. "I honestly don't have that much to pack. I did most of it before I left. I can finish mine tonight. I have the movers coming Sunday. When do you think we'll be heading back?" she asks.

"I was definitely hoping to leave no later than Monday. It's going to take most of the day to pack my stuff up, but tonight Luke wants us to have dinner with him at the little place off of East—Tuscans," I notify them.

I finish the last couple of bites on my plate. Kyle pours Kinsey and me some more coffee. "Mmm, I absolutely love that place!" Kinsey says, licking her lips. "You and Cody met th—" she stops mid-sentence. I close my eyes and shake my head. I can't believe she just said that.

"Who's Cody?" Kyle asks, looking between the two of us.

I sigh deeply. "We dated awhile back. Nothing special," I answer.

Kyle looks a little taken back, like he doesn't know how to respond to what I've just told him. There's nothing for him to be upset about. He has a past as well as I do. I've personally been stalked by his past.

He claps his hands together with a smile. "So what time do we need to be ready?"

I sigh in relief. The last thing I want to do is go into detail about Cody. "Luke set the reservation up for eight, that way we have enough time to get some things done," I answer.

Kinsey starts cleaning up the kitchen. "I'm dying for some chicken french! Kyle, you have to try it," Kinsey advises.

He laughs. "That's definitely my favorite."

"Okay, so Kinsey, you start here in the kitchen. I have paper for wrapping the breakable stuff over there, and Kyle, you can start in the living room. I'm going to conquer my room and then the den," I direct.

I walk over to my stereo system and crank up the sound

on 105.9. This is what I listened to growing up. We had a house off the beach when I was younger. During spring breaks and summers, the beach would be packed with tourists and vacationers; Myrtle Beach was always like that. I was only allowed on the beach during the down seasons. Luke didn't feel comfortable with me out there in the midst of strangers. I couldn't blame him, so I never argued.

On the off seasons, I would take my Walkman down to the beach with me, crank it loud, and watch the waves beat against the shore. It was healing and a good sort of therapy for me. Now, I can't wait to get away from this beach. It has too many memories from my childhood. I'm sick of them. I want to forget them.

We stay on schedule most of the day. It's now six thirty, and I stop to look around. I no longer see a home; I see walls and piles of boxes. I nod in satisfaction. Kinsey went home to change, and I jump in the shower.

Hands begin lathering my back with soap. I no longer flinch when he comes in; I expect it now. I turn around to do the same for him.

"So, are you ready to meet my brother?" I ask him.

He pours shampoo on his hand and rubs it over his head. Sometimes I wonder what the point is when he has such short hair, but it does smell delish when I'm kissing his neck.

"Yeah, why wouldn't I be ready?"

I don't think he realizes the seriousness of this. Luke

isn't just my brother. In ways, he's worse than any father when it comes to me. Cody learned this the hard way. Luke still isn't that keen on him. Of course, he felt bad about the way I dumped him, but he thought Cody was too perfect and just not right for me. After three years of being with him, I finally realized that too. Why settle for less? Why settle at all?

"He's overly serious. So, don't get too frustrated if he doesn't warm up to you right away. He doesn't know anything about us, either. I think we should keep it that way for now, okay?"

He smirks. "Okay, boss. You got it!"

He slides his fingers down my stomach and slips them over my sweet spot, through my slick folds. My eyes roll back, and I automatically arch my back, letting out a light moan and bringing my ass to his groin. He's hard and erect against me, just how I like him. He enters me without warning, fast and deep. I yell out from the jolt of pleasure it gives me. Kyle stays still, buried deep within me. He kisses the nape of my neck and nibbles on my earlobe as he waits for my body to adjust to his invasion.

I place my hands on the shower tile, and I begin to wiggle, giving him the green light to move. "Fuck me, baby," I whisper to him. Kyle immediately pumps into me, harder with every confident thrust, bringing me closer to that euphoric bliss.

He puts his lips to my ear. "Is that how you like it, baby? Do you like when I fuck you like that?"

Wow! Holy fuck! I love it when he talks dirty. It's such a turn on! I want to cream right here and now. My build up is about to overflow. I scream out his name as he moves his fingers in tiny circles over my swollen nub, and I begin to convulse around him. Kyle follows right after. We stay locked together until we can catch our breath. He showers me with light kisses until he finally slips out of me.

We get out of the shower. He gets dressed, and I finish getting ready. Kinsey has my car, so she comes back to pick us up.

We pull up to the restaurant; it's packed. But it's a Friday night, so it was expected. Luke is already waiting at the table as the waitress leads us to him.

He stands up with his arms open and a smile as bright as the sun. "Hey, sis!" He picks me up and twirls me around just as a father would do to his little girl. I embrace him.

He gives Kinsey a hug, and then I introduce him to Kyle. He shakes his hand like he would to an old friend. Luke doesn't seem reserved or in interrogation mode, which relaxes me a little. We all take our seats and order some drinks.

"Where's Justin?" I ask.

Luke rubs his eyes with his fingers. "He's in his own world. I asked him to come, but him and Valerie had already made plans."

"What's up with that?" Kinsey comments in disgust. "They couldn't hold off for one night to come have some drinks with us? He's way too attached to her. It's sickening."

The waitress comes over with our drinks. This glass of pinot has been calling my name. I take a sip and feel it glide down my throat. Just what I needed after this long day.

"So, Kyle, my sister here never told me how you met," Luke says. Oh no, maybe I was wrong in relaxing.

"Max just became partner at my parent's agency. They asked me to come help her move. I've been showing her around town, getting her acquainted with the area," he explains proudly. He looks adorable, too.

Luke seems impressed, which rarely happens. "That's awesome. It's nice to know she's in good hands. I'm looking forward to meeting your parents."

Luke takes a sip of his beer. Kinsey and I make some small talk on the side. "What are you girls whispering about?" Luke asks.

"Wouldn't you like to know?" Kinsey taunts.

Luke clearly looks annoyed. Ever since they met, Kinsey's been a pest he can't get rid of. Surprisingly, they never had any sexual chemistry together—thank God! I don't know if I could have handled that: my best friend dating my brother. No way. But I am concerned about him being so alone all the time. Everybody needs somebody.

We order our appetizers and entrees. "No, I guess I wouldn't. Never mind," Luke says, taking another sip of his bourbon. "So, tell me about Rochester."

Kinsey makes a guttural noise before sipping her wine. Kyle and I talk to Luke about the agency and the people who work there. Luke seems to be enjoying Kyle's stories. I notice that Luke keeps looking down at his watch as though he has somewhere to be or he's waiting for someone. Strange.

Our meals finally come after we start on our second drinks. I'm feeling warm and fuzzy inside. The smell from the lemon and garlic pasta is wonderful. I thought I would be full after the appetizers, but I didn't even put a dent in my hunger. I definitely worked up an appetite.

I excuse myself to go to the ladies' room. On the way back to the table, Kinsey tries to prevent me from heading back.

"Kinsey, what are you doing?" I ask as she places her hands on my shoulders, stopping me from walking any farther.

Her eyes are big, and she can't stop shaking her head. "I'm sorry Max. I didn't think Luke would do this."

"Do what?" I ask, aggravated. I push around her to go to the table. Something's up; this is not like her.

"Max, don't!" she yells. Now people are beginning to stare.

When I enter the dining area, I stop dead in my tracks. My father is seated at our table. The blood rushes to my head as my heart is pumping furiously. Luke stands up to try to explain.

"Stop! Don't come near me! How could you, Luke?" I

screech. I can't help but look at him and feel heartbroken and betrayed. Now the whole room is looking at me. Kyle immediately jumps up to stand next to me.

"Max, let me explain," Luke begs.

My father stands up. "Maxine, this wasn't his fault. I just wanted to see you. Can you please have a seat?" He gestures to the seat next to him.

Tears begin to flow down my cheeks. "You stay away from me!" I'm now hysterical. My father takes a step toward me, but Kyle stops him.

He puts his hand on my father's chest. "Don't move another step toward her. She doesn't want to see you," Kyle warns. Luke begins to walk in Kyle's direction. "We're leaving," Kyle continues. "You shouldn't have pushed her like this, Luke. You had no right!"

Kinsey grabs my shoulders and embraces me as we start to walk away.

"You don't know shit! Who the fuck are you?" Luke questions angrily.

Kyle stands his ground. "I know she already told you she didn't want to see him. I know that you bombarded her just now and made her feel like a fool in front of this whole room! You just don't do this shit," he growls.

Kyle storms away. He comes up behind me to help Kinsey get me in the car. I can barely breathe. The air has been sucked out of my lungs. Everything around me is whirling in blurry colors. My limbs are like jelly. If it weren't for Kyle being my support, I would have collapsed to the ground already.

He gets into the backseat with me and holds me tight, pressing me close to his chest. He kisses my forehead as I sob into his shirt. "Shhh, it's okay. I got you," he whispers.

CHAPTER THIRTY-SEVEN

Kyle

My stomach is in knots as she cries on me. I feel helpless. I should have just beat the shit out of her brother for what he just did. I didn't realize how bad the situation was until I saw her shaking. Her father must have done a real number on her growing up. She's trembling from just the sight of him.

I can't squeeze her hard enough. I want to make this all go away for her. I should have protected her somehow. Her father just sat there, so calm and collected. He must have known she was going to react like this. She hasn't talked to him since he left them. What makes him think she would want to talk to him in front of a room full of strangers?

She finally stops sobbing, but she's still trembling like a cold, wet puppy. We pull up to the house, and I lead her in. Kinsey takes her upstairs and helps her get out of her clothes so she can lie down. Now I'm the one shaking. Those five minutes keep running through my head over and over. I can't stop pacing; the rage is building up. I couldn't even protect her. How am I any good for her?

Kinsey comes downstairs after calming Max down. "How is she doing?"

She sighs and sits down on the barstool. "She's a mess. I can't believe Luke did that to her. That's just not like him," she says, shaking her head.

I sit down next to her. "Kinsey, she told me about the affair and her father leaving, but after what I witnessed tonight, there has to be more to the story."

"Yes, there is. But if I tell you, you have to promise not to repeat it."

I hold three fingers up. "Scout's honor."

"Dennis used to drink a lot. When he was home, he was drinking. Max's mother was never around. She was always shopping, out to eat, on girl trips—things like that. So, she was oblivious to what was happening. Not like she would have done anything anyways. When he was drinking, he liked to get physical."

My hands squeeze into fists. "Please don't tell me he touched her."

She shakes her head, and I exhale loudly. "He would have if it wasn't for Luke. Luke took the brunt of the beatings so Justin and Max didn't have to. They sat there helpless while he pounded on Luke."

"Shit. That fucking bastard. How the hell can Luke stand to be around him?"

"Dennis has been sober for over ten years now. They've made amends. Luke thinks it will be good for Max if she does too," Kinsey explains.

I get up to grab a glass of cold water. "Yeah, he might be right, but it should be on her own terms, not theirs!"

Kinsey holds her finger in front of her mouth, warning me to quiet down. "I know. That's why I don't understand what he was thinking. He's always so protective of her. He did look a little caught off-guard when Dennis walked in, but still. Luke should have told him to leave."

I lean my hands against the counter. "I wish I would have known. I should have done something more," I confess, beating myself up. "This has to be the reason why she always seems to be running. She's afraid to get close to anyone, and now I see why."

"Kyle, there was nothing you could have done. I tried stopping her, and she wouldn't listen. And she doesn't get close to people, because she doesn't want to feel disappointment and hurt. The farther away she is, the easier it is to let go. She needs you now more than ever. Don't disappoint her. Go upstairs and be with her. I'll come by in the morning," she directs.

I walk her out. "Okay, thanks Kinsey."

She turns to me before leaving. "I'm glad she has you."

I turn off all the lights and head upstairs. Max is still awake. I take my shirt and pants off and slide into bed with her, bringing her close to me. "I'm so sorry this happened, baby. I wish I could have done something to stop it," I tell her. I kiss her forehead; she squeezes me tighter.

"Kyle, there was nothing you could do. Thank you for being here for me, though. I must have looked like a crazy person to everyone else. Do you think I'm crazy?" she asks. She looks broken and defeated; a look I've never seen on her before. I hate her father for doing this to her. I don't care how many years sober he is. He's a coward for treating his kids like that in the first place.

I think she's amazing to be able to come up from a childhood like that and be so successful and unbelievably strong. I admire her. In my eyes, she's one of the strongest people I know.

"Of course I don't think you're crazy. Your brother should have known better than to put you in that situation. You were caught off-guard. That doesn't make you weak or crazy. It makes you human, Max," I express to her truthfully.

"That's what is so weird about this whole thing. My brother would never put me in a situation like that normally. So, why now?" she asks herself. I know she's just trying to straighten everything out in her head. It all happened so fast. "What did he say when he came in?"

"Well, as soon as we saw him, Luke looked a little confused. Kinsey immediately went to find you. Luke asked him why he was there so early, and your father asked where you were. You came in right after that. No other words were exchanged."

Max sits up, putting her face in her hands. "This just doesn't make any sense."

I rub her shoulders and coax her back down to lie against my chest. "You should get some sleep. You're exhausted." She nods, and I kiss the top of her head. I continue to hold her tight, wanting to protect her from the world. She's become *my* world. I need her just as much as she needs me.

I turn off the lights. It takes her a while to fall asleep, and even in her sleep she is uncontrollably restless.

"**W**hat the fuck is this, Maxine?!"

I jerk my eyes open, thinking I'm in a dream. There's a huge man standing over the bed, looking pretty irate. "Who the *fuck* are *you*?" he says. I quickly sit up and shake Max. She wakes from her sleep, rubbing her groggy eyes, still dazed and confused.

Finally she looks up. "Cody?" she questions with a rough, scratchy morning voice.

I stand up now. "Who the fuck are you, and how did you get in here?" I yell. I turn to Max. "Who is he, Max? Do you know him?"

She gets out of bed and yanks her robe over her, looking between us. It's clear that she knows exactly who he is.

"I should ask the same fucking question about you!" This dude yells back. "I'm her fiancé," he says so matter-of-factly.

I snap my head to look at Max. What the—? "Is this true, Max?" I walk to the chair and pull my pants on. I can see this isn't going to end well. Either I'm going to deck this dude in his face, or he's going to try and come after me.

I size him up. He stands a little taller than me, heavier built with broad shoulders and a thick neck. His hair is wavy and ashy blonde; he looks like a beach dude. I want to knock his face off.

"Yeah it's true!" he replies in a dickhead tone.

Max points to the door. "Cody, you need to leave right now! Why are you doing this? You're acting psycho," she screams. "Kyle, he's *not* my fiancé. He's my *ex*-fiancé."

Is she serious? She never mentioned that. If he's an ex, why is he in here freaking out? None of this is making sense, and I start to question everything.

"Were those really your brother's things in the medicine cabinet?" I ask. I fix my stance just in case he comes at me. I'm ready.

Cody laughs. "You mean the toothbrush, Degree deodorant, and the razor? Those are mine," he answers with a smart-ass smirk.

"That's what I figured," I reply. My heart crushes. I don't know who or what to believe. I look to Max. "There was no reason for you to lie. You could have just told the truth. Now I don't know if I can trust anything you tell me. I never lied to you about my past. I was an open book," I say, grabbing my bag and beginning to walk downstairs.

She runs up behind me and yanks my arm. "Kyle, please don't leave. I can explain," she says desperately.

Cody walks up behind her and grabs her other arm. "Let him go, Max," he demands.

She tries to rip herself from his grasp, but his hold is too strong. "Ouch, Cody. Let go. You're hurting me!" she yells.

Something inside of me clicks and a switch has been turned on by her scream. I see red, and even though I can't stand to look at her right now, I still can't bear to see anyone hurting her. Especially this dickwad.

I turn around without warning and deck him. I can hear the noise from my fist hitting his face. He stumbles backwards, almost losing his balance, as blood comes gushing out of his nose.

I watch as Max goes to him and then looks back to me with judging eyes. "What the fuck, Kyle? You didn't have to hit him!" she screeches.

Cody begins to come for me, but she begs him to stop. "You're lucky, you son of a bitch! If it wasn't for Max here, I would come beat the snot of you, kid!" he says.

Max continues to plead with him as he inches closer to me. I see where her loyalty lies. She's catering to him as though he isn't the cause of this all. I'm sickened by the sight of it. I turn to walk away.

She tries to grab my arm again. "Kyle, stop! Where are you going?" she asks.

"It's over, Max. We've only been having fun anyways, nothing serious, and now the fun is over. This is what you wanted anyways. I'm done! Go straighten your shit out, Max," I growl. I yank my arm away and then look to Cody. "She's all yours." I head downstairs.

I need to get away from this place—far, far away. I don't know what to believe, but I do know he still has a house key. That must mean something. Having a psycho ex is something I can believe, considering what we just left from, but Cody confronting us in bed seems questionable. I mean, she still had his shit in her medicine cabinet. That's not something she can forget about when she reaches for her toothbrush on a daily basis.

I get in my car just to take a ride. I shake off the pain in my hand. It's going to be sore by tomorrow. I don't know if I should go back or if I even want to go back. What the fuck is the point?

It's been thirty minutes since I left when my phone starts ringing. It's her. I hit the "Ignore" button. I slam my hand against the steering wheel. Why did this have to happen just as we were getting close? What else has she been keeping from me? There wasn't any reason to not tell me, and an engagement is not something to leave out about yourself when you're getting to know someone. What was the big deal if it was over anyways?

My phone rings again. I press "Ignore." God, why does this kill so much?

I just drive until my head's more scrambled than when I started. I shut my phone off. I look down at the clock, and it's one in the afternoon. I've been driving for four hours, and I'm already in Richmond, Virginia. I've been stuck in a haze, not realizing where I was going or how far I'd gotten.

What the hell were we doing anyways? This was all supposed to be for fun, right? It wasn't something that was meant for the long term. I'm too young for long term. I'm supposed to be in my prime. I'm supposed to be having fun, right? I need to go home and fuck the first girl I see so I can erase Max from my mind.

I don't know what I'm doing. I just know I need to get

home so I can think this all through. My heart falls into my gut just knowing she won't be by my side tonight. But I've gotten way too accustomed to her. I'm sure it will pass with time. The hardest part will be seeing her on a daily basis at work. But I never planned to stay at my parents' agency forever. I can manage it for now—I think.

CHAPTER THIRTY-EIGHT

Cody finally left after I came clean about my feelings. I was getting nervous when he was coming at me with closed fists. He's never hit me before, but he's never been that angry before, either. We argued and screamed. When he asked me why we couldn't try again, I screamed, "Because the man I love just walked out the door!"

It just came out. When I heard my own words, I slapped my hand over my mouth in shock. Cody just looked at me in disgust and finally walked out the door. I almost didn't realize he left, because I was still stuck on those words I said.

Holy shit! I tried to deny it to myself. At first, I thought I was just in the heat of the moment and letting my emotions get the best of me, but now that I've actually said it out loud, I feel it. I can feel it all the way down in my bones. I feel it through my heart, body, and soul. It's such a euphoric feeling but a frightening one as well. Now what?

I feel as though I've just had my closure with Cody. It wasn't the greatest closure, but it counted for something in my eyes. Now I need to figure out what my next step is with Kyle. Just because I have fallen for him doesn't mean he has fallen for me. I mean, look how easy it was for him to walk away without hearing me out. He didn't even fight for me; he didn't even try.

I feel nauseous out of nowhere. I keep swallowing back the saliva in my mouth. It's got to be the stress that has my stomach upset. As I take a step to go downstairs, the acidic vomit comes up my throat. I run to the bathroom and get sick all over. What the fuck? Really?

My eyes are spilling over with tears. I grab a towel to wipe my mouth and sit away from the toilet, feeling empty and exhausted. It's barely ten o'clock, and this morning has stressed me out to no end. I clean myself up and brush my teeth. I grab my phone off of the bed and head downstairs.

The only thing I want is to hear Kyle's voice. I dial his number but it goes straight to voicemail. I tried calling earlier, but he put me to voicemail then, too. I text him and wait. After an hour, there is no response. Where the hell did he go? Did he really leave me?

I thought maybe he would cool off and come back, but he hasn't returned, and it's been hours since he left. I call one last time, and he has his phone completely shut off now. If he had stayed, he would have heard Cody admitting he was wrong for storming in and that I had told him we were through before I left for Rochester, but Cody just didn't want to believe it. If Kyle had stuck around, he would also have witnessed my profound love for him. I feel lost and alone. I'm filled with all these feelings, and I have no idea what to do with them.

Geez, my stomach is still queasy, and I feel faint. I lie down on the couch with a bottle of water and call Kinsey.

The worst part is I still haven't dealt with what happened last night. I almost feel like if I think about that now, I just might explode into a meltdown. I did enough of that last night. I'd be crying right now if I still had any tears left.

Kinsey tells me she'll be right over. I know I can count on her to be here in minutes. We've always been like this. Nothing is too important to drop when one of us is in need of the other.

Not even ten minutes has gone by, and I hear my front door open.

"What the hell happened, Max?"

She takes a seat on the couch across from me.

"Everything. Cody decided to let himself in this morning while Kyle and I were sleeping. I forgot he still had a key." I rest my arm over my eyes.

She remains speechless for a moment. "How did he even know you were in town?" she finally asks.

"I guess someone he knew was at Tuscan's last night and witnessed my meltdown," I tell her.

She gasps. "Oh my! That's freaking crazy. So what did Cody say?"

I take a sip of water. "He told Kyle he was my fiancé. Kyle asked me if that was true, and Cody jumped in and said yes. I told him Cody was my ex-fiancé, but it didn't matter. He was hurt I never mentioned it. I also lied about Cody's things in the medicine cabinet. I completely forgot they were in there, so when Kyle asked me who they belonged to, I told him Justin. I shouldn't have lied about something so stupid, but I did, and now he thinks I'm lying about all of this!" I huff. "But that isn't the worst part."

"What else happened?"

"Kyle punched Cody right in the face," I tell her.

Her eyes pop out of their sockets. "What? Holy crap, are you serious?" Kinsey looks around. "Where's Kyle now?"

I remove my arm from my eyes to look at her. "He left."

"What do you mean he left? Is he coming back?"

I shake my head. "I thought he was going to, but he still hasn't shown up. I tried calling him and texting him, but he turned his phone off. I'm guessing he's on his way back to Rochester," I tell her. Tears begin to slide down my cheeks.

Kinsey comes over to sit with me on the couch. "Aww, sweetie, he's just upset. Give him some time to cool off. He'll come around," she says, trying to comfort me. "What about your brother? Have you spoken with him?"

More tears gush down my cheeks. "No! I don't even want to talk to him!" I screech.

She gets up to grab me a tissue and sits back down. "Well, I talked to Luke. He called me last night," she admits.

I pop up in my seat. "Wait, you did? What did he say?"

Kinsey takes a deep breath. "So, I guess your father was supposed to come in town last weekend, but he cancelled. He showed up at Luke's house Friday, unannounced. Luke had already made plans for dinner with us, and he told your father he could come by for a drink after you left.

Unfortunately, your dad didn't listen and showed up in the middle of dinner.

"Luke was pissed, but he didn't want to make a scene in the restaurant. After you left, he told your father to leave. He felt horrible. He felt like he failed you, like he didn't protect you. He had no idea of his father's plans to show up while you were still there. I think you should just call Luke. You'll feel better," she explains.

That makes sense. I couldn't understand why my brother would allow that to happen. He has always protected me from my father. Now I feel bad that I didn't give him the chance to explain. I just can't look at my father for even a minute, and it just baffles me how Luke can. How can he forgive a monster like that?

My father was horrible to all of us but mostly Luke. Sometimes I think if my brother can forgive him, why can't I? But I just don't know the answer to that yet. I can admit it's tiring holding on to so much anger. Sometimes I think it uses more energy being angry than it does to just forgive. I've thought of getting counseling with him and my mother, but just going back to those memories makes me want to shut down. I don't think I could relive it all.

I've done such great things in life without my parents; what could they possibly add to my life now?

"I will call him in a little while. I think I may have eaten something last night that didn't agree with me. My stomach feels crappy," I tell her.

Kinsey stands up. "Do you want me to pick you up

something?"

"No, I'm fine. I'm just going to make some toast."

"Okay, well you rest, and I'll get started on packing up the office."

I take another sip of water. "Okay, I'll be there within the next couple of hours."

I take a nap and wake up feeling rejuvenated, but my mind quickly drifts to Kyle, and my energy immediately deflates. There's a piece missing from my heart now, and the pain is utterly sickening. What the hell am I going to do? What if he doesn't answer his phone? Am I supposed to see him at work and pretend the two of us never happened?

I guess I'm going to have to prepare myself for the inevitable. It's going to hurt like hell to see him at work, but I took the risk, and now I have to deal with the consequences. I have to put my big-girl panties on and just deal with this. It may destroy me, but I've gotten through worse.

I go upstairs to freshen up, but before I head out to meet Kinsey at the office, I call my brother.

He answers on the first ring. "Max?"

"Hey Luke."

I hear a sigh of relief on the other end. "Max, I have been worried sick over you. I am so sorry Dad showed up. He promised me he wouldn't. I seriously wanted to *kill* him for that. How are you doing? Are you okay?" he asks, clearly worried.

"Luke, Kinsey told me everything. I'm sorry I didn't give you a chance to explain. He caught me off-guard. I wasn't ready to face him yet. I made myself look like a fool, though. I just couldn't hold myself together. I totally lost it," I admit.

"Who the hell cares what anyone thinks? I told Dad you needed time, but it's clear he didn't care what I thought. Max, I swear, I am *so* sorry! If I knew he would do that, I would have cancelled the dinner."

My brother seems heartbroken over this.

I put my shoes on. "He probably would have just shown up here anyways. You did nothing wrong, Luke. Don't beat yourself over the head about it, okay?"

"Max, are you seeing that kid Kyle?" Luke asks.

Now it's my turn to sigh. "We were more than friends if that's what you mean."

"I think he's a good fit for you. Anyone that stands up for you the way he did is good in my eyes."

Wow. I'm shocked. I've never heard those words come out of his mouth before. If he can make this good of an impression on Luke, I know my heart has made the right decision. Kyle is truly spectacular. My heart twinges with pain.

"Well Cody ruined it for us. He came in this morning like a freaking psycho!" I explain.

Luke sighs in aggravation. "What a dick! Listen, if it is meant to be it will be. Just relax and give it some space. Kyle will come around in time. Either way, you still have to see him at work. I guess that's why people say 'don't mix business with pleasure,' huh?"

I chuckle. "Yeah, you're right about that one. I have to get to the office to help Kinsey with packing. We might not be leaving as scheduled. I have get to the office to see how far behind we are."

"Okay, sis. Call me if you need any help."

"I will. Love you."

I smile. He can always make me smile. "Love you too, Luke."

I start the car, and as I pull out, I get sick out of nowhere. I slam my hand over my mouth, put the car in park, and quickly open the door to vomit outside. Thank God I have a napkin on the side of the door. I'm one hot mess. What the hell did I eat last night? I tried a little of everything, but I've never had a problem with that before.

I pull up to the office and grab a tiny bottle of Scope from my purse to wash out my mouth before I head up.

"Hey! How are you feeling?" Kinsey asks when I walk in. She's boxing up the bookshelves.

I dramatically plop down on the plush green chair and exhale. "Not good. I just got sick on the way here. Something I ate last night is not agreeing with me at all. I couldn't even hold the toast down."

Kinsey stops putting the books in the box. "Are you sure you're not pregnant?" she asks and then laughs as if she's just joking. I don't laugh. A light bulb clicks on.

Now that I think about it, I was supposed to get my

period last week. I've been totally preoccupied, so I haven't even noticed. This is not good. I can feel the blood drain from my face.

"Max?" Kinsey says, rushing to my side. My hearing is now muffled with a high-pitched ring in my left ear. "Max, your face just got pale as hell. Are you okay?" she questions, clearly worried.

I nod my head, unable to talk. I think I may be in shock.

"Kinsey, I never got my period last week. I haven't even realized it. Do you think I could really be pregnant?" I ask her, hoping maybe she'll tell me no.

She goes into the bathroom and grabs me a wet cloth. She hands it to me before she answers. "I think it's time to take one of those early pregnancy tests. You didn't use protection?"

I place the cloth over my forehead. "We did at first and then I guess we just got too caught up in the moment. We didn't really think much about it. Shit! That sounds so bad out loud, doesn't it?"

Kinsey laughs. "Yeah, it does. So don't repeat it."

I can't help but laugh. She's always way too honest. My mind is just running in circles. It's got be something I ate. There's just no way I can be pregnant, right? Wrong. I feel like I have just entered into a dream state, and I'm hoping I get to wake up from this nightmare.

"So, what do I do now?"

Kinsey stands up and grabs her car keys. "You take a pregnancy test. Come on. Let's go."

I take a deep breath and will myself to get up. With each step, I feel like I'm sinking farther and farther into quicksand; I'm headed into the abyss. What the hell am I going to do if I am pregnant? How the hell is this going to affect the new partnership? And more importantly, what the hell would Kyle say? Would he tell me to get an abortion? I've never been in this predicament before. I'm not too sure if I could even bring myself to get an abortion.

"Okay, you go in and buy it. I don't think I can even do that right now," I tell her.

Kinsey rubs my thigh as if to tell me it will be alright. "I'll go in for you, but if I see someone I know, you're going to owe me big time!"

It's always like Kinsey to crack a joke at this time. Thank God for her. I don't know what I would do if I had to do this alone.

We pull up to the drugstore. I wait in the car as planned. Once she purchases the test, we head back to the office. I take the same seat again as she opens the box and unwraps the test. She reads me the directions and then hands me the stick. I look at it, unable to move or coordinate my muscles. I can't believe I'm really doing this.

"Max, honey, it's not the end of the world if you end up pregnant. Even if Kyle won't take part in it, you still have me. And there's no reason you can't raise a baby by yourself. What are you so afraid of?" Kinsey asks.

She's right, what am I so afraid of? We both knew this could be a possibility without protection, and the pill isn't one hundred percent foolproof anyway. I suck it up, hold my head high, and head to the bathroom. After doing my business, I set the stick on top of the bathroom counter. Kinsey and I stare at the clock, and when the time's up, I peek over at the stick.

"Holy shit!"

Kinsey looks over my shoulder, gasps loudly, and covers her mouth. "Oh my God, Max. You're pregnant! Holy shit is right!" she yells, jumping up and down.

Everything surrounding me begins to blur into a black darkness with tiny specks of stars twinkling around me. I hear Kinsey's voice fading far in the distance, sinking deeper and deeper until she's almost nonexistent.

Splashes of ice-cold water smack my face and snap me out of the dark. I look around, confused. "What happened?" I ask. I'm now sitting on the floor against the sink cabinet.

Kinsey has a wet cloth against my forehead. "You passed out, Max. Are you okay?" she asks with panic in her voice.

She helps me up and sits me on the toilet. "I think so. I don't know what happened. I had this weird vision that I was pregnant," I tell her, snickering.

Her eyes grow big. "Um, Max, you are pregnant," she tells me, pointing to the positive stick.

I almost want to faint again. I pick it up to look. "What am I going to do?" I whisper, not taking my eyes off of it.

"You need to figure out what's going on with you and Kyle before you make any hasty decisions," she advises me.

I stand up and head back into my office to lie down on my couch. "I'm not having an abortion if that's what you think, but I'm not so sure I want to mention this to Kyle anytime soon. I can't be more than three weeks. Anything could happen between now and the second trimester."

"Yeah, I guess you're right. I have heard that. So, why don't you try calling him to see where you guys stand?" she suggests.

"No!" I snap. "He walked away from me! I didn't walk away from him. I would have never done that to him. I would have waited for him to explain rather than leaving him in the dust. I'm not making the next move." I sniffle now, obviously upset.

Kinsey squints her eyes at me. "Are you in love with him, Max?" she probes.

Shoot! I can never lie to her; she always knows. I put the cloth back over my forehead and close my eyes so I don't have to look at her. "No, why would you think that?"

"Because I can see it all over your face. Do you think he feels the same about you?"

"I don't know, Kins. I don't know."

CHAPTER THIRTY-NINE

Kyle

It's almost springtime. The cold weather is breaking, and the sun has been shining warmer each and every day. I love spring. It's my favorite time of the year. I would normally be breaking out the white tees and getting a fresh shave for every weekend's adventures, worrying about the next piece of ass. But instead I am in my pajamas, not showered, unshaven, and lying on my couch on a Friday night.

It's been two months since I left Max down in South Carolina. She never ended up coming back. She told my parents she had to tie up some loose ends before she was able to come back to the office, so she sent Kinsey in her place.

At first, I pretended like it didn't bother me. I would walk by Kinsey as if it was no big deal and she was just another regular employee. But as the days went on, I wondered where Max was and if she was ever coming back. My mother's only words were "she'll be back shortly."

I tried picking up the phone to call her many times, but I failed to press "Send" after I dialed. I wrote a million and one texts but never sent any of them. I guess I was too chickenshit to feel the wrath of what I had done to her. I just walked out on her and left her there, high and dry. I didn't even wait to hear the full story or find out if there was any truth to what Cody was saying or not. I was too blinded by my male pride to give her the benefit of the doubt as she allowed me to do so many times before with Beth.

As each day passed, I felt more and more like a coward, and I wouldn't have been able to stand it if she wanted nothing to do with me ever again. At least this way she hasn't said those words, so there's still always a tiny bit of hope, right? God, I need a shot of some good tequila.

I finally got the courage to speak with Kinsey one-on-one after a couple of weeks had gone by. I asked her how Max was doing; she just smiled politely, and told me to ask her myself. Man, I hated that answer. That vague excuse for an answer just ate me up inside. We once, not so long ago, would have laughed and joked with each other, but now Kinsey treats me as though she doesn't know me. I guess it's better than her ripping my head off.

Today, I decide to confront Kinsey one last time. There's no doubt about it that Max shared her feelings with her best friend. I just need to know what I'm walking into before I call Max. I need to prepare myself for the inevitable, whatever that may be.

I clock in to work. I stroll down to Max's office, which Kinsey now occupies, and knock on her door. She looks up at me with a look of revulsion. At this point, I know I am in trouble. I close the door behind me so nosey onlookers can't lurk, and I get ready for the explosion.

"What do you want, Kyle?" she growls.

I take a seat on the chair in front of her desk, fiddling with my fingers. I look down, trying to avoid eye contact. "I know I don't have any right to ask—"

"No, you don't," she snaps.

I look up at her. "I need to know how Max is doing," I finish.

She rolls her eyes. "I told you to call her yourself! You know, you're lucky you're even here in my presence. If my job wasn't so important, I would leap over this desk, rip your balls off, and feed them to you!"

My eyebrows lift halfway up my forehead in shock. I knew she was a tough girl, but I never knew how tough. "Okay, okay, I deserve that. But please, is she coming back?" I ask.

Kinsey is now rolling her pen through her fingers in thought. "I don't know, Kyle. You totally fucked things up. You could have at least been a man and called her to apologize. She knows you two weren't in a relationship, but she thought if anything you were at least friends," she explains.

I exhale loudly. She's right. I did royally fuck things up. The worst part is missing her like crazy, but I feel like that's my punishment. I deserve it. I just don't know if I can live with it any longer.

"Man, I know. That's what's killing me inside. I miss her just being around. I miss everything about her. I haven't been able to sleep in weeks because she's not by my side. Is that crazy?" I ask, knowing she'll give me the honest truth.

Her face muscles ease just a tad. "No, that's not crazy. Sounds to me like you really care about her—maybe more than you realize."

I just nod my head. There's no doubt in my mind that I care about her. Every time she enters my mind, my whole body aches. My heart feels like it's missing a piece, and my soul feels incomplete. That's the easiest way to explain my pain.

I stand up. "Thanks for the talk, Kinsey."

She smiles. "Oh, and nice job on Cody!" she adds with a wink and turns back to her work.

I don't feel like going home to an empty apartment tonight, so I make a U-turn and head to McGregor's. I know the bartender there, which is a definite plus when I'm trying to get wasted. I just want to feel numb for one minute. I've been feeling so much agony and regret during these last couple of weeks; I'm ready to just drink my sorrows away.

"Hey, Kyle. What brings you here without your crew?" Jenny asks. She pops open a Heineken and places it in front of me.

I sigh and run my hand over my head. "It's just been a rough day."

She pours us both a shot of Patrón. "Here, this will help." She slides mine in front of me with a wink.

We both raise our shot glasses and throw it down. The

liquid heat burns down my esophagus and warms my belly. It gives me comfort and lines my insides, which are waiting for more. I down my first beer; now I'm ready for my second. I wait for Jenny to finish with a customer.

"Let me guess, broken heart?" says a deep, rugged voice to my left.

I turn my head to look at him. I've seen this man in here before. He looks to be in his late sixties—worn down, one lonely soul.

"Uh, no. I'm just a man who needs a drink," I tell him. I try to concentrate on the news ahead.

He chuckles and takes a sip of his beer. "Believe me, I know a man that's hurtin' when I see one. I used to be one back in the day. Still am one," he tells me. He holds out his hand. "I'm Adam."

I put my hand in his and shake. "It's Kyle."

He takes another swig of his beer. "I've seen you here before. You always seem to be on the prowl. I know it's none of my business, but you look like shit, my man."

Is the guy for real? I huff and shake my head. "Yeah, like I said, bad day."

"It was forty years ago when I lost her. Her name was Jane. She was the love of my life, and I let her slip away. I had too much pride to tell her how I really felt. I got scared. A guy like me didn't fall in love. She was moving out of state for a job offer and wanted me to go with her. That was just way too much commitment for me, so I let her walk away," he tells me.

Man, this all sounds too familiar. "What happened next?" I ask.

"Nothing. When I finally realized what I had done, I tracked her down, but she was engaged to be married. She told me it was too late. I've never loved another woman after that. My heart still aches. The pain never goes away; it just gets manageable. If you love her, you need to go to her before it's too late," he advises me.

My blood is furiously pumping through my heart, making it pound against my rib cage. Shit! I look him over one more time. Will this be me forty years from now after I let Max slip from my fingertips? I don't want to let her go. I want her by my side for the rest of my existence. What if she decided to go back to Cody? What if I pushed her back to him? I would hate myself for not manning up and allowing that to happen.

I can't lose her. I won't lose her. I love her. I fucking *love* her! I stand up, grab my jacket, and pat the old man on the back.

"Thanks, man. You just saved me from making the biggest mistake of my life!"

I head to the door. "You go get her!" The old man screams across the bar.

I think I see Jenny smile.

CHAPTER FORTY

Can I get two scrambled eggs with cheese, home fries, a side of bacon—crispy—with white toast, and an order of french toast—a short stack? Oh, and an orange juice as well?" I hand the waitress my menu. "Thank you."

Justin whistles. "Wow. I'll have what she's having," he says. The waitress takes his menu and leaves. "What's going on, Max? Hungry much?"

"Yeah, I'm starving. Where's Valerie? Luke said you guys are inseparable," I tease.

He chuckles. "She just got promoted to bank manager, so her hours have changed. She's making some real good money now. We're looking into buying a house this spring."

Shock smears my face. "Really? That's a big step, Justin. What about marriage?" I ask.

The waitress brings our orange juices. "I actually wanted to talk to you about that." He goes into his coat pocket and pulls out a little black box. I gasp and cover my mouth with my hands.

He opens the box and a one-carat pear-shaped diamond sparkles in the light. "It's beautiful! When are you going to ask her?"

When I look up at him, I don't see my baby brother any longer. I see a handsome, grown man that I've missed out on getting to know these past couple of years. I'm so proud of him for doing the right thing. I just hope he knows what he's getting into. It's a big step.

"I don't know yet. I'm waiting for the right time. I guess I'm going to carry it around until I feel it's the perfect moment. I don't want to do one of those cheesy proposals or anything. I want it to be just about her and I and nothing else," he explains.

I'm impressed. "You've thought a lot about this, haven't you?"

"Yes. She's the one," he admits. "What about you? Luke mentioned someone named Kyle, is it?"

A huge pain stabs my heart. "We had a fling two months back. It was nothing serious." I shrug my shoulders while looking out the window. I don't want him to see the pain across my face.

The waitress comes with two huge trays of food. My stomach is doing somersaults. I barely wait for the plate to hit the table. I begin inhaling the food. Justin eyes me closely.

"What's going on with you, Max? You're acting like you're eating for two," Justin throws out there. I stop chewing and look up at him. "Holy shit! I'm right! You're pregnant, aren't you?"

I nod. I haven't told anyone other than Kinsey. I haven't even told Luke.

"Yes, I'm three months' pregnant. Please don't mention this to Luke. I don't want him hunting down the guy to kill him," I beg.

"Who's the dad? Is it that guy, Kyle?" he asks.

I sip my orange juice. I could really use a coffee right about now—or maybe a stiff drink. "Yes."

Justin finishes his bite. "Have you told him yet?"

"No."

"Then what are you waiting for?" he questions with his hands flaring about.

"I don't know. We sort of ended it before I found out. I made the choice to go on with the pregnancy, so I figure it's my job to raise it. Not his," I explain.

I push my plates away. I killed it all. They're spotless. "But Max, you're not even giving him a chance. You at least need to talk to him about it. If he wants nothing to do with it, then you're still left in the same boat as before." Wrong. I'll be crushed into a million pieces. I won't be able to recover.

My brother has become so wise. I'm so proud of him.

"I know. You're right. I'm going to have to figure it all out," I admit.

The waitress brings the check. I reach for it, but Justin is faster. "It's on me." He throws the money down. "Come on. I'll drop you home."

We reach my house, and I see a black Cadillac parked in front. My heart skips a beat. It can't be Kyle's. There's no way. I can't see inside, because of the tinted windows, but as Justin and I walk up to my door, I hear a car door slam.

"Max?" Justin and I both turn around. It's Kyle. He

looks at me and then looks to Justin. "I'm sorry. I must have come at a bad time. I can see you're busy," he begins to walk away, but I call his name.

"Kyle, this is my little brother, Justin. He is just dropping me off."

Justin walks down the steps with his hand out. "Great to meet you, Kyle. I was just making sure she got in safely. You two have lots to talk about, so I'll be on my merry way." He comes up to give me a kiss on the cheek and says goodbye.

My hands are shaking. I haven't been this nervous since I was dropped off at college for the first time. I unlock the door and step in. I don't even have to turn around to see if Kyle is behind me. I already know. Every nerve in my body is awakened. I'm no longer numb when he's around. I feel alive, and I also feel all the pain he left behind.

I take a seat on the barstool. I can't stand for this. I don't know what's going to come out of his mouth. He looks like he hasn't slept in weeks. He also looks just as nervous as I am.

I speak first. "Why are you here, Kyle?"

"I'm here to tell you that I'm sorry, Max. I should have never walked out on you like that," he says. I continue to look at him, flabbergasted. Does he really think his sorry will make up for it all? "I was an asshole. I *am* an asshole. I was completely in the wrong. I should have waited to hear your side of the story, but instead I let my ego and temper get in the way. I shouldn't have hit Cody either, but *God* it felt so good!" he admits. "I am so sorry, Max."

A tear slides down my cheek. He walks around the counter, lifts my chin, and gently wipes the tear from my face. I look him dead in the eyes, and I can see the anguish and remorse deeply imprinted on his face.

"I didn't tell you about Cody, because it wasn't important. I was with him for three years and only engaged for a few months. I realized he wasn't the one, and I broke it off with him. He just didn't want to accept it. I wanted to leave him in the past. I was ready to move on, Kyle. That is why I never mentioned him."

He drops his head, ashamed. "I should have allowed you to explain this then. I can't tell you enough times how sorry I truly am, Max. Please forgive me?" he begs.

I'm still so angry, but seeing him this broken kills me. "You hurt me, Kyle. I will accept your apology, but if you hurt me or walk out on me like that again, there will be no forgiveness," I inform him, making sure he understands. It's not easy for me to let someone in, especially after hurting me so much, but for some reason I believe what he's telling me. "So, what now though?" I ask.

He grabs my hand and places it with his. "I want you to come back with me. I want you to be with me, Max."

My heart picks up. "Be with you how?"

He makes sure to look me in the eyes. "Max, I'm in love with you. Being apart from you has been driving me crazy, eating me up inside. Please say you'll come back? You're my everything. I need you."

"Kyle, I love you too, but it's just not that simple," I confess.

His smile turns into a huge grin. "Wait, you love me too?" he asks.

I sigh. Is that all he heard? "Yes." I smile. "If you would have stayed longer when Cody was here, you would have heard the words come out of my mouth. That's the reason why he finally left, because I confessed that I am in love with you, not him."

He grabs my face and smashes his lips against mine. His lips feel like home. In his arms is where I'm meant to be. I can't get enough of him, but then I remember, there's still more. I push him away. Now I'm terrified. How is he going to take this news?

"Kyle, there's something you need to know."

He looks a little worried. "Whatever you have to say, we can get through it. I love you, and I'm not going to get scared away again."

I just have to say it. The words are stuck in my throat, terrified to come out, but I just have to say it. It's now or never.

"I'm pregnant, Kyle."

The blood runs from his face just as it had mine. "Are you sure?" he asks.

"Yes. I'm most definitely sure. I'm entering my second trimester, a little over three months," I explain.

I can't tell what he's thinking. He's like a blank page right now. He places his hand over my belly in amazement.

"You mean, I'm going to be a father?" he asks, his hand still on top of my stomach.

"Yes, you're going to be a father."

He looks up at me with tears in his eyes. He slams his lips against mine once more. He puts his forehead against mine. "I fucking love you, Maxine Leigh Daniels!" He grabs my hand to lead me off the barstool. "Let's go upstairs. I want to make love to the mother of my child."

CHAPTER FORTY-ONE

Kyle

It's officially summer. The windows are open, and the smell of flowers and barbecue is heavy in the air. I feel as though I have the world on a platter for the taking. Everything I thought I didn't want in life has happened, and I feel like the luckiest man on earth. I have the love of my life as well as a baby on the way. What more do I need? Life now feels effortless.

Max and I found the perfect house after two months of searching. I gave up my apartment, and Kinsey found a new roommate. Everything is finally working out perfectly. My mother's ecstatic about the baby, and my father is still getting used to the idea.

I've been watching her belly grow over the last five months, and it's the most fascinating phenomenon I've ever experienced. My daughter is growing inside of her. *Our* daughter! Watching her and feeling her move inside Max is the most beautiful thing I've ever experienced.

Max looks up at me. "Did you feel her?"

Her head is in my lap as she lounges out on the couch on our back deck, outside. "I did. She's so strong. I can't wait to meet her."

"Me either," she adds. "What are you going to do when she ends up with someone just like you?"

I close my eyes and lean my head back. "Kill him," I answer. She laughs with amusement.

I've had a secret for weeks now, and keeping it from Max is driving me insane, but I've been waiting for the right time to reveal it. Now seems like the perfect moment. My stomach is queasy, and I begin to shake as I gently move out from under Max, replacing my lap with a pillow.

"Where are you going?" she pouts.

I stand above her, kneel to one knee, and take the ring from my pocket. She sits up and gasps with her hands over her mouth. She gets more beautiful each time I look at her.

"Maxine Leigh Daniels, you struck my heart like a lightning bolt, so unexpectedly. Ever since, my world has been turned upside down—in the best way possible. I am *so* in love with you. I want us to be linked together in every way possible for the rest of our existence," I take a quick breath and gulp. "Maxine, will you do the honor of being my wife? Will you marry me?"

My hands are shaking as I wait. Tears are gushing down her cheeks. She leaps into my arms, her belly slamming into me first.

"Yes! Yes, I'll marry you!" My breath releases, and I stand up with her in my arms, carefully twirling us around in circles. "I love you, Kyle."

I stop and put her down to look into those baby blues. "I love you too, Max." I kiss her softly. My heart is filled with every amazing feeling possible. I am the luckiest man alive. She is my soulmate, the love of my existence—my everything.

About the Author

Shevaun DeLucia, author of the *Eternal Mixture* series, lives in upstate New York with her husband, four children, and two dogs. As a stay-at-home mom while her children were young, she fell in love with reading. She indulged in the small moments that took her away from the reality of her loud, rambunctious household, bringing her into a world of fantasy. When reading wasn't enough to satisfy her, she turned to writing, determined to create the perfect ending of her own.

Acknowledgments

Wow! I can't believe I am publishing my second book! It's so surreal. Just like the first, I feel like a proud mama. One preconceived notion has transformed into a novel. But none of this would be possible if it weren't for my dream team, always behind me!

To Scott Schisler—photographer of the book—what can I say? Your work is brilliant. Bravo! You've taken my creative idea and multiplied it by a thousand. I feel honored to have taken part in it.

And to Jinelle Shengulette—editor—you never disappoint me! It feels like Christmas every time I open one of your emails. I absolutely love working with you! Thank you for the tremendous time and effort you have put into this project. We have many more to come, and I can't wait!

Next, I'd like to thank Rachael Baltes and David Santa Lucia for your willingness to take part in my book cover. My vision of you two was right on, and you both looked amazing!

Jayded Playlist

Nothing Really Matters – *Mr. Probz*
Talking Body – *Tove Lo*
Sex on Fire – *Kings of Leon*
No Ordinary Love – *Sade*
The Heart Wants What it Wants – *Selena*
Sideways – *Sheryl Crow*
Me and the Old Man – *Neil Van Dorn Band*
Hanging by a Moment – *Lifehouse*
One – *Ed Sheeran*
Latch (Acoustic) – *Sam Smith*
Let her Go – *Passenger*
Wings – *Birdy*

www.ingramcontent.com/pod-product-compliance
Lightning Source LLC
Chambersburg PA
CBHW070102120726
47909CB00002B/477